FIRST BLOODS: BOOK ONE

BAD SEED

TRACY KORN

ANIMUS FERRUM
PUBLISHING

Preface

The man on the corner drank from the bottle in the paper bag, oblivious that he only had twelve more minutes to live.

The tingling at the base of Marcus's skull had already started, which was always the first sign the change had begun. It was pointless to run, to try and hide or lock himself up somewhere so he wouldn't kill again.

The adrenaline spike from trying to disappear before it was too late would only bring the change on faster, and it didn't matter who was in front of him once he'd gone completely Feral. He'd learned that the hard way.

This was just as well, he thought, watching the old drunk stagger back against the smooth concrete outer wall of The Citadel. *He probably didn't have any people, or he wouldn't be in the state he was in,* Marcus rationalized. One less piece of *Grind* trash, as the elites on the other side of the wall would say.

Ten minutes.

The itch started in the back of Marcus's throat—a prickle he knew wouldn't go away no matter how many times he swallowed or coughed—the incessant scratch of countless tiny barbs pushing through the lining of his trachea, the scientist at Wu Fong had told him. All the better to swallow his prey.

Marcus wished he'd never been told that. It was one thing to know he was a monster now, but he didn't need to be able to visualize it.

The drunk slid down the wall, his back propped against it as he took another swig from the bottle. He was surprisingly large for somebody who lived in the Grind, let alone someone who probably didn't even have running water or a regular roof over his head given the state of his grimy, tattered clothes.

Eight minutes.

Marcus's temples started to throb. In another few seconds he knew the pain would spread to his sinuses and jaw as the bones of his skull elongated and the tissues connecting them all stretched taut. The roof of his mouth started to go numb, soon to be followed by his gums, and he was thankful for at least that small mercy. The innumerable sharp, enlarged teeth he'd seen in the footage of one of his earlier changes haunted him to the point or paranoid terror—waking dreams of his arm or leg falling asleep only to transform into rows upon rows of gnashing and grinding canines, molars, incisors. Marcus began sweating, the salty rivulets from his brow stinging his eyes.

Five minutes.

The old drunk let the bagged bottle fall from his grip as his arms went slack, his legs outstretched straight in front of him. Marcus could see the holes in the soles of his shoes, one of them so far gone a wad of cloth had been shoved inside as a patch. Yeah. Marcus would be doing him a favor. He wouldn't even know it was coming passed out like that. It would be over fast.

Searing pain needled through Marcus's joints in waves. First, his toes and ankles, then his knees and hips, up every vertebra in his spine until it began to feel like he was standing on an open pyre, the flames licking higher and higher. His skin began to burn as it stretched, and though he knew how grotesque it was to watch the hair thicken on his arms, his fingernails darken and curl into claws, the absurd sight of it all took his mind off the pain. Marcus needed to walk—to start making his way across the street to the passed out drunk on the corner before his own body abandoned him and his mind dropped into a dark abyss where he was only aware of his own screaming. When he could no longer hear that, it would mean the Feral was already tearing someone apart.

Two minutes.

Marcus started to cross the street, every step like hot coals pressing into his feet. He heard his sternum crack and as his collarbones extended through his shoulders, ripping muscle fibers which didn't grow fast enough to accommodate. *Don't scream. Don't scream!* He told himself. The drunk had to stay asleep. Had to stay immobile. If he ran, the Feral would chase him, and it wouldn't stop if others were in the path. *Don't scream!* he shouted in his mind when the long snout covered in dark hair came into view where his nose had been. One more look at his hands and arms, covered in the same hair now and three times the size they had been with black talons curling to a point.

One minute.

The drunk flinched, and the startle was all it took to release a jolt of adrenaline into Marcus's bloodstream. Acid coursed through his veins, ice picks stabbed through his eardrums as he watched the arm—his arm, the Feral's arm—reach for the man in the same second he awoke. Marcus's screams gave way to an otherworldly growl that reverberated in his skull, blurring his vision and upending his equilibrium. The man dangled by his throat, clutched in the huge, hairy grip before his eyes. He tried to scream but either couldn't, or Marcus couldn't hear him over the sound of his own personal Hell surrounding him.

The Feral's other arm blurred before his eyes, instantly digging four gaping wounds over the man's stomach and chest. Blood spilled over the ground as the man jerked and writhed, and mercifully, the hurricane of demonic growling stopped and Marcus's vision finally went black.

Chapter 1

One drop, and it could really, finally end, I thought as I inserted the needle into the receiver port.

I stared at the bio simulation without blinking. Without breathing. *Ten minutes to full absorption.*

The olive leaf concentrate was a Hail Mary pulled from our catalog of proven antiviral organics. The others hadn't even made a dent in the virus's stranglehold—ginger, licorice root, calendula, even astragalus root and devil's claw... They would all make a more effective base for salad dressing.

Not even our newest arsenal of super organics proved viable: boju thistle from the rainforest of Peru, which was the active ingredient in the vaccine for both strands of herpes simplex; ichorapalm root from Malaysia, which completely reversed the ravages of HIV to NED—no evidence of disease—twelve years ago. And, of course, my most humbling defeat thus far was the latest: jicambi bark enzyme from the Congo, which replaced eighty-seven percent of antibiotics overnight because it temporarily supercharged the immune system.

But not this time.

As miraculous as all these organics were, no combination of new and old, no mixture, no extract, and apparently nothing in my experience as an Authorized Botanist here at the Citadel Pathology Center for the last four years had been able to stop the

novel HHV-1, *Human Hyperendochrine Virus*—
commonly called *Red Fever* since it tinged the victim's
corneas, teeth, and fingertips red as it progressively
decimated one biological system after another. The
only thing we could do was delay the inevitable for a
time.

Our synthetics were of no use either; in fact, my
colleagues had begun referring to the pathogen as
Goliath since nothing they did seemed to break its
stranglehold. It often only took a year after infection
for a person to become emaciated to the point that
even basic digestion and breathing were too much for
the body to handle. We'd isolated transmission to
direct contact with the blood, which was puzzling
since usually blood borne pathogens were also
transmissible through body fluids and mucus
membranes, but not this. We suspected unauthorized
medical treatment outside of the wall may be to
blame, but it was hard to prove since no one would
ever confess to receiving such a thing and then be
subject to devastating fines.

To make things worse, now, we had a new strain
of Red Fever on our hands that didn't present as the
debilitating sickness that Citadel scientists had been
researching for nearly a decade. At least, not in
everyone. It seemed transmissible in the same way—
direct contact with the blood—in our simulations, but
it didn't inhibit blood flow to internal systems, or
weaken cells, or slow the production of brain

chemicals. This strain did the opposite of these things and more, all at the same time. Instead of breaking down the body of some victims, the mutation seemed to rebuild it into something...*else.*

Everything we'd learned so far about this new variation of Red Fever came from working for the last six months on a rare Feral cadaver—a *Feral* being the rumored *werewolf*-like creature those outside The Citadel wall blamed for their increasingly frequent, fatal attacks over the last three years. To keep tensions in check *inside* the wall, the newsfeeds had attributed those gruesome deaths to a rise in crime among the Grind Lands scavengers, but after our index patient was taken down with a droid bullet to the head in the midst of an attack, the only media spin that had any traction now was emphasizing that Ferals couldn't get beyond The Citadel wall. Disgustingly, that was enough to let far too many people here sleep just fine at night.

One of the only things that helped me keep my resolve in the face of so much apathy and so many treatment failures was to put aside the terror of this mutation and look at it clinically, even with awe at just how complex a machine the body really was. The rate of physical growth alone in this cadaver was unfathomable, especially in terms of increased bone density, which must have been painful given the rate at which the bones amassed layers—essentially, self-fortifying. It was almost as if his body knew what would be coming next and needed to build internal scaffolding.

But it was the fourth and final stage of the infection that rendered this man unrecognizable as a human being with his elongated ears, nasal cavity, and jaw structure, plus a tripling and enlargement of the teeth. Bone spurs even grew through his fingertips like claws.

Here in phase four, this once normal, healthy man who was nearly my age quite literally became a monster. If the incubation data from this cadaver was conclusive, one minute, a middle-aged legacy chip adjuster could be collecting a few weeks from someone's life for an overdue bill, and in as little as eight hours, he could become lost in a Feral rage and take *all* of his next client's weeks. If the virus could hijack a young, healthy person, it could likely rewrite anyone.

In addition to a decade without a cure for the Red Fever wasting sickness, people beyond the wall had lived in fear of being torn limb from limb over the past three years. The numbers had only been increasing, and now we knew why. This creature in front of me was our missing link in treating the Feral Red Fever mutation, but until we could isolate the source of the virus or at least where this new strain originated, we were just shooting blindfolded.

The simulation finally finished as I twisted my lanyard impatiently in front of the computerized immuno-map. I waited for the virus to shrivel and writhe in response to my newest antiviral, to choke and suffer the way it made so many people living in The Grind suffer.

But it didn't. *Goliath* had only hijacked the healthy simulated cells and forced their mutated replication like it had already done a hundred times over the last six months. All the ligaments and tissues began turning red, and we were now officially back at the drawing board.

"Shit!" I said under my breath, then heard a beaker topple over behind me. It took me several seconds to realize I'd backed into a shelving unit, even as I watched the rest of the beakers topple to the ground. I braced for the deafening clatter and sighed. The last thirty-six hours were catching up to me.

I crumpled over the cool, metal countertop just as the familiar thud of an overly stuffed backpack hit the tile floor. Instead of his usual too-loud bellow, Scott's voice was thin and wary. "Frankie?"

I took a breath to collect myself before I turned to him. "What are you still doing here?" I asked, trying to keep my voice steady. "You'll miss your board defense."

"I just finished it" He handed me his new clearance badge, which read *Scott Jeffries, Authorized Citadel Pathologist.*

"Congratulations." I nodded, returning the badge. I rested my chin on the backs of my hands and all but fell asleep on the countertop. "The olive leaf enzyme is a bust, by the way," I mumbled. "Sorry I don't have better news for your last day as the intern whipping boy."

Scott smirked. "Just means now you'll have to share the credit when we find a cure." His dark brows crashed together as he tiptoed through the broken glass, struggling to contain a laugh. "What happened here?"

"Casualties of war." I gestured to the infection simulation. The holographic immune system display of my computerized patient was now completely red, even the bones…irreversibly *Feral*.

Scott scanned it and swallowed a groan. "So much for olive leaf." He tilted his head at me with an exhausted, sympathetic smile, and it struck me that just now, with his pale skin and dark features, he reminded me of a mime at the end of his rope—placid, but with something heartbreaking in his eyes. An incarnation of fatigue…of finally being tired of searching for a way out of his invisible prison. I wondered if I looked the same to him.

Maybe we all felt like that these days. Over the last ten years The Citadel had become a prison with Red Fever just on the other side of the wall in The Grind, where most people lived. But I didn't dare let myself feel sorry for those of us who got to go to sleep at night without the visceral fear that we would wake up as a monster.

"What happened? What was that crash?" Dr. Beck's pinched face twitched as his eyes darted around the room, his bald head shiny with sweat in the doorway.

"Sir..." Scott said, quickly looking again at the broken glass, then at his lab coat on the wall. He cleared his throat. "Uh, sir, I tossed my coat onto the hook and caught a beaker."

I rolled my burning eyes at the epic failure of his excuse. "It's my fault," I confessed. "It was an accident."

Dr. Beck glared at me and nodded absently. He straightened his lab coat. "How did olive leaf run on the Donovan mutation?"

Donovan? I thought, confused, until it dawned on me he was talking about the cadaver. "No effect," I said, defeated. I glanced up at the wolf-like face of the huge, hairy-bodied hologram and suddenly felt irrationally guilty for poking around inside him for the last six months. *Nice to meet you, Mr. Donovan.* I took a deep breath and fought to keep my eyes open.

Dr. Beck moved his glasses to the top of his balding head, his lean face lined with years of practiced condescension. "All right, get this cleaned up before you go home," he said, turning to leave the lab. "And Scott, good defense today. Welcome to the team."

"Thank you, sir," Scott answered, broom already in hand. He had most of the glass swept up by the time I

returned with a dustpan, which he took from me and finished the job. He put the broom and dustpan away and gave me a fierce side-eye. "How long have you been here, Frankie? You've been wearing the same clothes since the night before last."
I looked down at my red blouse, having completely forgotten what I was wearing at all. "I guess since the night before last?" I gave him a weak smile.

Scott shook his head at me and sighed. "And I suppose that's the last time you ate, too," he said impatiently. "Come on, I'm buying you dinner and then putting you to bed before you walk into traffic."

Chapter 2

Ivy's Pub was just around the corner from The Citadel campus, but I hadn't been there in weeks. Between staying late at the lab and the newsfeeds reporting new attacks, I just couldn't justify sitting around like nothing was happening. I didn't know how anyone else could forget what was happening, even for a little while.

"After you," Scott said, opening the gilded brass door to Ivy's, which had a long rope of winding, oxidized green leaves around the frame, although the door pull itself was polished to a high shine. Inside, holographic screens of sporting events and newsfeeds hung in the air throughout the pub. The rest of our team sat at our regular table, a pitcher of beer and various appetizers already served. The others waved us over.

"There's the man!" Blake Bingham got to his feet and opened his awkwardly long arms. "*Dr.* Jeffries… Well, who's going to get our coffee now?" he added, slapping Scott on the back. Jack and his girlfriend, Anita, stood and applauded, the lot of them looking like they'd stepped right off an insurance commercial —all backyard cookout casual and smiling until the scene inevitably cut to everyone knee-deep in basement water. How could these people have been working in the same lab as I have? How could they have been living in the same city and still be *this* carefree?

"Frankie, you look like shit..." Jack said with a slap of his own on Scott's back. His blue eyes twinkled as he raised a pint to his lips, which was exactly when Anita elbowed him in the chest. He spilled his beer down the front of his shirt, and I stifled a laugh.

"Jack..." Anita hissed through her angelic, kindergarten teacher smile, her tone of voice containing just the right amount of condemnation without *actual* chastisement.

Blake laughed. "Don't be a dick, Jack. *Some* of us actually work for a living." He raised a freckled hand to signal the waitress. Everything about Blake Bingham was indistinguishable from a twelve-year old, except maybe his height. He was taller than all of us, but the freckles, curly, red hair, and dimples made it impossible to take him seriously, even when he was insulting you. He pulled a few chairs over from an empty table and offered us both a seat. "Did you work through the night again?" Blake asked, passing me the bowl of pretzels in front of him.

"Anything else for you two?" the hovering server disc said as it got into position over our table. It lowered the pitcher of beer and two empty glasses it was carrying, then released its arms. Blake filled each glass from the pitcher and handed one to me.

"I'll have a burger and fries," Scott said to the hovering disc. "Frankie?"

"Uh, the same, please," I said, probably a beat too late as I watched the server disc folding and retracting its metal arms.

"If she's mesmerized by the wait-disc, she definitely worked through the night again," Anita said to the table, and the soft laughter drew my attention back.

"Sorry." I smiled and lifted my beer, which smelled like floor cleaner. I wasn't a beer person.

"The champ here just spent the last *three days and two nights* processing our latest shot at Goliath, but it didn't make a dent," Scott said, putting a little plate of various fried foods in front of me.

"No wonder you look like shit, Frankie." Jack kissed Anita quickly on the cheek and pulled her close before she could elbow him again. She tossed her halo of blonde hair and looked at me with faux-exasperation.

"It's OK," I smiled at her. "*You're* the one who has to live with him."

"Therese, can you turn that feed up, please?" Blake called to the closest live waitress, who had just taken a tray of drinks from Nick, the bartender. They both scowled at our table.

"Yikes, what's wrong with them?" I observed.

"Not fans of hockey?" Blake offered.

"They're training that new guy who doesn't look like he's slept in weeks. There, wearing the highlighter yellow," Jack said, pushing a hand through his thick, dark hair in amazement as the new bartender splashed himself while pouring a drink. "He's like a walking caution tape."

"He doesn't look well," I said, noticing the dark circles under his eyes and slightly sunken cheeks.

"Thank you!" Blake smiled widely at Nick when he turned up the holographic feed closest to him.

Whatever hockey game that had been playing on the screen was suddenly interrupted by images of a crowd gathered just outside The Citadel wall. My stomach sank.

"—one of the victims is reported to be alive, but in critical condition, John," the solemn female reporter said, cupping her earpiece. In the next second, her face fell. "I'm sorry, no… It appears the second victim of what is now a *confirmed* Feral attack has died from his injuries. The Feral is, unfortunately, still at large. Law enforcement personnel are compiling lists of missing persons from the last seventy-two hours in the hopes they will be able to identify the Feral with DNA from the scene of the attack. This brings the tragedies in the outer Portland area to thirteen this year as a result of the *Red Fever* mutation, two more than last year's total. John?"

"DNA from a stage four Feral…right," Jack shook his head at the feed and yelled at it across the table. "It's too far gone for DNA matching, John!"

The feed cut back to the studio anchor, his heavy brows drawn together and his lips pressed into a thin line. "Thank you, Gwen," he said with a decisive nod. "Fortunately, The Citadel Center for Pathology has just announced that it may have encouraging leads in controlling the spread of both Red Fever and the recently discovered variant in the outlying Portland area. Let us reiterate there have fortunately been *no* Feral attacks or Red Fever cases inside the Citadel wall. News Seven reached out to Dr. Howard Beck, Director of Epidemiology at The Citadel Pathology Center on their progress."

Scott leaned over to me. "Did you see a news crew when we left the lab?" he whispered. I shook my head.

"What we know is that the Red Fever variant seems to be caused by a virus that has a short incubation period," Dr. Beck said into the feed capture. "And our eradication trials have been promising, especially in organic antivirals. After today's progress, we're getting close."

The feed cut to a list of general health practices to reduce the chances of infection, none of which were particularly applicable since the Red Fever virus and the mutation didn't seem to be airborne or there would be far more cases by now, not to mention they'd be on *both* sides of The Citadel wall. I gaped at the feed in disbelief.

"He just told everyone we're close? As of *today*?" I asked no one in particular. "I told him specifically that my latest organic was a bust."

"It has to be damage control for the rioters outside the wall," Blake said, lowering his beer. "Think about it—imagine how much more panic there would be out there if he said we had *nothing*," he added, his freckled forehead wrinkling as he looked around the table for agreement.

My food arrived, but suddenly, I wasn't hungry anymore.

"Did you know the cadaver's name was Donovan?" I asked the table, then forced down a few of the fries in front of me.

Blake looked at me curiously and laughed a little. "You dug up his paperwork?"

"No," I answered. "Beck mentioned it just before we left today."

"Awkward," Jack said, stealing one of my fries and leaving an ice blue wink in return.

"Would you like to sit by her?" Anita leveled a glare at him.

"How could I kiss you from all the way over there?" he asked, giving her a peck on the cheek.

Blake rolled his eyes. "Beck probably has to vet all the cadavers to make sure we don't get the dean's sister-in-law in there or something," he said, pushing pizza sauce around his plate with a mozzarella stick. "You couldn't pay me enough to play politics like that *and* try to run the pathology center," he added, which I believed. Blake Bingham's trust fund ensured he would only work as long as it took to get credentialed in an authorized career field. I would be shocked if he stayed a week longer than necessary after the fund was vested in another year. Blake was a nice person, but he wasn't what you'd call a front lines kind of guy.

Jack blew him off. "How hard could Beck's job be? Don't run trials on important dead people. Don't spend the research budget on beer, and don't hire morons." He smirked at Scott. "Oh, shit…maybe it's harder than I thought," he said. Scott threw a fry at him, which Jack caught in his mouth. He raised his arms over his head in victory, and we all erupted in cheers.

"I'm sorry. He's worse than my students. And they're *five*." Anita shook her head at the rest of us and laughed. "Thank God we have the birth control mandate here. Ten years of *mostly* peace and quiet," she said, turning back to Jack.

"Hey, you know, our service obligation contracts are almost up." Jack wiggled his eyebrows at her. "Two more years, and then we can call the first one Jack Junior…*J.J.* for short!" He nodded, knowingly, but Anita just gave him a deadpan look. "Or, you know, *Anita* Junior." He shrugged, then mumbled to his food "Doesn't have the same ring, but…*A.J.* I guess A.J. works."

Scott cleared his throat. "Well, you got him to stop eating paste and putting crayons up his nose, right?" he said with an overly compassionate smile.

"Growing up is hard. He's lucky to have a professional like you."

Everyone laughed again, even Jack, his dark eyebrows raised in impressed acknowledgement. He threw a jalapeño popper across the table, which Scott unsuccessfully tried to catch in his mouth. It ricocheted off his chin and rolled to the floor.

Jack opened his arms. "I'm still the king. Still the king, boys and girls."

Blake snickered. "Frankie, what's up next from botanical?"

"I don't know. I was sure the olive leaf would be a stable enough base, but Goliath still tore through the cell walls like they weren't even there. I'm out of ideas," I said, and rested my chin in my hand.

"You just need some sleep. We'll start fresh tomorrow," Scott said. "It took decades before they cured AIDS, right? We have the framework identified, we know the stages of infection. Maybe we're just coming at it from the wrong angle."

"You know what, you're right," I said. "We're trying to wipe out the whole thing—eradicate Goliath's existence, and we don't even know where it's coming from. Do you have any leads whatsoever yet? This is like trying to find a needle in a haystack *in the dark*. What else do we know about the cadaver?" I fired, turning to Blake.

"Just what was on his legacy chip: twenty-seven-year-old male, normal lifespan prediction of eighty-nine years, minus the *seventeen* or something he was in debt." Blake raised his thin eyebrows and shrugged. "I mean, what else do you need? We ran a complete environmental workup. He was in good health. Dock worker in The Grind, I think, before he got a scholarship to The Citadel."

"He was a dock worker in *The Grind*?" I asked, incredulous that nobody thought this was important information.

Blake looked at me, surprised. "Yeah, like six years ago or something. He probably got infected going back home to see a girlfriend."

"Won't have that problem anymore thanks to the lockdown," Jack grumbled.

Scott nodded. "He's right. This guy turned stage four eight hours after being infected. There's no way to know where or how he picked it up before the lockdown was initiated."

I shoved a handful of fries into my mouth to buy myself some time before I had to reply. Jack chuckled and turned to Blake.

"What did the guy do here?" he asked casually. "He was on a scholarship for which school?"

Blake took a drink of his beer. "I don't know, Engineering maybe? I didn't memorize his intake paperwork," he said after he put the glass down.

"Can I see it?" I asked.

Blake smiled widely. "Well, I don't have it on me at the moment, Frankie."

I rolled my eyes at him. "You know what I mean."

Blake shrugged. "Didn't you get his tear sheet? It had all his environmental factors on it. We've run all the pollution screens, done all the random blood samples. The sheet says it all."

"It didn't say he'd been a dock worker in The Grind," I said, leaning forward.

"If you want to waste your time checking our work, Frankie, by all means," Blake raised his hands in placation. "Come to my office, and I'll show you the intake papers myself." He winked.

"It's not like that," I said. "I just need a new perspective. Like I said, I'm out of ideas on this. None of the antiviral organics have made any difference at all on this variant. At least with Novel Red Fever I could slow it down."

"If it makes you feel better, Frank, we're in the same boat with the synthetics. It's just the process," Jack said, taking a swig of beer. "Hell, we're all still learning about what the damn disease does. Nobody's expecting you to be a hero."

"*You know*, maybe that's part of the problem, Jack," I snapped. "Nobody seems to be in much of a hurry to do anything about this at all. How long do you really think Red Fever and this new variant are going to stay on the other side of The Citadel wall?"

Jack's blue eyes widened as a smile pulled at the corners of his mouth.

He started to lean in to reply, but was cut off.

"All right," Scott said with a long sigh. "Box!" he gestured to the wait-disc, which delivered a leftovers holder almost immediately. "If you were thinking about throwing your beer in his face, Frankie, you're out," he added, pressing his thumb into the print reader next to him to pay for our food. He slid my burger and what was left of my fries into the box as I looked at my glass, surprised that it really was empty. I didn't even *like* beer. Scott glanced down at me as he got to his feet. "Ready?"

I shrugged and nodded, then stood up too.

"I hope you get some sleep, Frankie," Anita said. "And don't worry, I'll take care of this one for you," she added with another elbow to Jack's chest.

"Ow! What?" he asked, laughing. "I wasn't going to say anything."

"Take the morning off, Frankie. You clearly already put in the time," Blake said sincerely. "I'll get the intake file ready for you on the cadaver."

I nodded to him and tried to smile a little, but I was still so frustrated with both of their apathy. "Thanks. I'll see you after lunch, then," I managed, and rose to leave.

It happened that fast—just long enough for me to turn my back to the bar I'd been facing a second before. I heard the deafening crash first...the glass breaking. And finally, the screams.

Chapter 3

I didn't have time to take a step toward the door. I didn't even have time to turn around to see what caused the sudden commotion. One minute I was upright, and the next, I was under the table huddled with Scott, Anita, Jack, and Blake. People were running toward the exit, but apparently they weren't getting out very quickly.

"What's happening?" I raised my voice above the screams. Anita turned to me, all the blood having drained from her face. Her eyes were wide and vacant as she opened her mouth several times to speak, but each time, she just wound up closing it again. Rivers of tears streamed down her cheeks as Jack held her close to him.

"I don't know, but we need to get out of here..." Jack said, looking around frantically. "We'll never get out the front."

More crashing glasses, breaking furniture, and in addition to the screaming, a growling, guttural noise that sent a chill through my entire body.

Something heavy hit the top of our table, which made Anita cover her mouth with both hands.

Scott started to move out from under the table, but stopped when a broken bottle covered in blood crashed onto the floor just beyond us. Anita's scream ripped through her clasped hands, and we all scrambled to our feet toward the door.

"Go to the kitchen! Out the back!" Blake shouted as we tried to make our way through the crowd of people who were either running or fighting.

More crashing. More glass breaking. More screaming. It was all blending together.

In the reflection of the mirror behind the bar, I saw the new bartender's face, his mouth spilling blood onto his yellow shirt. He easily threw off the men trying to restrain him, but it took a little more jostling for me to see that his mouth wasn't bloody because he'd been hit with anything. The blood came from the throat of the motionless man he kept *biting*.

"This way!" Scott pushed through the crowd, making a path to the kitchen where a few cooks were already running. We followed them through the back door, which led to the alley. They scattered, and we made our way toward the other end of the street, opposite the people pouring from Ivy's entrance.

It was only a short run back to the lab. We locked the front doors behind us and crouched behind the reception desk.

Jack tapped his temple and within seconds, the police queue displayed in front of his face, but it was just static.

"What is your emergency?" a woman's voice said, even though there was no picture.

"Ivy's!" Jack nearly yelled. "The bartender there went crazy! He killed someone!"

"We have officers and droid units already in route, sir. Are you currently at that location?"

"No, we got out."

"Do you need medical attention at your location?"

"No, we're OK. Just get to Ivy's!" Jack said, then lowered his hand to disconnect the queue.

Anita crumpled into him and began crying. Scott and I exchanged glances.

"What just happened back there?" he asked everyone.

"The bartender looked normal..." I said, not sure what, other than being well on his way to becoming Feral, could have enabled someone to do that—to tear someone's throat out...to throw grown men halfway across the bar.

"He must have had some kind of psychotic break," Blake pushed his hands through his curly red hair and blew out a long breath.

"It's all right," Jack said, trying to comfort Anita. "The police are probably already there."

I turned to Blake. "Or he just wasn't manifesting the physical signs of stage four yet."

Jack fired a steely glare. "He looked like he was fully fucking manifested to me! Didn't you see the *trachea* he was pulling out, Frankie?" he barked, which made Anita sob even harder. "I'm sorry...it's all right. I'm sorry," he said, patting her hair and holding her closer.

"That's exactly what I'm talking about! He's infected. He has to be. I'm going back," I said, standing up.

Scott grabbed my wrist. "Are you nuts?"

"If he's that violent and hasn't even mutated yet..." I trailed off. "If that level of violence starts before the visible physical changes, people need to know. We need to quarantine him."

"Do you think you're just going to walk back in there and ask him to follow you back to the lab here? Maybe record a little Q & A with your lens feed as you chat on the way?" Blake gaped at me. "There will be droids and live patrols everywhere. You won't be able to get a word in, let alone a foot back in those doors."

"There's only one way to find out," I said, making my way outside.

"Frankie!" Scott shouted. "Goddamnit!"

"I'll be all right!" I keyed in my door code and pushed through the turnstile. The sidewalks were crowded with onlookers, and a barricade was in the process of being set up around Ivy's from what I could see a few blocks away. I started running toward it.

I turned down the alley we'd come through on the way out, which, miraculously, hadn't been closed off yet.

"Frankie! Wait!" Scott called from behind me.

I looked over my shoulder and saw that he was a few yards back. "What are you doing?"

"Having a heart attack at the moment," he gasped.

"How are you so in shape and so out of shape at the same time?"

"Because I never have to sprint down the block with dumbbells, Frankie," he huffed, bending to grip his knees. I rolled my eyes and pulled the back door to Ivy's open. "Hey!" Scott shouted after me.

"What? Hurry up with your asthma attack then!" I called back and went inside with Scott a few feet behind me.

There was no more crashing or screaming coming from the dining area. The kitchen was deserted, but nothing seemed in disarray beyond how the cooks had left everything in mid-prep.

I inched toward the window of the swinging door, but quickly abandoned my plans to peek through it when I saw it was opaque with blood. My stomach lurched.

"This is a bad idea," Scott said, pushing the handle of a long kitchen knife into my hand. He pulled a cleaver from the blade block on the counter behind us and moved to the side of the opposite swinging door. We inched the doors open at the same time and when there was just enough space, we darted to the edge of the bar and crouched low.

Live patrol officers were taking pictures of the massacre while several Sweeper droid units were calculating the trajectories *of the body parts*, based on the green laser arc geometry and maps taking shape in the air above our heads.

"Holy shit..." Scott exhaled, then covered his mouth with his hand. Behind the bar, pools of blood and I didn't even know what else covered the floor, but there was no trace of the bartender, dead or alive.

"He must be gone," I whispered.

"Just when I thought this couldn't get worse. We are *not* going to try to find him, Frankie," Scott said, his voice sharp and urgent.

"I know that. I'm not stupid! We'll have to try to get back to the lab." We only waited another few seconds before trying to make our way back through the swinging kitchen doors, but we weren't quick enough.

"Hey—stay there!" one of the live patrol officers called to us. We almost started to run, but two Sweeper droids rounded on us and flashed a still scan, which momentarily blinded me.

"Dr. Scott Julian Jeffries, Dr. Francesca Leigh Mason, please remain calm." The Sweeper droid's deep masculine voice was comforting at the same time it was a little intimidating. "Please remain still as I scan for injuries."

"*Julian*?" I whispered to Scott. He closed his eyes in a long, exasperated blink and took in a deep breath.

"No critical injuries found," the Sweeper droid continued.

"You two were in here when all this went down?" a mustached officer asked, sliding a narrow camera into his shirt pocket. We nodded. "Want to tell me what the hell happened?"

"Thank you, Officer Roarke." A tall, lean woman with cropped, dark hair came out of nowhere and moved quickly past the officer. "It's all right. You're both safe now. I'm Eve Adams, Crisis Management. Let's get you out of here."

"Yes, we were actually…just trying to leave," Scott said, taking a step toward the swinging kitchen doors.

"OK, we'll go that way," Eve nodded and gestured for two of the live patrols to go ahead of us.

"No, I mean, we're fine. We don't need escorts or anything." Scott held up a hand to the advancing officers. "We're just going to go home."

Eve smiled gently at him like Anita smiled at Jack—a smile that said what a really excellent effort he'd just made with putting all his words in order correctly.

"Of course, of course," Eve said softly. "We'll make sure we get you home right away." Scott and I exchanged glances as the officers moved several steps in front of us, each of them opening a swinging door. Another officer followed behind us.

"You're taking us *home*, right?" I pressed.

"Yes, we're just going to get some coffee into you first and make sure you're..." she trailed off and glanced at the tablet she pulled from the pocket of her tailored jacket. "...and make sure you're not too traumatized to return to work at the pathology lab," she added, smiling that kindergarten teacher smile again.

"Like he said, we're fine. We just want—" I tried to insist.

Scott sighed. "Save your breath, Frank. Either we go with her and pass whatever test she wants us to take so The Citadel isn't liable for us potentially offing ourselves from untreated PTSD or something, or she puts us on a medical suspension and hospitalizes us until we pass it."

"How do you know that?" I asked, looking back and forth from him to Eve. "How does he know that? Is that true?"

Again with the kindergarten teacher smile and *this* time, complete with wrinkled forehead and doe eyes. "I'm afraid so," she said with a little nod. *Of course* there was a little nod.

Scott glared at me as the officers escorted us out of the building to a waiting patrol car in the alley.

Chapter 4

After an impossibly long psychological evaluation at the police station, Scott and I were finally taken home. I scanned all the newsfeed links as soon as I was alone and again the second I woke up, but there was nothing about what happened at Ivy's last night. I flipped through one newsfeed after another the whole way to the lab and didn't hear a single word about this latest attack.

I walked into Blake's office at five after twelve not knowing exactly what to expect, but it definitely wasn't his crooked smile.

"You look rested," he said sarcastically.

"I could say the same for you. How long were you here last night?"

Blake looked around the room conspiratorially. "Well, by the time I was able to hack into the medical feeds—"

"Wait, what? You can do that?" I interrupted.

He just blinked stupidly at me a few times. "It wasn't long before they uploaded your *psych* eval clearances, so at least we knew you two hadn't become human piñatas...which was nice," he said, smiling genuinely this time. "But it was too late to go home given everything that had happened, so we slept on the couches in my office. Jack took Anita home this morning. He just got back."

"How are they?"

"He's fine. She's as good as can be expected. Rattled, but..." he shrugged.

"Did they catch him? The bartender?" I asked. "He wasn't there when Scott and I went back... There's nothing on the feeds, which is odd."

"Couldn't tell you," Blake said absently. "I'm too exhausted to care right now." I must have stared blankly at him a beat too long because after another few seconds, he abruptly started talking again. "Oh! I was going to give you those intake documents." He started tapping away on his keyboard and scanning his screen. It was curved to meet his peripheral vision, so I couldn't even glance at what he was sorting through. "Here we go. Just sent it to your station. Let me know if you have any questions," Blake added. "Now, if you'll excuse me, I forgot to cancel a lunch date, and now it's too late," he said, his rusty eyebrows drawing together in mock pain.

I nodded awkwardly. "Thanks again, Blake."

"No problem." He hung up his lab coat, and I followed him out of his office. He shut the door behind us and disappeared down the window-lit corridor while I veered off to my part of the lab to see what our cadaver's intake file said.

I looked into the retinal scanner and once it unlocked, I navigated to my inbox. As promised, the file was at the top of the new messages. I blinked twice while staring at the file in order to open it, then waited for the pages to arrange themselves in augmented reality. When they were finished, I reached into the screen and pulled out the file to flip through.

The first page had the standard legacy chip information.

Name: Marcus Donovan DOB: March 18, 2099
Natural Expiration Date: June 29, 2184
Legacy Debt: 17 years 9 months
Actual Death: May 11, 2126
No Next of Kin.

"Is that the Donovan file?" Scott asked, crossing to me from the pathology side of the lab.

"Yeah. Sorry, I didn't see you over there," I answered. "How are you?"

"Tired," he said, giving me a long side eye.

I winced. "Sorry about that whole thing. I shouldn't have gone back there."

"Ya think?"

I smiled. "So, next time, dinner is on me. Though, obviously Ivy's will be out of commission for a while."

"You didn't see the feeds, huh?"

"No, there's nothing. I've been scanning all morning. I would have gone down there but I woke up too late."

"That's just it," Scott said. "There's not a word about it, and the place is open today. Spotless inside. I went down there about an hour ago. It's like nothing happened."

"That's impossible…" I said, touching my temple to bring up the channel feeds again. One after the other was still nothing but advertisements, sports, and the newsfeeds that *were* reporting were posting weather updates and stock trades. "*How*? Why are they burying this? Who cleaned all that up?"

"Blake thinks it's damage control. People are already on edge about the Feral reports outside the gates," Scott said, taking a seat next to me. "Something like this would ruin local businesses. Nobody would leave their flats."

"But people were there last night. They'll talk."

"Maybe what, fifty people out of how many thousand live inside the wall?" Scott raised a dark eyebrow.

"Someone had to record what happened on their ocular lens," I added, tapping my temple again to pull up the social media widgets. Scott waved a hand in front of my face, which made me blink before I could pull up the digital projection.

"Don't bother—I checked all the Authorized platforms," Scott handed me a coffee. "If anything was there, it was scrubbed as fast as it went up."

"Someone is dead, Scott! And the guy who did it is apparently still out there."

"I know, calm down." He said, then lowered his voice. "I was there too, remember? Maybe Blake is right and they're just handling it all quietly."

"People need to know there's a threat out there—here, inside the wall! That had to be a Feral attack, Scott."

"We have no evidence that the bartender was a Feral." Scott shook his head. "For all we know, he just snapped under the pressure of his first night on the job. Easy enough to see that with Nick and Therese already out of patience when we got there. And no, before you get any ideas, they're not at Ivy's today. I checked."

"Did you ask about them? How are they?"

"They only had a droid staff. No live service today."

"Well, that's understandable." I nodded. "Did you recognize anyone there last night? Any friends we can call?"

Scott shook his head. "We weren't there too long. The only people I noticed were Nick and Therese."

"OK, well, we can't be the only people who are—"

"Frankie." Scott held up a hand. "Can we just let it go? Yeah, it's some trash that they're massaging it all like this, but I get why. There would be mass panic."

"There *should* be mass panic, Scott. There's a murderer walking around out there somewhere who might be our only chance at breaking the code on Red Fever."

"Or," Scott held out both hands like he was presenting me with something. "They already have him in a nice, padded box." He smiled. "So since that's a possible thing in the world *too*, and we'll never know one way or the other, can we just get back to work now? You know, stuff we can actually control? What's happening with the Donovan sheet?"

I sighed. "The only thing I've noticed in the five seconds I've had it up so far is that he died a few months after his twenty-seventh birthday."

Scott blanched as he read the file over my shoulder. "Almost eighteen years in legacy debt? I thought he got a scholarship to The Citadel?"

"Could have been medical bills? Lawyers? Maybe he was a gambler, who knows?" I said, sliding him the virtual cover page. "And no next of kin listed. Says here he started at The Citadel on a conditional scholarship—he had to apply every year? Why would they only give him a year at a time?"

Scott shrugged. "He was from The Grind, right? Maybe they're all admitted conditionally."

I shook my head and glared at him. "They're *not* all admitted conditionally. I've never heard of anything like that. Especially not to the Engineering school. If they're not sure about you, they just don't take you."

The next page was very sparse. Just a few records of medical procedures, but they weren't performed by an Authorized medic, so there was no record of where he'd gone for the service.

"Unauthorized medical fines could be part of that legacy debt. But otherwise, it looks like he was pretty healthy," Scott observed. "Just a few shoulder dislocations and some nicks and dents. He was a dock worker?"

"Yeah, here it is," I said, flipping the virtual page. "He worked for six years on the docks right outside The Citadel exterior gates."

Scott furrowed his brow. "What about his secondary school registry?"

"Says he stopped in his third year at Portland Prep. But that's—"

"Hang on," Scott interrupted. "So he goes from being a dropout to being a longshoreman to getting a *scholarship* to The Citadel's *engineering* school?"

I nodded. "I think some of his file must be missing. Did the Sweeper droid's bullet damage his legacy chip at all?"

"Not according to the coroner's report," Scott answered. I turned quickly to look at him over my shoulder. He blinked at me for a second before vehemently shaking his head. "No, Frankie. It's impossible. It's been six months. Who knows if they still even have it down there."

"There's only one way to find out," I said with a smile.

"I really hate when you say that," Scott grumbled as I closed the intake file and logged off, then headed down to the morgue.

Chapter 5

It was much too cold for comfort in the morgue and smelled equally of ammonia and nauseatingly sweet air freshener. The cement floor was polished, and the overhead fluorescents were as unforgiving of the living as they were the dead.

"Hi, I'm looking for information on someone named Marcus Donovan. He came in about six months ago," I said to the gaunt man who was just closing one of the wall units. I marveled for the briefest second at how his chin, ears, even his fingertips all seemed to end in a taper like some kind of wraith. The irony wasn't lost on me, and I stifled a smile.

"And you are?" the man answered in a surprisingly low voice that was just as sharp as his features.

"Sorry, Doctor Francesca Mason, Botanicals Consult to the CPC," I answered, holding up the ID at the end of my lanyard.

He eyeballed it from where he was standing and looked me up and down.

"And what is it that you want to know about Mr. Donovan?" he asked, turning to walk in the opposite direction. I followed him.

"Well, I know the cause of death was a shot to his brain, but—"

"Actually…" the man said, as he typed away at a standing desk in the corner of this steel and concrete dungeon. He didn't say anything else for several long, awkward seconds. I cleared my throat, but still, the wraith said nothing.

"I didn't catch your name?" I said, just because the silence was making me crazy.

"That's because I didn't give it to you." The man didn't look up from his typing as he answered, and I closed my eyes in a long blink to keep from rolling them. I guess small talk was the first thing to go when you hung around dead people all day.

"All right, well, if you'd *like* to give it, I'm all ears," I said, stupidly.

He sighed. "Crenshaw, Charles."

"Charles…"

"Or Mr. Crenshaw," he said, still without looking at me.

"Mr. Crenshaw…" I repeated. Good Lord, how long was this going to go on? "You have quite the memory then, Mr. Crenshaw. You remember the details of a cadaver from six months ago just from the name…"

"This one was hard to forget, as I'm sure you already know, Dr. Mason," Crenshaw said, still typing so slowly it was all I could do to not crawl out of my skin watching him. "Here we go…" he finally said.

"Oh good, you found him?"

"No," Crenshaw added. I pressed my teeth together and forced a closed-lip smile. He still didn't look up at me before he went on. "Something else. The Donovan file is already up in Pathology."

"*What*?" I asked, struggling to keep the exasperation out of my voice. "Why didn't you just tell me that when I asked the first time?"

Crenshaw typed like each of his fingers had to recharge on the upstroke of pushing a single key. "You asked for information," he said. "Not the file."

I took a deep breath. "Right… You were about to say something about his cause of death? It wasn't the bullet to the brain?" I asked in the most neutral possible voice I could muster given that I was about fifteen seconds from screaming at the top of my lungs.

"That's right. It was a heart attack," Crenshaw said.

"A heart attack after he was shot in the head?" I narrowed my eyes in disbelief, and at this, Crenshaw finally stopped typing.

He stared at me blankly, his sunken eyes and cheeks catching every shadow in the fluorescent light. "He had the heart attack just before he was shot in the head."

I almost asked him how he could possibly know something like that, but then I remembered Donovan's legacy chip. "You must have cross-referenced the timestamp of the Sweeper droid's shot with the legacy chip's last second?"

Crenshaw's thin lips twitched, which I took as a smile. "You might have a future in the morgue, Dr. Mason."

I raised an eyebrow at him. "Someday far off, I hope, so long as I stay out of debt and oncoming traffic," I laughed. Crenshaw's infinitesimal smile withered…like my soul for every second I spent talking with this man. "Anyway," I began again. "I guess that means his legacy chip was intact? No damage from the bullet?"

"Clearly," Crenshaw answered, his expression unchanging.

"All right, well thanks for your time then. Just one more thing? You didn't happen to get anyone in here since last night with a…throat wound, did you? Or maybe a smallish guy in a yellow shirt with blood all over his mouth?" Crenshaw stared at me without so much as an eyebrow flinch. I nodded slowly. "All right, well, I'll just go find the chip records for the rest of what I need on Donovan then. Thanks again," I said, trying to hold the smile I'd been forcing.

Where was the body from last night? And why hadn't Blake just given me Donovan's legacy chip report along with the intake paperwork if it was already up in Pathology? I wondered on my way back to the lab. Blake wasn't back yet when I checked his office, but Jack darted behind me and grabbed his lab coat from the rack.

"Hey, Frank. Thanks for not getting eviscerated last night. That was super thoughtful of you."

"Sorry," I said sheepishly. "I was sure that bartender must have been in some pre-Feral stage. He was gone by the time we got back to Ivy's, though. You OK? How's Anita?" I asked, scanning again for Blake.

"I'm fine. She's better. I gave her some anxiety meds," Jack replied.

I nodded at him. "Don't you think it's strange there's nothing on the feeds about any of it? And Scott said that Ivy's is open today. Completely cleaned up like nothing happened."

Jack nodded. "Well, yeah, damage control. Bad press like that right now would be more dangerous than some rando psychopath who couldn't pour vodka."

"I don't think that's all he was, Jack."

"Which you made abundantly clear when you ran back there like a completely different, yet equitable psychopath." He smirked. "Anyway, what are you doing in this neck of Hell?"

I smiled at his surly comment. "I need to get the rest of the paperwork on this cadaver. Blake gave me the intake file for Donovan. I just need the legacy chip report from him. Do you know where it is?" I said, looking at Blake's wraparound computer monitor.

"Uh, well..." Jack followed my eyes to the desk. "Maybe." He went into Blake's office and logged onto his computer with a retina scan. "Donovan, you said? First name, Marcus?"

"Right, that's him," I answered.

After a few seconds of typing, and then a few more, Jack nodded. "Sent it to your station," he said, logging off Blake's computer.

"Great, thanks!"

Jack waved me off and walked back to his station. I rushed back to mine to check the legacy chip file. Scott caught my eyes as I darted behind my keyboard.

"That was fast. How did you get anything that quickly from Crenshaw?" he asked, rolling his chair over to my computer.

"You know *Crenshaw*?"

"Well, yeah, unfortunately. Two years as a pathology intern whipping boy means you get all the gopher errands."

"Oh," I laughed under my breath. "Actually, the legacy chip report was already here in pathology. Blake just didn't give it to me when he gave me the rest of the intake file for some reason," I said, pulling up my messages. "Here it is."

I opened the report and scanned through the credit logs, then the immunity reports where I would be able to see every cold, every allergic reaction—basically anything that might make a blip on his predicted lifespan.

"What are we looking for?" Scott asked, leaning in.

"I don't know. If we assume he went Feral eight hours after exposure, he got infected…wait, where is it?" I asked out loud when I didn't see any interruption in his immune system logs from six months ago. "There's nothing there?" I kept scrolling back until a drastic dip in levels appeared. "Oh my God," I looked up at Scott. "*Three years?*"

"That's impossible," Scott looked more intently at the graph. "That has to be a rendering error."

"No, look," I turned back to the display and clicked on the first dip in the graph. "August second, 2119. See how the trend line is about even all the way back through his life? But on August second everything jumps up to this new trend, where it stayed until he was shot and killed."

"Frankie…" Scott laughed.

"Marcus Donovan was Feral for three years, Scott." I met his dark, squinting eyes. "He was about to graduate from The Citadel then, right? Maybe he had an internship after that too," I said, returning to scroll through Marcus Donovan's purchase records and life credits. "Two days' credit? What's that?" I asked, pointing to the screen.

"Looks like an *acts of nature credit*," Scott answered. "I don't remember any storms that claimed casualties in the last few years, though."

I shook my head. "No, I do remember. There were two attacks in The Grind on the same night about three years ago. It was the first time there had been more than one in the same day, remember? Scott, do you know what this means?"

Scott looked at me blankly for a second, but then realization dawned on him. "Wait, yeah. That was in The Borrower's Report. We all got that ten-day credit because neither of those victims had any next of kin."

"No! Scott—"

"What? Don't you read The Borrower's Report?" Scott asked.

"*No*," I said with a shudder. "That thing creeps me out. I'm going to die when I'm going to die. I don't want to know when it's coming. But look—"

"Wait, you don't know your expiration date? I thought you had to borrow credits to pay for your last year of tuition?" Scott asked. "That's five years from your life right there."

"I don't know, OK? They said social percentage for being a civil servant will take care of it." I said. "But that doesn't matter. Scott, this mutation has been around for three years, not six months like we thought. This changes everything."

"How?"

"Because! It means all those attacks outside the wall the past three years really have been Feral attacks. Maybe there can be *acts of nature* credits or whatever paid to those families since—wait, what's this?" I pointed to a line near the bottom of the screen. "I keep seeing this vendor pop up. Raphael's... Why do I know that name? Whoa…" I counted the number of times the name *Raphael's* appeared. "Donovan had *sixteen* charges from this place, all in the six months before he died. Isn't Raphael's the name of the tea place they put in the old bakery?"

"I think so," Scott said. "So he liked tea. A lot, I guess."

"He spent a year of his life in legacy credits on *tea*?" I asked, incredulous as I did the math. "Who puts *tea* on credit?"

"Nobody, but apparently he was a regular," Scott said. We exchanged glances. "Frankie, no."

I smiled at him. "Got plans for after work today?"

Chapter 6

Scott and I finished our shift at 5:00 p.m. and hung up our lab coats. We were nearly to the elevator when we heard Blake calling after us.

"You're both clearing out early today," he said.

"It's five—that's not early," I replied, turning around to face him. "That's how late we're scheduled."

"For you two, on time is early," Blake chuckled. "What's the occasion?"

"For what?" I asked a little too abruptly. I felt my throat tightening as Blake's nearly invisible brows twitched, but I wasn't sure what I was trying to hide. So what if I wanted to follow up on Donovan's last hours pre-infection? "I mean, we're just..." I trailed off.

"It's our anniversary," Scott said, quickly slipping an arm over my shoulder. My blood ran cold. *What did he just say?* I forced a static smile to conceal the shock that I knew had to be all over my face.

Blake's furrowed brow relaxed and his eyes widened. "*Oh...*" he said, more than a little surprised, but at least it put a hard stop to his small talk.

"Yeah, one whole day—it's official," Scott said. Blake's brows furrowed again. "One...*day?*"

Scott shrugged. "We wanted to wait until my internship was finalized before making anything official. You know how people talk. And then with everything last night…it just wasn't the right time to say anything." He nodded for emphasis.

"*Right*. Yes, makes sense," Blake gaped at us like a naked parade was tromping through the lobby just behind us. "Well, congratulations," he added, seeming to settle into the new parallel universe he'd found himself in. I wished I could say the same for myself.

"Right, so, *honey*… We should go if you want to make it to the tea shop you love so much," Scott said, giving my shoulder a squeeze. I laughed through a stiff smile.

Blake looked at me, surprised. "Tea? Well, now I know what to get you for Christmas," he added with a decisive nod.

I forced a laugh and put my arm around Scott's waist, digging my fingers into his ribs. "All righty, well, I'll look forward to that. See you tomorrow, Blake!" I said, turning to leave before this small talk *in fact* killed me. Scott was vibrating with laughter the entire way out of the building. "I actually hate you. What the hell was that?" I said as the elevator closed behind us. "Have you lost your mind?"

"Sorry, it's the first thing I thought of to shut down his questions."

"That's what came to mind first? A one-day anniversary?" I closed my eyes, still partly in denial. "How about it's your niece's birthday and you wanted my help picking out a present? Or I'm selling you a couch and you're picking it up today?"

"Selling me a couch? That's better than this is our one-day anniversary?" Scott asked, giving me the longest blink that mankind has ever recorded.

I heaved a sigh as the elevator doors opened, and we made our way to the street to hail a car.

Scott and I managed to snag a driverless hover car, which had just been rolled out for public use in The Citadel.

"Yes!" Scott said as the car slowed. "I've been wanting to try one of these."

"Good timing, too," I added. "I think the tea place is going to close soon."

The door of the silver hover car slid open seamlessly for us, then slid closed behind us.

"What do we do?" Scott asked. "Just tell it where to go?"

"Thank you for choosing Norstar. Where can I take you?" Scott and I exchanged impressed glances at the disembodied female voice.

"Raphael's, please," I said.

"Raphael's Imported and Exotic Tea on Tempest Boulevard; is this your destination?" the car's voice asked.

"Yes," Scott answered, turning to me with a goofy grin.

"Please secure your safety belts and your trip will begin," the car prompted. Scott and I both sighed and fastened our seatbelts.

The car started moving, but I only knew that because everything around us started moving. To sit in the car itself felt like we were still parked on the curb.

"I'm definitely never taking the metro taxi again," Scott said, leaning back into the smooth interior, which seemed like it was actually starting to warm. "This thing is heated!"

I chuckled at his excitement, but looking out the window at the people walking by—especially the particularly athletic man who had just entered a building—I could only think about which of them was either the next victim of Red Fever, or the next Feral.

The front door to Raphael's was behind a tall, iron gate surrounded by carefully landscaped, flowering trees and bushes that lined the path to the entryway. Inside, we were met with the intoxicating smell of spices and citrus, which I'd assumed was from the large baskets of loose tea leaves directly in front of us. That is, until I noticed two large orange trees with white flowers in bloom on either side of the door.

Flowering pots and climbing vines lined the perimeter of the small sitting area to our right. Some of the vines even seemed to be dotted with differently colored berries. Dwarf trees stood in the corners with small, dark red fruits, and prints of sunbursts over mountain ranges decorated the walls. We followed a large, burgundy rug to the inviting stretch of tea-filled baskets and looked around for an attendant.

Scott pointed out a little table in the seating area to our right, and we took off our coats.

It couldn't have been a full minute before an elderly Chinese woman approached us with two narrow, red menus.

"Welcome to Raphael's Tea House," the woman said in a soft, but enthusiastic voice.

"It's beautiful in here," I told her, almost overcome by all the foliage.

The woman smiled again and lowered her eyes. "We try to make a paradise for you. Specials today are house mandarin blend—very good for clarity," she said with a nod to me. "And pomegranate ginseng." She leaned in and whispered conspiratorially to Scott. "Very good for *stamina*." She winked. Scott's face flushed.

"The specials sound wonderful," I said before Scott could protest. "We'll have those."

His eyes widened at me, and I had to stifle a laugh. The older Chinese woman's face lit up just before she gave us a little bow.

"Cute," Scott said, giving me a deadpan look once she left.

"Hey, after what you pulled back there with Blake, fair is fair," I said, taking in the surroundings. "*Look* at this place. I wonder how they keep up with all the watering it must take. And look at the skylight!"

Above us, the center of the ceiling was a giant antique window, the sun pouring through it so brightly I could only look at it for a few seconds. "This place is awfully big just for a few tables and that storefront, don't you think?" I asked, remembering the outside of the building.

Scott scanned the rest of the seating area and the front counter. "I suppose. There must be a little kitchen or something back there—maybe even an apartment."

I nodded as the Chinese woman returned with a tray holding a few cups and two small pots. She placed the darker pot in front of Scott, and I could already smell the citrus coming from the one she set in front of me.

"This has mandarin in it you said?" I asked.

The woman gave me a small nod and smiled. "House secret blend."

Scott inhaled the steam from his pot. "These smell amazing."

"Wait until you taste." The woman poured the first cup for each of us out of our respective pots, and after a beat, she made a gesture for us to drink.

I hadn't been much of a tea drinker, but that was all about to change. The taste was several times more intense than the smell, and after just one sip, I felt more awake than I had in weeks. It was like all my senses had only been on half power before now.

"Wow." Scott met my eyes, his dark brows raised in surprise too. He looked at the tea in his cup, confused before turning back to me. "That's good," he said, evidently at a loss for more words.

"Enjoy." The Chinese woman smiled, her silver hair shifting in the bun she wore as she gave us another small bow.

"Yes, it's the best tea I've ever had. Could I buy a pound of this to take home?" I asked. She nodded, and with another small bow, turned to go to the front counter where the baskets of tea were displayed. "Oh, but could I ask you a question first?"

She turned back to me. "Of course."

I pulled out my tablet and found the Portland docks ID picture of Marcus Donovan, pre-transformation, from his file. His face was lean, but his long neck and muscular shoulders suggested he was wiry rather than skinny.

"Do you remember this customer?" I asked, showing the woman the picture. Her delicate smile withered slowly, but she didn't look away for several seconds. When she did, her smile bloomed again disingenuously.

"Sorry, no," she said, a quick bow this time as she turned to leave.

"Wait, please," I called after her. "He came in here all the time and bought tea. Are you sure?"

The woman looked at me intently for another several seconds, her lips fixed in a smile. Finally, she seemed to decide something, and her careful smile softened as she glanced again at the picture.

"Ah, yes, of course," she said, quickly this time. "Very sunny boy. Green sunshine blend—good mood tea—his favorite."

"Did you know anything about him?" I asked, but she just shook her head and bowed yet again before heading back to the counter. I glanced at Scott and blew out a breath. "What does that even mean, *a very sunny boy*?"

"That he was happy?" Scott shrugged. "She said he liked their *good mood* tea."

I picked up the menu to see if I could find the name. Surprisingly, it wasn't listed. "There's nothing called *Green Sunshine blend* on this menu," I said, looking up at Scott.

"I'll find out." He got up and went back to the counter, but the old woman wasn't there anymore. In her place, a younger Chinese woman stood arranging the different sachets near the register.

"You had the pound of House Special tea?" she asked him, and it took him a second to process what she'd said.

"Oh, right. No," he answered, then gestured at me. "I mean, yes, and the two pots there." He pressed his thumb into the credit reader. I started to protest, but he ignored me. "Hey, do you have a tea called—"

"Hi, sorry," I interrupted. "Could you take a look at something for me?" I crossed quickly to the counter and showed the younger woman Marcus Donovan's profile picture. "You don't know this man, do you?"

The woman looked at the picture for several seconds with a furrowed brow like she was trying to place him. "I think that's the guy who used to do our deliveries?" She smiled coyly at Scott, and if I didn't know better, I'd think she was actually flirting with him.

"Do you know about how long ago that was—I mean, the last time you saw him?" I pressed.

The younger woman looked up in thought for a second before she looked back at Scott. "I don't know, a few years ago I think?"

"All right, thank you very—" Scott started, but I cut him off again.

"Do you know why he stopped working here?" The young woman pulled back a little, but didn't have a chance to answer before the older woman came out from behind a curtain I hadn't noticed before. She fired a barrage of words in Chinese at the younger woman, who quickly scurried behind the curtain. The older woman bowed several times to Scott and said several more things in Chinese to him, to which he politely smiled and nodded.

"Thank you for coming to Raphael's," she said to us with a tight smile, then she pushed the bag of tea at Scott. She nodded a few times, and with one last small bow, returned behind the curtain.

Scott shook his head, and suddenly, the exotic plants surrounding us seemed to make everything feel claustrophobic. We quickly left the shop.

"What was all that about? You speak Chinese?" I asked as I scanned for a car to hail.

Scott pushed out his bottom lip. "I mean, my skills spoke for themselves I think?" he said, grinning.

A car finally pulled over for us, this one, unfortunately, not the hover variety.

"Where to?" the driver asked.

Scott nudged me, but my mind was racing with questions about the tea shop and why Marcus Donovan suddenly stopped working there—why the old woman tried to pretend she'd never seen him before, and how he was even working there to begin with if he was supposed to be studying full time at The Citadel.

"Who's the owner of that tea shop?" I asked the driver, who would likely know all the news inside The Citadel walls. He looked at me curiously in the rearview mirror.

"Who owns *Raphael*'s tea shop?" he asked with a snicker. "Probably Raphael."

I sighed. "The gate wasn't there a few years ago. Something changed, come on."

The driver shrugged. "Beats me. I'm a coffee person."

Scott rolled his eyes. "We can just go home. We tried, right?"

"Not yet," I answered. "Let's go to the engineering complex. Maybe we'll find out something there."

Chapter 7

It was well after dark by the time we got to the engineering complex, and all the tech labs were surely closed.

"So, your plan is to show a dead guy's picture around and see if anyone knew why he was making deliveries for the tea place," Scott stated more than asked, then thought for a second. "Frankie, who cares? What does it have to do with him turning Feral?"

"Because it might tell us where he got infected," I answered. "Why is this such a stretch?" I pulled my tablet back out and found Marcus Donovan's picture again as we approached the door to the engineering complex.

Scott slowed. "It's just weird for us to be showing up six months after the guy's been dead to ask questions about him."

"Do you have a better way of finding out how he got infected?" I asked, stopping just before we opened the large, glass door to the complex. Scott opened his mouth to say something, but then shut it again and took a deep breath.

"After you," he said, resigning to open the door. I smiled at him.

The engineering complex was surprisingly warmer than the medical complex. Colorful geometric paintings hung on the walls and overstuffed couches and chairs surrounded a fireplace at the far end of the foyer to our right. A few people were sitting on the furniture reading as we approached the young woman behind the reception desk.

She made eye contact and gave us a wide, plastic smile. "Can I help you?"

"We're from Medical," I said, trying to return her smile. "And we're working on leads to help us with a research issue. Do you remember this man?" I showed her the picture of Donovan.

"I think that's Marcus Donovan." The woman nodded. "Is he back now?"

"Back from where?" I asked.

The woman blinked at us. "Field assignment somewhere abroad I think. He left like, three years ago." She tried to smile, but her wary gaze kept darting from Scott to me and back again.

"Who told you he was abroad?" I asked.

"The registrar from the engineering school," the woman said, her smile melting. "So we could reissue his room. Is something wrong?"

I darted a glance at Scott.

"How did he get a field assignment before graduating?" I asked.

The woman's face went blank. "Uh, well... It's usually the result of an industry request," she said, looking from me to Scott. "At least in engineering. He must have impressed his boss."

"His boss? He had a job here?" I asked, surprised.

The woman nodded. "Not here. He did some handyman work at the Wu Fong Pharmaceuticals building. Do you know when he's coming back?"

Scott pressed his lips together, neither of us apparently knowing how to answer this one.

"Thank you for your time," I said to the woman with a nod.

Scott gave her a gentle smile. "I'm sure someone will be in touch."

We left the engineering building and started walking the few blocks to the medical staff apartments. My head started aching all over again.

"What Citadel student has time for not just one part time job, but two?" I asked, shaking my head.

Scott sighed. "I was just wondering the same thing. I've barely had time to keep up with my labs. Maybe it was a work-study?"

"A handyman work-study at a *pharmaceuticals* building? For an *engineering* major?" I narrowed my eyes. "That doesn't make any sense. They would put him to work doing something in his field. He wouldn't be clearing drains and delivering tea." I shook my head again. The ache was starting to build in my temples, which was a clear sign I needed to put this away or I wouldn't be sleeping much tonight.

"Maybe he was trying to pay off his legacy debt," Scott said over my shoulder.

"No. Working as a Citadel engineer would have raked in plenty of social percentage. Maybe even the whole seventeen years he owed."

"Then maybe he was just a restless guy." Scott chuckled. "Are you going all detective on me now?"

"*What*?"

"Frank, come on. We're just trying to find out where he'd been so we could triangulate a point of infection, right?"

"Well, yeah," I said over my shoulder as I crossed the street to the medical staff apartments. "But there's clearly a lot more going on here than Donovan's intake report suggested."

"Frankie!"

Scott gripped my shoulders and threw me to the ground an instant before a black hover car whizzed by. I couldn't even really see it until it slowed down, but then it turned around and came at us again. I scrambled to my feet and ran the final steps to the sidewalk of the building as the hover car made another outrageous pass.

"What the *hell*?" I said, turning to face Scott, whose face was flushed.

"Are you all right?" Anderson, the white-haired building attendant asked, helping us get through the doorway.

"It turned back on us after it missed!" I babbled. "Did you see that? It was like it was *trying* to run us down."

"I don't trust those things," Anderson said, adamantly. "Driverless robot death traps," he mumbled, shuffling to the reception desk to pour some water. "Are you both all right?"

"I'm fine—I wasn't as close to the middle of the street," Scott said, then looked me up and down. "You OK?"

I nodded. "Just a little rattled."

"I'll make a report," Anderson said. He put a finger to his temple, and a few seconds later, the hologram image of an officer appeared in front of him.

"Citadel dispatch, this is Bev," the officer said.

"One of those robot death machines just tried to run over a few doctors. *Doctors*!" Anderson chided. "Do you think we can afford to be light on doctors around here lately?"

"Sir?" Bev questioned, tilting her head in the display. "What robot death machines are you referring to?"

"The cars! Those flying robot cars that drive themselves!" Anderson's voice was sharp and tight.

"Are you referring to hover cars, sir?"

"Yes! That's what I just said. One of them just tried to run them down."

"I see that you're queuing from—no, you stay put, princess," she interrupted herself to look over her shoulder, then turned back to the screen feed. "Sorry, all kinds of strange things going on tonight."

Anderson sighed. "Well, go get that car before it kills someone!"

"I have your address. We'll send a few Sweeper units to the area, sir," Bev said.

"*More* robots!" Anderson shook his head and blinked the display closed. "They think robots are going to fix everything."

"We're all right," Scott said, patting him on the back. I smiled at how things had turned to us comforting Anderson rather than him comforting us. But at least I wasn't rattled anymore.

"If the Sweepers come in here and want a statement, could you just buzz us down?" I asked. Anderson nodded after a beat, his face and throat blotched red.

Scott walked him back to his chair behind the reception desk. "We're *all right*. Just a runaway wire or something no doubt," he added, and I noticed him gripping Anderson's wrist and checking his eyes. Anderson nodded again. "All right, we're heading up then. Just take some deep breaths for me first..."

Anderson took a few long breaths and exhaled slowly. After a few seconds, he was visibly calmer. Scott poured him a glass of water from the pitcher on the reception desk. He took a sip, and the blotching on his face and neck started to fade.

"Thanks. All right, I'll buzz you if the police robot shows up. Have a good night," Anderson said, taking another swig of water. Afterward, his coloring was back to normal.

"Thanks, Anderson," Scott said, maneuvering to see his eyes again. Satisfied, he motioned for us to go.

"Is he all right?" I asked as we rounded the corner.

Scott blew out a breath. "He'll be fine. I was hoping he wasn't about to have a heart attack."

"What a day..." I added as we approached the elevator. Scott's room was still on the bottom floor since he'd just completed his program less than a few days ago.

"Oh, this is yours," Scott said, fishing my bag of tea out of his jacket. "A few cups of this and you might just find the Red Fever cure tomorrow," he added, handing me the tea with a wry grin.

"Thanks." I reached for the tea with an unsteady hand.

"You sure you're all right?" he asked.

I nodded as I pushed the button on the elevator, but I couldn't shake the feeling that what just happened was more than a technology glitch.

I turned back to him. "That car turned around to take another pass at us, Scott. Why would it do that?"

The brave expression he was trying to put on slowly wilted. "Maybe we should just... I don't know..." he trailed off. "We've just been asking a lot of questions the last few days. And that woman at the tea shop clearly didn't want to talk to us about Donovan."

"Which is *exactly* why we need to keep asking questions," I said. "Something is going on here, Scott. First, they sweep everything under the rug at Ivy's, and now we find out that Donovan was obviously into something that wasn't recorded on his intake paperwork. Maybe whatever that was had something to do with how he got infected."

Scott's expression hardened a little. "Frankie, I think we're getting in over our heads." He sighed.

"Maybe that's what it takes," I responded just as the elevator doors opened. I stepped inside, pressed my lips into a flat smile, and let the doors close between us.

Chapter 8

"You look like shit again, Frank," Jack said from across the room as I made my way into the Pathology lab the next morning.

I waved at him without looking over. "Thanks, Jack."

"You'd look like shit too if a hover car tried to kill *you* last night," Scott said from our station. I dropped my bag at my desk and gave him a flat stare. He smiled awkwardly. "I mean, not that you *do* look like shit. Because you don't. I'm just saying *he would*…um, look like shit." Scott cleared his throat and took a sip from his travel mug. He quickly looked away and pulled up the image of our Feral cadaver, Mr. Donovan.

"You picked a smooth one." Blake patted my shoulder and crossed behind me. I was confused for a second until I remembered Scott's idiotic idea to make Blake think we were a couple celebrating our *one day* anniversary yesterday.

"You're here early." I groaned, glaring at Scott.

"New kid on the pathology team," he said, smiling proudly, then blinked several times. "Apparently, I still have to start the coffee."

Blake raised his mug to Scott, and we all chuckled.

"You really get chased down by a hover car?" Jack asked from the other side of the lab.

"Guess they're not quite ready for the public after all." I fell into my chair, avoiding eye contact with Scott. "What did I miss?" I gestured to Donovan's internal systems images, which were already loaded.

"Just starting a corticosteroid inhibitor," Scott said, injecting something into the receiver port of the simulator. "Here we go."

"Didn't we already run everything for adrenals?" I asked.

Scott half-shrugged. "Jack had an idea that Goliath affected the pituitary like Cushing's disease."

"Which, of course, we can't verify because half the pituitary is gone thanks to that Sweeper droid bullet," Jack added. "I should have sent that thing over the wall when I had the chance."

"Well, batter up. If this works, you can slam the whole fleet in a press release," Blake said as the absorption timer on the simulator counted down to zero. I didn't breathe for several seconds as we waited for the network systems to turn green, indicating that we'd finally brought down Goliath—that after years of research, Red Fever was officially cured.

But that wasn't the case this time. Again.

"Come *on*..." Scott groaned as the bones and ligaments started darkening to pink, then red, until every system was mutated.

"Are you fucking *kidding* me?" Jack shouted from the other side of the simulation. "Well, that's it, kids. There's nothing left to test."

"On the contrary, Dr. O'Dell," Dr. Beck said, rounding the corner to our station and to get a closer look at the simulation. "Whatever that was made it at least one round before it failed. Increase the levels and run it again."

Blake let out a low whistle as he watched. "Something's up," he said under his breath.

"Cushing's treatment? Interesting." Beck angled his head as he glanced up at the Feral cadaver simulation in front of us. "Still, the media pressure for results is only getting worse. We need more avenues." He nodded matter-of-factly as he handed a file folder to Scott and another to me.

Inside the folder was an itinerary, a set of boarding passes, and a mobile account authorization disc for five thousand credits.

"What's this?" I asked, leafing through the materials.

"Field assignment," Beck answered. "You and Scott are going to follow up on a lead that came in this morning for a plant off the coast of Florida. Seems it might just be the big brother to jicambi bark." Beck gestured to our folders. "Please imprint the discs so you can access the spending account. I'll file the registrations with Human Resources this afternoon."

I met Scott's eyes as he started to press his thumb into the palm-sized disc from his folder. I did the same with mine, and we both handed them back to Beck.

"Did I hear that right?" Jack asked, crossing to us. *"They're* going into the field?"

"There's a lead on a *plant,* Jack," Blake said. "Botany means plants. Frankie has to go."

Jack gestured to Scott. "He's not a botanist."

"It would be good for Scott to get his hands dirty," Dr. Beck cut in, nodding to Blake and then to Scott.

"My hands have been clean for three years—look how clean!" Jack held up his palms. "I love dirt. Plants and dirt. Sign me up."

Beck grinned. "I need experienced people here to continue working other directions," he added with a quick nod, then slapped Jack on the back as he turned to leave. "Increase your levels and rerun the Cushing's test. That's promising."

Jack mumbled something and leaned in to read the papers in my folder. I stared blankly at the itinerary in front of me, reading the same line over several times before the words actually processed.

"Wait, this says the plane leaves *tonight*? Dr. Beck!" I shouted after him and even jogged a few steps, but he'd already left the lab.

"Unbelievable," Jack said with a sigh.

"Well, you heard him," Blake added. "Take the day and go get organized."

Jack laughed. "Yeah, get your bikini packed."

I leveled my eyes at him. *"Really*?"

"I'm serious! You're going to a tropical island," he said, raising his hands in defense. "Can't be dusting pollen and picking leaves or whatever the entire time, right?"

He looked to Blake, who begrudgingly agreed, and they both refocused on the simulation display.

"Does your itinerary say you leave tonight too?" I asked Scott, just to make sure.

He nodded. "Eight on the dot with Horizon Air."

"What kind of notice for a field assignment is that anyway?" Jack asked without looking up from the simulation report.

"Beck did say the lead just came in this morning, though I've never heard of anything moving *that* fast around here," Blake replied, squinting at the circulatory system simulation, which was starting to coagulate in places. He grimaced and waved a hand at the hologram. "OK, reset that before I puke. And you two beat it before I find a way to invite myself on your tropical getaway. Jack, bring the rest of your Cushing's data over here so we can log all this."

Jack huffed and started back to his station. "You're making the coffee while noobs is gone!" he called back over his shoulder to Blake.

Scott signed out of his computer and hung up his lab coat. I hadn't even had a chance to put mine on, so I just grabbed my bag and read more of the itinerary.

"This says we won't be back for a week?" I said to Blake.

"We'll be *fine*, Frankie." He drew out the words. "Have fun. You deserve the break after everything this week. Just try to watch out for rogue hover cars." He snickered.

I smiled at him and walked with Scott to the elevator, but something didn't feel right. Dr. Beck wasn't in his office as we passed, so I couldn't even ask him for more details about the trip. I leafed through the folder again.

Scott turned to me as soon as we were behind the elevator doors. "What just happened?" he asked with a quick head shake and a laugh.

"I was about to ask you the same thing," I said after a beat.

"What's wrong?"

I shook my head. "I don't know. Maybe it's just that Donovan was sent on a *field assignment*, at least according to his residency hall record. The woman there didn't even know he was dead, Scott."

"That's true." Scott's smile faded as he looked at me carefully, then nodded.

"So what do we do?"

"What *can* we do?" he asked, his voice suddenly tinged with exasperation. "I don't know, Frankie. To be honest, maybe we're just being a little paranoid." He sighed. "What happened at Ivy's was insane, but they let us walk away after a psych eval. If someone had it out for us, wouldn't they have done the deed then?" he asked, shaking his head.

"There was nothing on the feeds at all about Ivy's. It was like nothing had happened the next day," I pressed. "How is that normal, even in a city this big?"

"Actually, getting everything back to status quo again makes sense the more I think about it," Scott started. "We'd have chaos if people knew something like that happened inside The Citadel wall."

"OK, how do you explain the way that woman in the tea shop couldn't get us out of there fast enough. And what about that hover car last night?" I asked.

"Yeah, that was all weird, but come on, Frankie. Do you really think people are trying to kill us?" he asked with a chuckle.

"What makes you so sure they're not?"

"Frankie..." he sighed and pushed a hand through his dark hair. "I want to find out how to beat Red Fever as much as you do, but maybe all these hours we've been pulling are starting to take their toll, you know?" he asked, meeting my eyes. "Are you OK? Really? Because I'm not. It's been months on end at that lab. And with the climate out there thanks to the media reports... I got caught up in a little paranoia too. Anybody who's been keeping our schedule would. This field assignment couldn't have come at a better time if you ask me."

The elevator doors opened unceremoniously in front of us, and I had to squint at the sudden blast of sunlight that beamed through the wall of windows.

"Ugh…" I said, raising my hand to shield my eyes.

"There! You see what I mean?" Scott laughed. "We're like vampires here."

I chuckled at this, and my nerves dialed down several notches. "Maybe you're right," I agreed.

"Sorry, what did you say?" Scott asked as we got out of the elevator.

I rolled my eyes. "*Maybe* you're right."

"One more time?"

"Don't push it," I said, cutting in front of him to move through the turnstile door.

"Nice, OK, no problem—I'll just wait here to see if you burst into flames," he shouted behind me. "Thanks for taking one for the team, Frank!"

I laughed again and waited for him on the sidewalk with my arms outstretched, the sun beating down. He emerged from the door a few seconds later squinting.

"How about that? Not vampires," I said, suddenly remembering how much I had to do now. I groaned.

"What, you *want* to be a vampire?"

"No." I smiled. "I just remembered we still have to get home and pack. I hate packing."

"It's better than listening to Jack's chewing all day," Scott said, emulating the noise. I shook my head at Scott as he raised a hand to hail a car. Almost immediately, a hover unit started coming our way, and we exchanged knowing glances. He waved it on. "We'll just get a live-drive."

***

A molecular scanner and a few dozen clean slides, along with an extra set of boots, some clothes, and several pairs of socks was about all I could fit into the one carry-on bag we were allowed to bring with us. The itinerary said we'd have provisions from one of the local doctors once we got there, but I didn't want to take any chances.

Scott met me in front of our building in shorts, a T-shirt, a ridiculous, floppy hat, and with a duffle bag that looked like it was about to burst at the seams. I had no words, so I just gaped at him.

He shrugged in confusion. "What?" I shook my head when he widened his eyes at me. "Beck said we were going to a tropical assignment, didn't he?"

"I guess I just wasn't expecting the tourist hat there." I tried to stifle a laugh.

"Hey, I burn easily, Frankie. Don't judge me." He feigned indignation and moved past me to hail another car, which, again, came almost immediately.

We rode in relative silence during the short trip to the airport, which happened to be just enough time for the unsettling feeling to fall over me again.

Chapter 9

The turbulence on the flight to Florida only frayed my nerves even more, but at least we were finally on the ground.

Like Maine's, The Citadel's Floridian campus also included their airport compound, but despite everything being identical—the same smooth and featureless buildings, the same narrow streets—everything felt more militarized than collegiate here. Except for the docks, this campus was also sealed off from the surrounding slums that, at least from what I could see as we were landing, resembled the lawless expanse of The Grind. I wondered what they called those lands here.

Scott and I were driven through the outer city gate to the docks just as the sun was breaking on the horizon. The only ship in port looked like an iron tub that could have only been held above water by divine intervention. A line of small port windows lined the algae-tinged hull, and a wide, rusty ramp seemed to lay over the dock like the tongue of this huge, dying ship.

"The Morningstar..." Scott read the chipped, black scrawl on the side of the hull. "That's us."

"The itinerary didn't say anything about this being a shipping barge," I added. "What is this?"

Scott and I walked up the ramp and were met by several scurrying deckhands who were pulling on ropes and securing huge, stacked crates.

"You'll be Jeffries and Mason den? It's an early mornin' fer ya," a man said in a thick, tropical accent. We turned to find a tall, very tan, older man smiling at us, his open shirt tails blowing back with the breeze coming off the water.

"Or a very late night," Scott replied after a second. "I don't think I slept at all on the plane."

He gave us another huge, brilliant smile. "Well, ya might find a few more hours once we launch," he said. "Should make landfall again around midday. I'll show ya to yer cabin."

"One cabin?" I asked, probably too abruptly.

"Afraid der's not much in de way of modesty aboard dis old girl. But she'll do for a place to lay yer head should the need carry ya off."

We followed him down a set of metal stairs, which led to a narrow corridor of open bunks, crates, and at the end of the corridor, a small galley with large steel pots hung from the ceiling.

"Is this your boat, *Mr...*?" I asked as the man slid open a door and stepped out of our way.

"People call me Alistair," he said with a slow grin, then chuckled. "And no, no. I'm just de hospitality." He extended an arm to show us into the room. "Please, make yerself at home den. We'll be shovin' off promptly," he added, then disappeared down the corridor.

The cabin was very small, just enough room for a set of bunk beds with dark, woolen blankets, a trunk, and a writing desk with a rickety chair. A portal window was positioned just above the writing desk, and I imagined given the darkness of the corridor, a window like this must have been a luxury.

"What do you think this boat carries?" I asked.

"Could be anything this far south." Scott shrugged. "Doesn't matter I guess as long as they have some food aboard. I'm starving."

I hadn't been hungry until he said something, and as if on cue, my stomach started growling. I groaned and looked longingly at the pillow.

We made our way back up the stairs, and to my surprise, the shoreline had already disappeared. I definitely wasn't tired anymore.

"How are we this far out already?" I asked, confused even more when I noticed all the deckhands were gone too.

"I didn't even hear the motors kick on to take us out of port," Scott added as he crossed to the railing. "Frankie, look at this. We're already pretty deep."

I followed him to the railing and peered over the edge, shaking my head. The water was black and opaque. We *were* already deep. "I don't understand. Maybe we should ask someone how—"

"That's exactly your problem, Frankie," Scott interrupted, seizing my upper arms. "You ask too many fucking questions."

I struggled against him as he tried to *push me* over the railing. He pinned my forearms against his chest and wrapped his other arm tightly around my waist. I felt my feet leave the ground as he lifted me, so I tried bringing up my knees to create some space between us.

"What are you doing? Let me go!"

"I tried...to help you!" he said, struggling to keep me restrained. "But you had...to keep pressing..."

"Get off me!" I bit his shoulder as hard as I could, which made him cry out. He dropped me, but grabbed the back of my hair before I could run. He closed his other hand around my throat and squeezed so tightly that I saw stars for a second. I tried to gouge his eyes with my fingers, but there wasn't enough space between us to get around his arms. I slapped his back and tried to kick, but I had no leverage bent backward over the railing.

I found his elbow and pushed up as hard as I could, hoping to at least distract him for a second. The boat shifted at the same time by some miracle, and the displacement gave me the momentum I needed to lock out his arm. He let go of my throat and hair for just a second, but that's all I needed. I darted under his arm and ran back toward the stairs... If I could get to the galley, I could find a weapon.

I didn't get more than a handful of steps before an arm closed around my throat and hauled me in the opposite direction toward the railing again. I couldn't get my feet under me long enough to do anything, so I stopped trying altogether and gripped handfuls of Scott's shirt. I bent my knees and pulled up my feet hoping to offset his balance, or at least loosen his grip enough that he'd have to stop and reclaim it.

He didn't fall, but he did stop long enough for me to twist out of his hold. I was free for about a second before he hit me in the face, causing stars to appear all over again.

"I wasn't supposed to leave any marks on you!" he said, hitting me again. I lost my balance this time and fell hard on the deck, seized by a fit of coughing as I gasped for breath.

Scott dragged me back to the railing and lifted me up. My vision was blurred, and I couldn't get enough of a breath to offset the panic I felt. He was going to throw me overboard.

"Scott!" I coughed. "*Why?*"

"Do you think I wanted to do this? Low man on the totem poll, that's why!" he said, pinning me against the railing. He gripped the back of my hair again and held my wrist in his other hand. "Oh, man. You really do look like shit now."

"Just tell me...*why*..." I managed, the tinny taste of blood filling my mouth.

"I told you already. You ask too many questions. Goodbye, Frankie," Scott said, pale in the pre-dawn moonlight. I reached for something, anything to grab as he forced me backward over the railing. I gripped his collar, gravity took hold of me, and somehow, Scott and I both began falling toward the churning, black sea.

I lost all sense of direction in the dim light when I slammed into something hard, but it wasn't the water. It was solid.

My right leg felt like it was on fire, and as I reached for it, I felt the coarsely woven deck ladder wrapped tightly around my thigh. It must have been caught on the way down.

I managed to pull myself up and loosen the rope, but not completely. It was dark, but I could see the blood dripping from the point of contact, the sharply twined weave biting into the bare skin just below the hem of my shorts.

I squinted against the mist and thrashing water all around me and tried to reach my temple to queue Citadel security since there was no one else I could call. They would send someone, I was sure. I pressed my temple a few times, but only saw flashes of a scrambled display. We were too far out from shore.

I tried to leverage myself up on the leg that wasn't caught, but a stabbing pain shot through my ribs where I'd smashed into what I now realized was the side of the boat.

"Help!" I shouted toward the deck, but between the roar of the engines and the crashing water all around me, I didn't hold out much hope.

"No one is coming, Frank!" Scott shouted, appearing in the sea spray below. He was climbing the rope ladder, but his shoulder was bleeding through this soaked gray T-shirt.

"*Who is making you do this*?" I screamed to Scott as he got closer, terrified he would grab hold of my foot and pull me down.

"You, Frankie!" he called back to me, then choked as a small wave slammed into him. "Your stupid questions! You couldn't...just do your job!" he yelled between coughs.

Another few feet and I thought I might be able to kick him with my free leg, but putting all my weight on my injured leg gave me tunnel vision.

I blinked hard to keep from passing out. "Help!" I shouted again into the sky—again, without answer.

Scott slashed at my leg with a knife I didn't know he had, the entire sleeve and half the front of his gray T-shirt now marred with blood. I gripped the rope ladder over my head and drove the heel of my free foot into the center of the stain. Scott dropped the knife, and when I kicked him this time, he fell several feet before he caught the rope ladder again.

"Help!" I shouted once more, but Scott's screams drowned mine out. Half his body was in the water, the pace of the boat pulling at him...or so I thought, until I looked more closely. Sharks were lunging at him, biting, swallowing, and lunging again until the screaming stopped and Scott let go of the rope ladder.

I watched, frozen in horror for several more seconds as the sharks surfaced a few more times, their jaws gnashing at nothing, before they finally disappeared again under the surf.

The adrenaline coursing through me was like rocket fuel, forcing my hands and free leg to move much faster than I could possibly control. I fumbled through the weave of the rope ladder until I managed to untangle my thigh, the flesh torn and bleeding from the friction. I looked away—looked upward toward the railing and started to climb.

The deck lights suddenly flickering just a few feet from me nearly made me lose my grip as I pulled myself over the railing. I landed hard on the deck below, and pain seized my whole body as I lay on my back.

Lightning ripped across the sky, which somehow seemed to be getting *darker* instead of lighter in the pre-dawn hours. The flash forcing my eyes closed, and the crash of thunder that immediately followed left a ringing in my ears. Seconds later, large, warm drops began pummeling me as I listened to the waves crashing below.

Chapter 10

I tried to queue for security again, but again, only saw the same intermittent signal. It was useless. I needed to get back to my room, or at least to a first aid kit, but I couldn't bring myself to move. My head ached more with each drop of rain that hit me, and my vision began to tunnel. I couldn't let myself pass out, not with everything so upside-down here. I thought about calling for help again, but I began to suspect the boat seemed deserted now for a reason.

I rolled to my side and pressed up on my forearms until I could get my good leg under me. Slowly, I got to my feet and made my way back toward the narrow stairs that led to my room, which might as well have been ten miles away for all the strength I could manage. I just had to regroup behind a closed, locked door so I could try to think.

My head was pounding and spinning at the same time and it was hard to breathe through my nose. I hoped nothing was broken—that thought was the first to dive bomb me in this sporadic moment of clarity, and then the floodgates opened. *What if Scott wasn't acting alone? What if the crew of this ship was in on it?*

My palms were burning, but there wasn't enough light in the corridor to see what kind of damage was done. I moved as quietly as I could back to my room and slipped inside the door, latching it behind me. I didn't want anymore surprises tonight.

Moonlight came through the small porthole, illuminating the room just enough for me to pull the chain on the wall sconce. *What happened to dawn?* Someone had set a tray on the desk across from the bunkbeds, which made me instinctively check the latch on the door. I was alone—Scott was dead. I was safe.

Scott was dead... I thought. I turned my palms over and saw the deep rope gashes across each of them, then blew out a breath and lifted the lid of the tray in the hopes there was at least some water there. In fact there were two bottles, along with two wedges of cheese, an entire sliced pineapple, grapes, and a whole baguette.

My stomach lurched and my head swam with ideas—*two bottles* of water and enough food for two people...delivered while Scott and I were out of the room, while Scott was supposed *to kill* me? The crew couldn't have been in on this. The idea was stabilizing, so I held onto it and sighed in relief, though my hands still shook. I needed to focus on something else...cleaning up, treating these wounds, getting off this boat.

And go where? I thought, but the weight of that unknown answer was too heavy for now.

I looked around for some kind of first aid kit without any luck, but then remembered the lab supplies I'd brought in my bag.

I pulled out several pairs of socks, the alcohol swabs, and took the small tube of iodine out of the molecular scanner, cradling it all carefully in my arms over to the desk. It wasn't much, but it was better than trying to squeeze pineapple juice into the wounds, the citric acid in the juice being the only antimicrobial alternative in this little room.

I poured some of the water over the burns on my hands, then clenched my teeth as I applied the alcohol swabs. I wrapped a thin wool boot sock around each one and tied as tightly as I could with my teeth and other hand. By some miracle, all the swabs stayed in place for both wrappings.

The deep rope burn that had gouged my thigh was going to be another story. I didn't have a sock long enough to wrap it, so I fished out a cotton tank top and folded it to use as a padded dressing. I tied two socks together as a bandage and braced myself for the imminent burning as I dripped the iodine into the wound.

The pain was blinding for a second, but it passed soon enough, though my hands wouldn't stop shaking. A wave of nausea crashed into me, and I took a seat in the desk chair.

I took a few deep breaths and forced myself to eat a piece of the cheese, then decided to try to queue for help. Again, the signal was intermittent. I really was alone here.

I glanced across the room and saw Scott's bag still on his bed and rose to open it. I fought impatiently with the zipper as if his orders to murder me would somehow just be folded nicely in an envelope right there between his underwear and razor.

There was no envelope, but I did find his itinerary folder and opened it. The first several pages were identical to the contents of my folder—an itinerary, ticket stubs—but attached to the back inside cover of the folder was a sealed, plastic sleeve. It was hard to see in the dim sconce light, but it looked like the sleeve contained three microscope slides—one tinged red, one blue, and the other yellow. I blinked in an effort to read the labels: *IS-1, IS-2,* and *IS-3.*

IS was a lab code, but we weren't working on anything with that tag. The number sequence suggested each of the slides was a new formulation of whatever *IS* was, but since the slides were vacuum sealed, I gathered *IS* probably wasn't innocuous.

I pulled the sleeve from the folder and held the slides up to the wall sconce to get a better look, and a scrap of paper fell to the floor. *Plan B* was handwritten on the back when I stooped to pick it up, but that's all I could see for a minute as the room took a spin. I leaned against the wall and waited for the whole-body surge of pain to dissipate before I could focus enough to flip the paper over. After a few shallow breaths, I read the writing on the front: *Captain Robert Monroe, Intake Officer. NWA Maritime Penal Facility.*

Below this was a set of coordinates, but no other information. *There was a prison somewhere at sea?* I thought. *Is this where we were really going?*

My head was pounding with the effort to piece everything together, but the one thing I did know was that I couldn't go home now. I couldn't risk that Dr. Beck was somehow behind all this, or even Blake... *Jack?* I couldn't imagine Jack would have known anything. Wasn't he just as surprised as I was about the field assignment? He even tried to get Beck to send him along.

Scott said I just didn't know when to stop asking questions...this was all because I started looking into Marcus Donovan's life? So after two years with Scott, two years of mentoring him, he was that easily turned against me?

They must have threatened him, I thought. I wanted to believe Scott didn't have a choice—that it wasn't just about money or the promise of a promotion.

The pressure in my head had become crippling, and I had to put everything else aside for now. I made my way back to the desk chair and grabbed the full water bottle to hold it against the back of my neck. It was cool, and the sick feeling that had come over me started to dissipate. I needed some sleep, if only for a few hours, but I knew enough from my medical residency that I probably had a concussion, and sleep would have to wait.

All right then, I'd wait. It's not like I could just jump off the side of the boat here in the middle of the ocean. I needed to rest, even if I couldn't let myself sleep. *Just sit here for a little while.* I thought distantly as everything blurred, and I felt myself starting to fall.

***

Either the pain in my head or the breeze on my face woke me, but it was too bright to open my eyes. I squinted, trying to make sense of the sounds all around me: a woman crying, waves crashing, some kind of knocking, and a strange, low buzz.

"I said it's pretty!" a grating female voice said to my right. I turned toward it and forced my eyes open the rest of the way. When the whitewash of the brightness faded, an older woman with whole sections of her hair missing barked at me. "You're supposed to say thank you!" she informed me, but it took me another few beats to realize she was even talking to me.

"OK! Thank you!" I said, hoping this would calm her. We were sitting on some kind of built-in bench with a series of armrests that stretched the length of the boat, only this boat wasn't the same one I'd boarded. All of us were shackled to our seats, dozens of haggard or dangerous looking people dressed in filthy clothes.

"It's pretty!" the woman to my right shouted in my ear again, this time lunging at me. Bands of light appeared around her wrist shackles and her waist like some kind of laser seat belt. She lunged again and was shocked back into position.

I jumped, but tried not to move too much in fear that similar bands would appear.

"What is this?" I called out, but everyone just looked at me. Some laughed, at least until a man in a black uniform turned the corner and began walking our way.

"This is my ship, little raccoon!" he said, leaning back against the deck wall, no railing to be found.

"How did I get on it? I was in my cabin. I'm supposed to be going to an island for a field assignment! I'm a scientist!"

"Well," the man started with a chuckle. "I have good news and bad news for you, little raccoon. Which one should I give her?" he asked the group of people also strapped to their chairs.

An indecipherable mix of shouted answers filled the air, and my head started to pound again. The man raised his hand, and the group slowly quieted.

"I have credentials. I can show them to you," I insisted before he could say anything else, but he ignored me.

"The good news...you are going to an island."

"Yes, Snake Island. That's where I'm supposed to go."

"The bad news is that it's not Snake Island." He grinned.

"If I could just show you my credentials. I'm a botanist. Please, there's been a mistake!"

"Murder is a mistake, yes! Even for botanists!"

"What?" I blinked at him, and the reality of the last twenty-four hours came flooding back. "No, Scott tried to throw me over the ledge. I didn't kill him. The sharks killed him!"

"It's pretty!" the woman to my right shouted, snapping her rotten teeth at my shoulder. Her seat shocked her again. "Say *thank you*! Say *thank you*!"

"Seems she likes your jacket," the man in black said with a nod.

"Where are we going?" I asked, but with a sinking feeling, I remembered the folder. The scrap of paper. *Plan B was the prison at sea?* "You're Monroe..."

His face lit in surprised amusement. "My reputation precedes me!" he said, and offered a sweeping bow.

"No, listen to me... This is a set up. I didn't do anything wrong," I said, but Monroe only smiled and held out his hands when a chorus of others started repeating the same thing.

"Did you get sterilized?" the man on the other side of me abruptly asked, his eyes wide and unblinking as he glanced from me to the woman who liked my jacket. "I didn't see *either* of you when we got sterilized!"

"That's just the gents, you lucky bastard. Easier access!" Monroe laughed so hard he coughed.

"We all got those Venetian disease shots, though," the woman to my right nodded. "I'm spring clean now!"

"*Venereal!*" Monroe shouted to her, triggering more laughing, more coughing. I closed my eyes and willed the pounding in my ears to get stronger just to drown it all out.

Chapter 11

"Home, sweet home, Scrapper Island Penal Colony!" Monroe shouted over the crashing surf as we approached an island. People came out from the trees and gathered on the shore, cheering and hooting. Monroe laughed, and a ball of ice seemed to form in my stomach. The prison wasn't on the island. It *was* the island.

The boat came into port and anchored, but the restraints pinning our wrists and legs to the seats remained on.

"They can't just leave us here," I said to the woman next to me. She narrowed her vacant eyes, the motion wrinkling the scar that ran through her other eyebrow and down her cheek. I turned away from her and shouted to Monroe. "You can't just leave us here!"

He smiled at me. "What do you think *penal colony* means, little raccoon?" he asked.

The woman next to me threw her head back and cackled, showcasing the handful of black and broken teeth she had left in her mouth.

"Why aren't there any guards on the beach?" I asked, ignoring her. The woman laughed even harder, which served just as well to confirm my fears. There were no guards here—no laws other than the one governing every other wild place: You're either predator or prey.

Cylindrical Sweeper droids rose out of cutouts in the ship deck, each droid extending a metal rod at us. The instant our restraints snapped off, the metal rods crackled with the same electric display from the laser restraints I saw earlier. This only made the people standing on the beach hoot and cheer louder.

"Disembark without issue, or you will be incinerated," the Sweeper droids said all at once, and the reverberation of it lingered in my teeth. I stood up hesitantly with everyone else.

Monroe referenced a holographic tablet as we shuffled past. "A supply boat comes once a month to pick up the dead," he shouted over the beach noise as he looked up at each one of us, checking something off his tablet as we passed. He paused and frowned when he looked up at me, then did a double take at his tablet.

"I told you. I'm not supposed to be here," I insisted again.

He leaned in slowly and smiled almost imperceptibly. "Maybe you'll last the night on Scrapper Island after all." He straightened and returned his attention to his tablet.

"Please!" I called to him again as we moved toward the docking ramp. "There's been a mistake!" A second later my whole body seized and prickled. I stumbled and fell into the man in front of me. He grumbled and shoved me backward into the woman behind me, who started cackling all over again.

"Disembark without issue," the Sweeper droid repeated, the rod it extended still sparking.

We moved more quickly down the ramp into the shallow ocean water, which was warm, but I winced as the saltwater soaked through my makeshift bandage above my knee and burned the cut beneath it. *I would boil some of the seawater...find antiseptic plants*, I thought, desperately trying to distract myself with a mental list of what might be growing this far south.

A few of the Sweeper droids directed us to line up on the beach and face the trees. Face the *people* who seemed more like a pack of wolves just waiting to attack.

"Clasp your hands behind your heads," they said in unison again. My stomach sank at the thought they were going to execute us, but several seconds passed, then several minutes. None of us dared turn around until the people who had come from the foliage started moving toward us. I risked a glance behind me... The Sweeper droids were already back on the boat, which was starting to leave port.

I turned back frantically to the people who had come from the foliage. They started to circle us, most of them looking like they'd been here for decades. Men and women alike had the same long hair that was bleached and brassy from the sun and salt. Deep grooves ran rivers around their mouths and sunken eyes, though, only a few of them looked old enough for time alone to have done this.

There were far fewer women than men among the others, but everyone wore the same frayed T-shirts and pants of varying lengths. If clothes were on that monthly supply ship, it certainly wasn't often. It was then that I started to realize why they were circling us.

"That's my jacket," a voice said abruptly, but I couldn't tell where it was coming from until a tall, square-faced woman emerged slowly from the crowd. Her long, dark hair looked like it could catch a spark and light like a brush fire just from the friction it created by falling over her shoulders. "I said, that's my jacket," she insisted again, stopping just a foot from me. I was frozen where I stood.

Two other women, smaller, but no less intimidating, sprang forward and began pulling my jacket off. I tried to pull my arms out, but they took it as resistance. One of them hit me in the back of the head, and the other hit me in the stomach so hard I lost my breath and dropped to my knees.

Fighting broke out all around me as I doubled over, still unable to get more than a fraction of a breath. Sand sprayed over my arms and cheeks as I pressed my forehead into the ground and tried to make myself as small as possible.

"Come on, come on," another woman's voice said close to my ear. Hands moved around my ribs, under my arms, pulling me up and away from the chaos. I blinked several times to try to clear my vision of the blurry flashes and burning tears, but it was no use. We started running once I finally got my feet under me, the whipping branches and vines starting new lines of burning scratches on my bare legs.

"Where are...we going?" I managed, coughing between the words.

"Hold on," she said as we started descending, the already dense foliage seeming taller the further down we went. In a matter of three or four steps, the branches, grasses, and vines were well above our heads.

The path we were on opened to a small clearing that backed into a high-reaching layered rock wall. A few more steps, and we were *inside* it. The woman unceremoniously dropped me onto the leaf-layered ground, and finally, in the mottled light, I could see the expanse of stone walls that slanted up and back. We were inside a mountain.

I turned and saw that the woman who brought me here was tall with straw-like blonde hair. She was small, but etched in lean muscle.

"You're safe here," an older woman said, seated with her legs crossed on the ground near a raging fire pit. Her eyes were wide and dark, and her gnarled fingers were dexterously weaving differently colored shells into her long, salt and pepper-colored braids.

Another woman came through the rock wall opening behind us and stopped abruptly when she saw me. Unlike the smaller woman with light hair, she was tall and dark, squarely built like the woman who had just taken my jacket. I flinched instinctively when her hands went to a weapon on her hip, which looked like a large, wooden corkscrew.

"It's OK," the woman who had helped me said. She held up a hand to the darker woman, then turned back to me. "I'm Gia. And that's Rita. She won't hurt you."

Rita reluctantly let go of her weapon, but her scowl remained. "You just got her from the boat?" she asked.

Gia nodded slowly. "Poppy and Mack took several more—older ones," she finished, then turned back to me. "What's your name?"

"Francesca, but everyone calls me Frankie," I said.

"This is Mae." Gia gestured to the older woman seated near the fire. "This is her place."

"Our place," Mae corrected with a wide, nearly toothless smile, though she didn't look away from the fire.

"They said this is a prison island?" I asked. Gia nodded. "Why did you help me?"

"Because you wouldn't have lived through the night if she hadn't," Rita answered instead, her expression hard and fixed. "The blonde ones never do."

I turned to Gia, confused.

"I wouldn't be here without Rita—she came for me when I landed too," she explained. "There are others like us, though."

"Where are they? Poppy and whoever you said?" I asked.

"Close by." Gia nodded for emphasis, apparently registering the panic in my voice. "You're safe here, like I said. We all take care of each other."

"You were with them, though…on the beach?"

"Rita and I go to the beach with a team whenever there's a prison ship and we…*intervene*."

They exchanged glances and each smiled widely at this. I didn't know what *intervening* entailed completely, but for now, I didn't care.

Mae gave me a large wooden bowl full of water, which I drank so quickly I nearly choked.

"What brings you to us then?" she asked, which I thought was a strange way to put it—like I was just in the neighborhood or something.

"I don't know," I said, coughing a little. "I was supposed to be going on a research trip to an island off the coast of Florida. But the boat I got on yesterday wasn't the boat that brought me here."

"How's that again?" Rita's eyes narrowed in scrutiny.

"I don't know, that's what I'm trying to tell you," I said. "I only fell asleep for a few hours, and my cabin door was locked. But I woke up on the prison boat strapped onto this bench with all the others on deck," I trailed off because it sounded even stupider when I said it out loud. "I was set up. I boarded the first boat at dawn. A few minutes later we were in the middle of the ocean and it was sunset. Someone tried to kill me then, and when that didn't work, I passed out and woke up on the prison boat. I know I sound like a crazy person..." I babbled.

Mae chuckled to herself in the corner. "New boat with nobody on it," she said, oddly underwhelmed.

I stared at her blankly. "How did you know that? At first there was someone...Albert? I don't remember. He greeted us on the first boat. There were some deck hands then too, but soon everyone was gone."

Mae's dark eyes lit like a match. "Luz got ya, child," she said in a breathy voice.

"*What*?" I shook my head. "Who's Luz?"

Mae yawned. "A queen, a queen, a river clay queen," she chanted, stretching high above her head, which made her sleeves slide down her thin, dark arms. She leaned back onto a makeshift bed and continued her sing-song verses. "A queen of a dead world...died on the eighth day. A queen, a traitor queen, all her sisters say..."

"I don't understand," I said, but she was asleep a few seconds after her head hit the fur pillow next to her. I looked to Gia. "What did she mean? Who's Luz?"

She took my bowl and dipped it in a bigger bowl full of water, then handed it back to me with a small loaf of hard, coarse bread.

"It's just one of the stories she tells," Gia said, tossing me a heavy fur. She stretched out on another one along the perimeter of the cave. "She never sings the whole thing, but she always mentions *Luz*."

"She thinks someone named *Luz* moved me to a different ship in the middle of the night?"

"Have you seen your face?" Rita said, her eyes already closed as she lay back on her bedding. "It's probably safe to assume you missed a few things these last twenty-four hours."

I raised my hands to my cheekbones and winced in pain as I remembered Scott's blows. Suddenly, Monroe calling me *little raccoon* made sense.

"I know I was only asleep a few hours," I said absently. "And the door was locked..."

"I think Rita means to say maybe the boat you got on was the prison boat all along," Gia said through a yawn. "Things get jumbled. Go to sleep, Frankie. We'll need to go back to the beach before dawn."

I started to protest again, to tell them I'd boarded the boat with Scott, but I stopped when I realized that would be a much longer story than anyone, including me, had the energy for right now.

I tried to take a bite of the bread that Gia had given me, but it proved to be too painful. I dipped the small loaf in the fresh bowl of water, then chewed as little as possible as I watched the last of the sun fade through the narrow rock wall opening.

Chapter 12

I didn't remember falling asleep, but I opened my eyes from the corner of the cave where I'd watched the light slip away the night before.

Everyone was gone, even Mae, the older woman whom I was desperate to see again so I could ask her more about whoever *Luz* was. Did Gia say they were going back to the beach this morning? I got to my feet with considerable effort and slowly made my way outside.

It must have been very early because there was a haze covering most of the dense foliage. The air was cool, but thick with humidity, and the forest was alive with chipping and clicking. Orange and blue bird of paradise flowers jutted up from the dense carpet of green to my left, and enormous banana plants, their leaves longer and wider than any I'd ever seen, draped over my head like a canopy of giant umbrellas. They shaded a narrow dirt path that led to the small clearing we came to last night, and here in the daylight, I could see the hidden steps that were carved into the earth. They led up into a thick cross section of leaves and branches that I had to push my way through in order to get to the beach beyond.

I was afraid to go too far after what Gia and Rita said last night, not to mention, what if I couldn't find my way back?

"Take one more step, and you'll be dead before you hit the ground," a man's voice said. I froze in place, but scanned the ground for some kind of weapon—a rock or a sharp stick. I heard his footsteps approaching and clenched my fists. "It won't be painless, either," he said, his voice low and menacing.

"Stay away from me," I tried to shout, but my voice sounded brittle and weak. I clenched my teeth to steady my nerves. "I'm here because I killed someone. A *man*." I exaggerated, still not as loudly or as forcefully as I intended.

"Just one?" he said in the same, low tone, which was quieter when he spoke again. "Stop talking and stop moving."

"Stay *away* from me," I said anyway, but it came out half whispered. "I'm *warning* you," I tried to sound more menacing, this time forcing the words through my teeth.

"You must want to die," he said thinly. "I suppose I can appreciate that." I felt him touch my shoulder and spun around to hit him in the throat, but he was taller than I thought. He caught my arm and threw me to the ground behind him. I scrambled to get to my feet before he could get to me again, but he wasn't even facing me.

I didn't understand what was happening until I saw the huge yellow snake striking at him from a branch high above our heads. It missed, but recoiled and struck again, this time connecting with his shoulder.

It extended from the tree until it touched the ground where it coiled again, raising itself up at least two feet in the air. But the man didn't move. He didn't fall backward or run. He just waited for the snake to strike again.

"Back up!" I called to him, but he still didn't move. The snake reared back again, though instead of striking, its golden, horned head bobbed, then lowered until it started swaying. I thought it was some kind of snake charmer trick until the mass of bright yellow coils unraveled and collapsed sideways, twitching a few times before the snake lay still on the ground.

The man pushed it with his *bare foot*, but it didn't move.

"It's dead. Pay attention to low branches from now on," he said without turning around, then started to walk away.

"Wait!" I called to him. He stopped, but still didn't face me. "I'm sorry... I thought you were—"

At this, he turned around and met my eyes. His were dark under the weight of heavy, drawn brows, which gave him an expression I couldn't place.

"I'm not like them," he said, but it wasn't a plea for understanding. It sounded like...a *warning*.

Blood started to seep through the shoulder of his open button down shirt. It was frayed at the edges and the sleeves were long gone.

"That snake bit you? OK, I can help," I said, looking around for a bolo tree, or even penny flower —both of them grew this far south. I could make a poultice of the bark or the leaves to draw out the venom, and I would need at least a few handfuls because he wasn't small. I held out a hand to the man while I scanned the foliage. "Try to be still. Moving around will just speed up the poison. I can treat the bite, though, don't worry."

"What's on your hands?" he asked casually.

"What?" I quickly glanced at the filthy rags the thin boot socks had become, the ones on my thigh having disappeared to reveal the rope burn from the ship. "Oh, bandages. Well, kind of. It's a long story— ah! Tobacco!" I almost shouted as I crossed the small clearing and used the end of my shirt to pick several of the long, waxy leaves. "These will help draw out the venom."

"You're a doctor?"

"Botanist," I answered without looking at him. When I had about a dozen leaves carefully cradled in my shirt, I picked a nearby caladium leaf and rolled them up inside it. "Now, I just need sea water," I added, turning back to him, but he was gone. "No... no, no, no. Hey! Come back!" I shouted into the wall of vegetation all around me. "I can help you!"

"Help yourself by shutting up," Rita hissed as she came through the curtain of branches and leaves to my left. I jumped halfway out of my skin. "Why are you out here?" she asked, tossing me a coconut. I caught it, but the tobacco leaves scattered at my feet. Gia emerged next from the foliage with a line of three large fish slung over her shoulder.

"Pays to go early. We can cook these inside so there's no smo—*whoa*," she said, stopping in her tracks and staring intently at the ground in front of her. "Nobody move... That's a djin snake."

Rita pulled out a slingshot and started loading a rock.

"No, it's dead!" I said, holding up one of my poorly-bandaged hands.

Both women gaped at me.

"*You* killed it?" Rita asked, lowering her slingshot.

"No, it just kind of...died," I said, realizing I must have missed something. "It was in the tree, then it struck the man, and then it was on the ground trying to strike at him again. It all happened so fast."

"*What* man?" Gia scanned the perimeter warily.

"I don't know," I answered. "But it would have bitten me if he hadn't stopped me. Listen, it bit *him*, though. I need to find him so I can try to draw out the venom with those tobacco leaves."

"That's a *djin* snake." Rita glared at me. "If it bit him, he's dead now."

"That's basically what he said it would do, but he was OK. I mean, he was bigger. Lean, but tall, you know? The poison would have taken a minute…" I tried to explain. "He was *right here* a second ago. I can make a poultice. Help me find him—he was just here!"

"That's impossible," Gia said, using a long stick to hold down the snake as she passed.

"I told you, it's dead," I repeated.

"They can still strike for a few minutes sometimes," she said, gingerly moving toward me. "I've seen it."

"You want me to believe a dead snake can still strike, and you won't believe that I can still help that man? Come on, we don't have a lot of time. He can't be far!"

"Seen it more than once," Gia said. "You get maybe a minute after a djin snakebite, then you start shaking and foaming at the mouth. That's it."

"No, listen. He *wasn't* shaking or foaming at the mouth yet. If you're not going to help me, I'll go by myself," I said, turning to walk, but surrounded by the forest, I realized I had no idea which direction he went.

"There's no one within the perimeter, Frankie," Rita said, coming back through the branches behind me. I didn't even know she'd left.

"Did you say there were tobacco leaves?"

"Uh, yeah." I pointed at them. Rita gathered them from the ground. "Don't touch those with your bare hands!" I warned, and she dropped the leaves.

"Why not?"

"They have to be dried before you can handle them."

"How do you know that?" Rita asked again.

"I told you, I'm a botanist—see the purple in the middle of the yellow flowers?" I pointed to the sunny side of the clearing. "Regular tobacco's flowers are just yellow—the purple means this is a more potent variety."

Rita nodded to Gia. "So we dry them. Maybe trade them," she said. "Make a fire."

"No, stop," I said, shaking my head. "You can't dry them like that or you'll make everyone sick. They have to be hung up for weeks."

Rita narrowed her eyes at me in disbelief. "Do it then," she said, unrolling several pulls from the ball of string hooked to her belt. She used the edge of her corkscrew weapon to cut it, then handed the length of it to me. I sighed and gathered up the leaves in the caladium while Gia and Rita made their way back to the stone wall opening.

It was quiet again, save the forest noises. I looked over at the bright yellow snake that was still motionless in the grass where it had fallen over. If there was ever any doubt it wasn't dead before, that doubt left me now. I hoped the man who helped me was all right, wherever he was. Maybe he hadn't been bitten? Maybe it was just a different wound that had opened up?

"I can still help you," I said, raising my voice just enough in the hopes that if he were still out there, he would hear me.

I wondered who he was, what he'd done to wind up on this island. There was no answer even after I called out a few more times, but standing there just then, I still did not feel alone.

Chapter 13

I finished stringing the tobacco leaves under a thick tree branch, which wasn't easy to do since I'd removed the socks I was using as bandages and slid them over my hands like gloves. I needed to clean the burns on my palms and the cut on my leg, and I really needed to take a look around to see if I could find some aloe or witch hazel, though I thought it was likely too far south to find the latter. I took one of the banana leaves I'd seen earlier, which would make a decent bandage. And if I could find some yarrow…

I let my mind wander with the possibilities of all the unknown medicinals on this island, but the oppressive reality that I was unjustly, mysteriously relegated to a penal colony in the middle of the ocean fell over me again. *Was I going to spend the rest of my life in that rock with Mae, Gia, and Rita? Who else was involved if I was moved to the other ship after Scott was killed?*

My head started to spin again, and then it began pounding. I needed to do some damage control. This would all get a lot worse if these burns and cuts got infected. One thing at a time.

It didn't take long looking around the clearing before I found not only several bright yellow blooms of yarrow, but also a white willow tree. I blinked repeatedly to make sure I was really seeing the thin, feather-like leaves. A few bark scrapings would work almost as well as aspirin, and I would crush the yarrow and make a salve for my hands and leg. I got to work collecting just enough for what I needed and went back into the cave, for lack of something better to call it.

Someone had made another fire near the back wall, but the smoke wasn't going up. It was being pulled back, deeper into the cave. I didn't know how that was possible since there *was* nothing deeper.

Mae emerged just then from what seemed to be the edge of the rock wall, and I gasped in surprise. Rita and Gia looked at me curiously at first, but then chuckled.

"Freaked us out the first time too," Gia said, placing a fillet of the fish on a makeshift rack that looked to be made of…bones.

"Is that *human*?" I gasped again.

"Nobody they knew, don't worry," Mae said, taking long skewers and running them through the ends of the strips of fish that Rita was cutting, then rubbing with what looked like salt. "Those bones were here when Mae found this place," Mae said, startling me with the reference to herself.

"She talks like that sometimes," Gia said in a hushed voice, then shrugged. "She's been here fifty-three years."

I caught my mouth falling open in disbelief and closed it quickly. That was over double my entire life.

"How long have you both been here?" I asked after another minute.

"Six years," Gia said.

"Nine," Rita answered without looking up from her work. She had an emblem tattooed on her shoulder that I saw for the first time—a diamond with numbers or letters that were hard to read.

Neither of them looked much older than I was, which meant they must have only been teenagers when they arrived.

"A lot of people here are ex-military," Gia said, noticing me staring at Rita's tattoo. "Too much time and energy spent training them just to execute them for whatever they did, especially with all the civil wars in the states." I nodded, knowing all too well, thinking of all the unrest in The Grind back home.

I glanced at Mae. "Fifty-three years..." I said in disbelief. "That's about when the walls went up in Maine," I added, but then regretted even broaching the topic.

"In Boston too," Gia said. "But not right away. At first it was just getting into the universities—paper walls most people couldn't get past. They kept building housing and more buildings to serve that population until it eventually turned into its own little city," she continued as she moved the fish over the fire. "After a while, the concrete walls went up, and you were either a productive member of The Citadel community, or you were a *leech* on The Rim."

I stared at her. "That's exactly what happened in Portland," I said, trying to keep the surprise out of my voice. "We call it The Grind outside the walls."

"So you *were* inside?" Rita asked, her voice tight.

"Well…" I started, not sure what the best answer here would be, but my head was pounding too hard to come up with something other than the truth. "I worked at the Center for Pathology. I was trying to find a cure for the virus that was mainly affecting people outside The Citadel," I explained, feeling the need to justify myself for some reason. Rita just huffed.

Gia nodded perceptively and handed a bowl of cooked fish to Mae. "And some of us were just fighting in the wrong place at the wrong time with the wrong people," she added with a half smile, which I took to mean that was all she was going to say about that.

"You come to Scrapper Island for two reasons," Mae said, suddenly attentive, her round, dark eyes fixed on mine. "They either won't kill you or they can't," she finished matter-of-factly, then burst out in raucous laughter. I tried to laugh along with her since Gia and Rita just chuckled and shook their heads, evidently not fazed.

"How did you get here, Mae?" I asked, but she just started humming to herself.

"She doesn't remember," Gia said with a shrug. "Been too long—she thinks she was born here."

I nodded, suddenly feeling restless. I needed to make myself busy, so I crossed to the back of the cave, which was somehow full of sunshine, and put the yarrow, willow twigs, and bark on a flat rock jutting out conveniently from the wall. I remembered the wooden bowl full of water they'd given me the night before, and brought that back to my new workstation too.

From this angle in the cave, I saw another wall running parallel to the one I was standing next to and several shafts of light filtering through from somewhere above.

"Oh…" I said out loud, realizing this is where Mae must have come from. "What's down there?" I asked.

"We store wood back there. It opens to the top of the mountain," Gia said, putting another fillet of fish on the fire. I stiffened.

"How do you keep animals from getting in up there…or people?" I asked, craning my neck to see how high up the walls went.

"No predatory animals on this island anymore except for snakes," Rita said. "But if they're stupid enough to fall through the crag, they land in the spikes."

"The *what*?" I asked, straining to get a better look as I crushed the yarrow against the side of the wooden bowl. "Whoa," I said, finally seeing the sharpened sticks arranged in a little death pit that must have run the width of the crag above.

I swallowed hard during the awkward silence and cut a few small pieces of the fresh willow bark to chew on, hoping the pain in my head and everywhere else for that matter would subside sooner rather than later. I used the remaining water in the wooden bowl I'd been given the night before to rinse the burns on my hands and the cut on my leg, then washed the thin wool socks in the little that was left. I let those dry by the fire, spreading some of the yarrow paste over each wound in the meantime.

"What is all that?" Rita asked, glancing at me.

"It's yarrow flower. I picked some right outside," I answered. "It helps prevent infections. These strips are willow bark. They help pain."

"Any of that stuff jog your memory?" she asked.

"There's nothing wrong with my memory. I'm telling you, I didn't do anything to get sent to a penal colony. I was just trying to find out what was making people sick."

Gia pulled the fish off the fire and began cutting it into portions. "What kind of sick?"

"People were wasting away at first, then there was a variant to the virus that made them lose their minds —become violent," I explained. "In some cases, they even...*changed* into a kind of animal. At least that's how it looked."

"People got sick, violent, and then turned into animals?" Rita asked, arching a dark brow.

"*Yes,*" I insisted. "I was asking too many questions about one of the cases, and people from my own lab tried to kill me."

The willow bark *had been* working until I started trying to prove myself again. I could feel the pressure behind my eyes and the pounding in the back of my head starting to increase again. I carefully turned my sock bandages over so the heat from the fire could dry the other side and tried to relax.

"It's not that she doesn't believe you," Gia said, handing me a bowl of fish. "There's something like that here, too. Something on the island."

"Salamanders…salamanders," Mae said to herself as she chewed.

"No, Mae. That's not salamanders." Rita chuckled. "It's fish."

"Something like what on the island?" I asked Gia, unsure if I'd heard her right.

"Something that leaves bones lying around in the jungle," Gia answered. "Human bones."

I looked at her cautiously. Rita rolled her eyes. "It's just the boa constrictors. Don't listen to her ghost stories."

"*Just* the boa constrictors?" I nearly choked on the bite of fish in my mouth.

Rita shrugged. "What else could just leave bones?"

"I was supposed to go to a place called Snake Island for my field assignment," I said, curious how far away we were if this island apparently had so many snakes.

"They're sisters," Mae spoke up again, tipping the edge of her bowl up to her mouth to reach the last bits of fish.

"The islands are sisters?" I asked.

Gia shrugged in what was apparently confirmation. "Monroe said our closest landfall was a thousand miles in any direction—that's why they made this island a penal colony."

"They built her boats and set her free..." Mae chanted. "Closed up Eden and opened the sea..."

"You said that's good for infection and pain?" Rita asked, ignoring Mae's little song.

"This?" I startled, glancing at the yarrow and willow bark. "Yes, it's helping already, actually."

"Make some more, and come with me."

Chapter 14

I bandaged my hands and leg again once the wool was dry, then went back into the clearing and folded more yarrow and another strip of willow bark into a banana leaf. Strangely, the bright yellow body of the djin snake was gone.

"You're sure that snake was dead?" I asked, scanning the ground. "Because it's not here."

I followed Rita as she pushed through the curtain of foliage. "Bird might have grabbed it up. Otherwise something else probably dragged it off," she said. "Food is food, and most things here aren't picky."

"Where are we going?" I asked, since we were only about a hundred steps from the front of the rock cave but it was nowhere in sight. "I can hear the beach," I added.

"That's where we're going."

My stomach tightened at the idea of seeing the people from last night again. "*Why?*" I insisted, but then remembered the yarrow and willow bark she had me bring. "Who's hurt?"

"Probably somebody."

The fallen leaves and trees soon gave way to white sand, and the breeze from the ocean hit us. Looking out, the jungle wrapped the length of the island in both directions, and the ocean seemed to stretch into eternity.

A group of people were sleeping on the beach, and still others in a line of shelters that utilized the standing coconut trees as corner posts.

"Those are the people from last night? I didn't see the shelters when the boat docked," I said, then looked around for the boat dock, which was also gone.

"That's on the other side of the island," Rita said. "Storms come in too hard on that side, so everybody builds back here."

We walked past the unconscious woman who took my jacket last night. She was sprawled over a tattooed, muscular man with the same diamond insignia Rita had, only this one was on his chest and larger. I didn't say anything out of fear it would wake them up, and I didn't want to deal with the imminent confrontation that would follow.

The older woman from the boat and a few other faces I recognized were all huddled together at the end of the row of shelters, a burned out fire in the center of them. We slowed when we came upon another shelter, this one on stilts and reaching back into the jungle.

"They were on my boat," I said to Rita as we passed the sleeping people. At least, I hoped they were sleeping.

"Poppy's crew picked them up," she said, taking a huge step onto the platform. *All this elaborate work and they couldn't make steps?* "Come on." Rita extended an arm, but there was no way I could just jump up there the way she did with my hands and leg in the state they were in. I sat on the edge and swung my legs up, then leveraged to my feet by hooking Rita's forearm.

"This is all one shelter?" I asked as we made our way down the long, winding floor that, like the walls, looked like young, tied-together trees. "Wait, are we going up?"

I couldn't tell where we were with the dense foliage obscuring my view of the ground, but the effort of walking was definitely getting harder.

When it finally leveled off, a wide, open room full of sleeping people spread out in front of us. There were only walls on one side with the entire front of the room opening to an uncovered deck, which overlooked the treetops and was surrounded by a wooden rail.

We had definitely gone up.

A tall, cat-like woman with shiny, vine-patterned scars over the dark skin of her arms and chest turned to us. Her tank top was frayed, but surprisingly not torn like everyone else's clothes, and the uneven crop of her shorts made it clear they used to be pants.

"Who did that to her?" the woman asked, agitated.

"She came that way off the boat," Rita answered. The woman nodded and looked me up and down. "Did Monroe do that to your face?"

I'd forgotten about the black eyes I apparently had. I brought my hands to my cheekbones and checked to see if they were still painful to the touch. The willow bark had helped some.

"No," I said, not sure how to even begin the rest of the story.

"She said someone tried to kill her before she got on the boat," Rita summarized, and I was grateful.

"Did they get what was coming to them?" the woman asked me.

"Uh, yes. He was eaten by sharks."

The woman nodded, satisfied, and looked back at Rita. "Is she the only one you got off the beach?"

"Yeah. Gia pulled her from the shore. She can treat injuries—we brought supplies." Rita nodded to me and glanced at the rolled banana leaf sticking out of my back pocket. I grabbed it and showed the woman the yarrow and strips of willow bark inside.

"You can read the plants?" the woman asked.

"I've never heard it put that way, but yes. I'm a botanist. Or...I was..." I answered, still not having really processed that I was on this island, or how long I might be here.

"Follow me."

Rita and I followed the woman around the corner to a smaller open room. Inside this one, another woman, broad and dark-haired like Rita, was sweating in a hammock. Her cheeks and eye sockets were bluish, slightly sunken, and a wash of dread pushed over me in a reflexive reaction to the appearance of Red Fever. But that couldn't be here, not on an island in the middle of the ocean. *Could it?*

"Mack?" Rita said, rushing to her side. "What happened?"

The woman in the hammock tried to laugh. "Poppy, you let her in here?" she asked through a cough. "I don't have my face on."

"Here's the seawater," a lanky man set a large bowl down and quickly stepped out of the way.

The woman who escorted us—apparently, *Poppy*—dipped a compress into the bowl of water on the floor and let it drip into the wound.

"You're using seawater to clean that?" I asked, apparently too abruptly.

Poppy looked up at me. "The salt helps," she said a little defensively.

"Damn it, Mack. What happened?" Rita asked as Mack sucked in air through her teeth as the seawater drenched what looked to be a puncture wound on her shoulder. "Did Burgess do this? I've been waiting for an excuse to kill that bastard."

"Somebody beat you to it," Mack said with a weak chuckle, still without opening her eyes. "We got about nine out..." she trailed off.

"Frankie, come here," Rita said, gesturing to Mack's shoulder. "Can you fix that?"

I moved closer and saw that the wound was small, fortunately, but red and inflamed. It didn't look deep since it wasn't pooling with blood, but the thick, white discharge it emitted wasn't a good sign. A cool breeze was also coming directly off the ocean, unobstructed by trees, but sweat was still beading on Mack's forehead. I felt her cheek, which was hot to the touch.

"She has a fever, which means her body is fighting an infection," I said, grimacing at the shoulder wound again. "I can try to treat it, but I need some boiled water—not seawater—and more of this to start," I said, holding up a sprig of yarrow flower and one of the strips of willow bark. "This is from a tree with long, sweeping branches. The leaves look like feathers."

"Take Burns with you," Poppy said with a nod to Rita, then nodded to another woman. "Maria, get a bowl of water from the pit fire."

"Wait—" I said abruptly, noticing that the bloodied corner of Mack's shirt was marred with a spot of something black and sticky, almost like grease. I examined the compress, but there was nothing like that on it. "This just happened to her last night?" I checked the wound again, this time noticing traces of the same black substance still under her skin.

"On the beach, when the boat came in," Poppy said. "What's the problem?"

"Do you know what this black stuff is?" I asked. Poppy shook her head. "And the cloth was clean before you used it on her?"

"*Of course* it was clean." Poppy scowled at me.

"OK, I just had to check because I think there might have been something on whatever cut her," I said, but the seawater was more likely to blame.

"What?" Rita asked, reaching to examine Mack's shoulder.

"Don't touch it!" I almost shouted. "I don't know what it is yet—it could make you sick too. It may have come from the seawater. How long have you been irrigating her wound with it?" I turned to Poppy.

"Since she came off the beach," she said, her lips tight. "We've always used seawater for wounds," she said, narrowing her eyes defensively again.

"I don't mean any offense," I said. "I'm sure it has worked in the past, but maybe the ship from last night spilled something into the water this time," I couched, not even wanting to discuss the untold microbes she could have introduced into Mack's bloodstream. Poppy's brow arched, and her mouth relaxed enough to suggest she was at least thinking about the possibility.

The woman, Maria, from before brought me another bowl of water, this one smaller.

"Rainwater," she said with a nod. I smiled at her and took the bowl carefully, the stone sides warm to the touch.

"I'm sure one of those assholes just tipped an arrow in something. Who did this, Mack?" Rita asked as I rinsed, then applied the yarrow paste to Mack's wound. "Who were you fighting?"

"Burgess..." Mack laughed. "But he's already dead."

"If he's not, he's going to be," Rita said. "Burns, Maria, come with us," she added. A broad shouldered, middle-aged man and another tall, athletic woman came forward from the small crowd.

"Just find out what they used on the weapons," Poppy said, taking a step into Rita's path. "Don't engage."

They started to leave, but Rita abruptly stopped and turned back to me. "Frankie, come on!"

"I'm going?" I asked, stupidly as I rushed to finish applying the rest of the yarrow paste I'd just made to Mack's shoulder. "You said they kill blondes!"

Mack laughed in her hammock, which gave way to a bad coughing fit.

"Just keep your mouth shut and don't make eye contact," Rita said, then turned to the man with us. "Burns, stay between her and the shacks. Maria will watch the perimeter."

We were down the timber ramp before I knew it, the white sand already nearly blinding in the morning sun.

The people from my boat were still asleep at the foot of the ramp. I sat down and slid off while Rita and the other two just jumped the four feet to the sand below.

We walked along the edge of the jungle for several minutes before we came upon a group of people in various stages of consciousness. The woman wearing my jacket and the human tree she was sleeping on didn't wake up as we passed them and the ramshackle huts, which didn't look to be more than a roof of palms held up by tied-together timber walls.

"Burgess!" Rita shouted, startling all three of us walking near her. People began waking up as we passed, hurling a variety of descriptive words at our backs. "Where's Burgess? I have a little present for him!" Rita shouted again.

I looked at Maria to my right, but she was too busy keeping an eye on everyone else between here and the shore to notice.

"What's the present?" I turned to Burns, who was also oblivious to me. "I'm not the present, right?"

"Burgess, you asshole! Where are you?" Rita yelled down the beach, tipping someone out of their hammock as we passed. The man crashed to the ground and started slurring curses. Rita was unfazed. "*Burgess!*"

"You lost, *amazon*?" a man's voice said. A second later, a bunch of green coconuts dropped out of a tree in front of us, followed by a lanky, balding man with a small, homemade axe in his hand. He landed on his feet and slung the little axe over his shoulder.

"Fuck off, Ross. Where's Burgess?"

The man looked me up and down. "Well, he didn't do that to her, if that's why you're here."

"That's not why I'm here," Rita said. "Just go get him."

"Can't help ya," Ross answered, then hammered the axe into one of the coconuts. He scooped up the other two in his long, leathery arm and licked his lips when he passed me. "I'll tell him you stopped by, though," he said with a greasy smile.

Burns kicked the back of Ross's knees, which sent the coconuts rolling down the beach as he fell to the sand. Maria retrieved the little axe and tossed it to Rita, who quickly drove a knee into Ross's back and brought the axe behind his ear.

"I'm going to tell you nicely one more time, and then I'm going to cut this flytrap off and wear it around my neck," Rita hissed. *Go. Get. Burgess.*"

"I can't! You bitch! Get off me!" Ross shouted, and people started to stir. Rita sighed and made a quick cut on the back of his ear with the axe. He screamed. "I can't! I can't bring him to you!"

"Why not?"

"He's hurt!"

Rita got to her feet and smiled. "Well, you should have led with that, Ross. I would have been in a much better mood. Take me to him."

Chapter 15

Ross stood up and touched the blood behind his ear. He swore again at Rita, but led us further down the winding path of huts without protest.

We made our way to one of the bigger structures, which was more of a shell than a hut with three log cabin-like walls, the fourth wall doubling as a window made of long branches that rolled up and hooked onto the roof. This hut was also built on stilts and had a wood floor like Poppy's camp.

"Give me back the axe now," Ross said, reaching for it.

"On our way out," Rita answered. Ross glared at her, but didn't argue. He just sat down on the beach while the rest of us approached the open hut. A man who had been sitting on the stoop sprang up and held out something that looked like a small sickle. I winced, realizing it was a rib bone, sharpened and fastened to a wooden grip.

Another man was lying flat on a raised platform inside. His face was also gaunt with bluish bruising under his eyes and cheekbones as he lay there unconscious. He was sweating like Mack had been. I scanned him for obvious signs of injury, but didn't see any. *Two like this now...it can't be Red Fever, can it?* I thought, my mind suddenly racing.

"You don't look hurt to me, Burgess," Rita said, though I could tell the man's appearance was a surprise to her. "Wake up! What did you put on your weapon last night? What was that black shit?" she said, taking several steps toward him.

The man with the bone sickle moved quickly into her path. "What do you want, *amazon*?" he said through broken, black teeth.

"Burgess poisoned Mack last night," she answered, unfazed by his weapon or his teeth. "Where's the black grease he made?"

"What grease?" The man glared at her.

"The grease he put on whatever he used to stab Mack!"

The man with the sickle took a step toward Rita, kicking over a large shell of bloodstained water that I was sure originated from the sea. Burns and Maria moved forward, and it was only a matter of time before this got really bad.

"Where's his wound?" I shouted, sure that he had one now. The man with the sickle looked down his long, crooked nose at me. "I'm a botanist—I know about medicinal plants. I might be able to help him," I said while I had his attention. He stared at me warily for another few seconds, but then walked back to the man lying down and pushed his shirt open.

He pulled back a soaked rag on the man's throat to reveal *two* punctures like the one Mack had, only these were both oozing the sticky, black material that I'd only seen traces of in Mack's wound. Burns and Maria both gasped as Rita and I exchanged glances.

"That's the same stuff," she said to me with a nod.

"What the *hell*?" The woman wearing my jacket stumbled up the beach to us, followed by the large tattooed man she'd been sleeping on before. She caught my eye and smirked, shoving her hands into the pockets.

"What happened to Burgess last night?" Rita asked her. "You were on the beach with him when the boat came in."

"I got what was mine and left," she answered, opening her arms. "Tell Gia she's lucky I had a date or I'd have taken those pretty short pants too," she said, leaning back and groping the tattooed man. He pushed her forward, and she fell into the sand.

"Somebody here has to know what happened!" Rita shouted.

"Something else was on the beach," Burgess said, his voice ragged.

"What did you say?" Rita moved back to his side, her hand gripping Ross's axe.

"It took the girl..." Burgess mumbled again. His eyes were still closed, and the wound spurted more of the black, sticky grease.

"What girl? Mack?"

Burgess started coughing, and some of the black grease started running from his nose. He coughed more as it collected in the corners of his mouth.

"What the fuck?" The man with the sickle stumbled backward as Burgess began coughing so hard he fell off the raised pallet to the ground. He got to his hands and knees and looked up at us through blackened eyes, as if the whites had been flooded by the same sticky grease that was pouring from his mouth. He screamed as all four of his canines elongated and sharpened, which sent even the man with the sickle running.

Burgess caught his leg and dragged him back. The man lashed at him until the bone sickle shattered, which only seemed to anger Burgess. He dove at the man's throat and began biting him, ripping him apart just like the bartender back at Ivy's. It wasn't just the microbes in the seawater. *It was here. Red Fever was here…*

"Run… *run…*" I tried to shout, but it came out in a cracking, thin voice.

In seconds, the man was torn limb from limb, and Burgess was covered in his blood. He turned to me, but despite Rita's efforts to pull me away, I couldn't make my legs move. Burns grabbed me around the waist and lifted me off my feet just as Burgess lunged at me, but he only got two steps out of the hut before he was suddenly engulfed in a fiery mass.

Everyone scattered, and before I knew it the four of us were running. It seemed like a matter of seconds before we were jumping onto the rising walkway to Poppy's large shelter and collapsing over the threshold at the top.

"Mack!" Rita raced back to where we'd left her.

I followed as quickly as I could, turning the corner just in time to see Rita pull the bloodied cloth from Mack's shoulder. I braced for the oozing black fluid to pour from her wound like it was with Burgess. But instead I saw the clean, dry yarrow paste I'd made still over her wound. I moved into the room and saw that the beads of sweat on Mack's forehead were also gone. I touched her cheek, and while it wasn't cool, it wasn't hot anymore either.

"I think her fever broke," I said in disbelief.

"She's all right?" Rita asked, her face flushed with exertion. "*Does that mean she's all right*?"

"I don't know," I said anxiously. "But she seems better."

"She should drink some coconut water since she's been sweating."

"Dehydrated…" Maria, the woman who had brought the rainwater exhaled, relieved. "That's why she looks like that." I wanted to believe that more than anything, but I couldn't shake the bone deep certainty that both Mack and Burgess had what the bartender at Ivy's had. I only hoped Mack was having more success in fighting it off.

"What the hell happened over there?" Poppy bolted in behind us.

"Get her some coconut water!" Rita commanded. "Maria…go!"

"Come out with me—hurry up," Burns said, still out of breath as he led Poppy out of the room.

Mack turned her head to us and opened her eyes. "You're still here?" she yawned. "If you're going to hover, at least get me something to eat. I'm starving."

Rita laughed awkwardly. "You feel better, though? No more coughing?"

Mack shook her head. "I feel like I could sleep for a week, but I bet that's still better than she must feel," she glanced at me. "Who did that to your face? Burgess—that asshole? I should have gone back and chased him down after we got our lot settled," she rambled. Maria returned with a split-open coconut, which Mack nearly spilled all over herself as she tried to drink.

"It wasn't Burgess, or any of those assholes this time," Rita said.

"Then who did that to her face?"

Rita shook her head in frustration. "She just came off the boat that way. It's a long story," she said, waving a hand to skip ahead. "Mack, look, I need you to tell me what else was on that beach last night with you and Burgess? What attacked him?"

"*I attacked* him." Mack laughed weakly. "That asshole was dragging her off. Cara!" she called out, but then her brow wrinkled for a second like she'd forgotten something. "Cara will tell you," she finished, abandoning whatever she seemed unsure about.

"What *else* was on the beach with you, Mack? This is important."

"You were there!" she chuckled at Rita and closed her eyes. "Didn't you see all the people scrambling off the boat? What's wrong with you?"

"Listen," Rita sighed in exasperation. "A little while ago, you said you thought Burgess was dead—that something *beat you to killing him*," Rita explained. "He *is* dead now, Mack, but not before he turned into this...I don't even know. This *creature*. He said something else was on the beach—something that apparently put two big holes in his throat just like the one in your shoulder."

"This?" Mack slurred, gesturing to the wound. "That was a cheap shot he got in when I pried him off Cara from the boat," she added, but then her eyes darted to the ground. She frowned as if she were replaying the whole thing. "Come here, *Cara from the boat!*" she shouted, sounding drunk, and I wondered what exactly was in that coconut water she had.

"We have to lock down," Poppy said with urgency in her voice as she came back into the room with Burns.

Rita waved her off. "Mack, are you sure Burgess did that to you? Are you sure it wasn't someone—*something* else?"

"Burgess was dragging Cara off!" Mack's brows furrowed as she frowned, her eyes still closed. "Until he tackled him..." She slurred again, her expression contorting like she was trying to look away from something.

"Who tackled him? Did he have a weapon?" Rita pressed.

"Now, there's no more time," Poppy insisted, grabbing Rita's arm and ushering her backward out of the little, open room. "Tell me what the hell happened out there. I told you not to engage!"

"Burgess…" Rita started. "He just caught on fire, after he—" She stopped abruptly, lost for words.

Poppy took a deep breath and blew it out slowly. "That's what Burns told me about that, and the black grease. There's going to be chaos for days down there. And they're going to blame us."

"Why?" Rita said. "Everyone saw him change!"

"Doesn't matter. You were there, so they'll find a way. They'll try to come for you and Mack."

"Let them try," Rita said through her teeth.

Poppy shook her head. "Don't be stupid. I'll call a quarantine until we can determine if that black ooze is anywhere else. That will buy us a little time. Go back to Mae's and stay out of sight until this dies down. I'll send word about Mack."

Rita nodded reluctantly, and we made our way down the ramp and back through the jungle. My mind raced with the possibility that even though I knew better, I somehow could have brought Red Fever here. Mack and especially Burgess's case were too similar to the bartender's. Too similar to the effects of novel Red Fever, but also to the mutation with their violence. *Would Mack become violent next?*

I had no answer for the tar-like substance beyond something in the water reacting with the infection. "Damnit, I just need one slide on an imager!" I shouted into the trees. I should have said something to Poppy…I should have warned them. My head was starting to pound again, and I realized I was suddenly alone. It was impossible to have any sense of direction with all the trees and vines blending together with no demarcation whatsoever, and Rita apparently wasn't in a tour guide mood. "Hey!" I called up to her. "How do you know your way out here?" She didn't answer, so I called again, but there was still no answer. "Rita!"

I stopped moving and listened, hoping I could hear her, but the only thing within earshot were the jungle chirps and hoots, and then far in the distance, the screams from the beach.

Chapter 16

I walked for what must have been hours, but was no closer to finding Rita or the cave. I'd even tried to head back to the beach after the screams had stopped, but somehow even that eluded me. I hoped beyond hope that I'd been wrong about Mack.

The sound of the ocean was also eclipsed by the different chirps and calls that were echoing through the jungle, and I knew if I didn't find my way soon, I would be out here in the dark.

Rita had to notice I wasn't with her at some point, even if it took until she got all the way back to the cave. We'd made our way to the beach in what seemed like maybe ten minutes, so surely she could just double back and find me.

Of course, she'd find me. I just had to wait it out and try not to get too far off the path.

Only, there was no path, and I had no idea how far I'd already wandered.

Panic ebbed and flowed in my thoughts. I was sure Red Fever, or some variety of it was here on this island. It was getting dark out, and Poppy said the people from the beach would be coming for us. I had to stop aimlessly wandering. I had to think.

The cave was at the bottom of a huge rock mountain, right? And there was a crag at the top where the smoke from the fire came out. It seemed like the only chance I had was to somehow get above the trees enough to get oriented again.

I got a foothold in one of the banyan trees, the wrapping, winding bark making it look like the whole thing had just stopped spinning. The deep grooves made it easy to grip, even with the burns on my hands protesting. I'd inched about halfway up, just enough to see a break in the jungle canopy, and nearly shouted in relief when I saw a huge, rocky rise jutting through the blankets of green ahead. It would be a long, long walk—longer than the initial walk from the cave to the beach—but at least I knew which way to go now.

I started to make my way back down the tree, and stopped like I'd been turned to stone when a flash of yellow caught the corner of my eye. A horned djin snake was coiled into a spring about four feet away, vibrating with anticipation.

"*Shit...shit...*" I whispered before remembering what the man in the clearing had said about not talking and not moving, but it was too late.

The snake struck out at me, snapping just to the side of my head. I heard the pop of air next to my ear, and the next thing I knew I was falling, landing, and falling again until I finally stopped moving.

I couldn't breathe. Each time I tried to pull in a breath, it just wouldn't come through the invisible barrier that had shut off my airways. I opened my eyes, and everything I saw was ringed in a black edge that was only getting larger. I blinked repeatedly because that's all I could do, and after a few seconds, the black was replaced by burning tears and coughing.

Coughing was almost breathing... I tried to sporadically suck in small gulps of air until I could almost control it. I clawed the ground making fists with my hands because I couldn't seem to get any other part of my body to move, and then I saw the bright yellow snake coming in and out of focus on its way down the tree.

I gasped for air, feeling like it was entering my lungs as if through a clogged sieve, the sharp pain yielding only wisps of oxygen that weren't enough. I dug my nails into the ground, clawing until I managed to roll to my side. I coughed again, painfully, but it meant more air.

I imagined the snake was sliding down the smooth base of the banyan tree by now, feet from me, then inches, and something inside me jolted.

I pushed to my feet and began running as fast as I could, vaguely aware of pain radiating up my side.

I ran until I couldn't see the banyan tree anymore, and I had no idea which way I'd gone.

My heart pounded in my chest. Every inch of my skin felt like it was on fire, and I was aware of every insect, every displaced leaf.

Twigs broke somewhere behind me, and I didn't think, I just started running again. I ran until the adrenaline wore off and my lungs burned, my throat burned, and my legs were a crosshatch of bleeding, searing lines—the flogging of the jungle floor.

I was irrevocably lost now, but in the instant I almost completely lost hope, I heard water flowing. A sweet scent filled the air...almost jasmine, almost honeysuckle. I followed the sound of the water to a large boulder wall that was wet to the touch, but the surrounding ground was dry.

Dry, and littered with bones.

I should have flinched, but the sweet smell filling the air was so calming. I could almost taste the cool water, could almost feel it on my skin. I followed the trail of water to an opening in the boulder several yards up, but despite the daunting angle, I started climbing.

The higher I went, the louder the bubbling water sounded, and the stronger the sweet floral smell became. My muscles burned, my side felt sharp with each breath, but I didn't care.

I climbed faster, slipping a few times, but pulled myself up despite the pain in my hands. Finally at the opening, I crawled on my hands and knees through a trickling stream, but my skin began tingling to the point that I had to stop and examine my palms. I pulled off the wool wraps and brushed off the yarrow paste to find that the deep burns were disappearing. They looked just like sand being washed away.

I blinked hard and rubbed my eyes, and my face also began tingling. It was suddenly easier to breathe, easier to see, and the pressure that I'd become accustomed to in my head *finally* dissipated. The slashes on my lower legs were gone when I looked, and with growing anticipation, I untied the damp sock bandage around my thigh. The yarrow paste had been mostly washed away, and in its place was unmarred skin. I washed the rest of the paste off, and in seconds, the tingling sensation began healing the rest of the cut. It, too, just seemed to wash away like elaborate sand art.

I got to my feet and followed the stream. It grew louder, rushing, until I turned a corner into another opening with a single, enormous tree sitting in the middle of several shafts of sunlight. The root system reached out like huge fingers into the stone below, and the branches were heavy with white flowers that gave way to a pear sized, spiky red fruit I'd never seen before.

The trunk seemed to be dripping with water from the rushing little falls that cascaded down the stone wall behind the tree, but when I looked more closely, it was viscous...

"Sap?" I said out loud. My voice echoed. I reached for one of the fruits hanging on the branch, and as I did, *it* reached back for me.

"I'm starting to think you do have a death wish." The man from the clearing walked through the stream behind me.

I jerked my hand back from the fruit feeling like I'd been caught trying to steal something.

"You..." I said, noticing the faded blood stain on his open shirt. "How did you get up here?" A line of dark hair ran from the center of his chest through the muscles in his abdomen, which flexed with each step he took through the trickling stream.

I took a few steps back, and he stopped. He bent and cupped his hands in the water, splashing it on his face and pushing it back through his loose dark hair.

He glanced back over his shoulder. "Same way you did."

The leaves behind me rustled over my shoulder, and the anxiety tightening my chest relaxed. I took a deep breath of the sweet air. "Are you following me?"

"Come away from the tree," he said, extending an arm to me. "Hurry." His heavy, dark brows arched in and upward again like they had in the clearing outside Mae's cave. He took a few more steps toward me, but then stopped when I only moved back. "Please," he said. "It's not what it seems."

The sweet almost-jasmine, almost-honeysuckle smell was palpable in the air. It filled my head and made me want to fall into a bed of the leaves and flowers.

"Then what is it?" I said, letting my eyes close as my voice echoed softly in my ears.

"A monster," the man said, jerking me away from the tree. A high-pitched wailing sounded all around us and the ground started shaking. "Come on!" he said, leading me back through the opening I'd come through.

"Stop!" I yelled when he didn't slow down at the threshold. I tried to break away from him, but he pulled me to him and jumped off the ledge.

Branches whipped past us as we fell, but in the seconds I thought we would have before we would crash into the ground, we just stopped falling. All the jungle noises stopped, the scream in my throat, silenced. Instead of air not being able to get in this time, the sound just couldn't come out.

His skin was warm on mine, his throat on my cheek, and the only thing I heard was a deep, resonating heartbeat half a second before the world rushed back into place around us.

We stood there without moving, his arms wrapped around my shoulders holding me tightly to him. He smelled like woodsmoke and seawater, the scent competing with the intoxicating florals still in the air around us. I suddenly felt my own heart pounding against my forearms, but the scream that had risen in my throat had slipped away. His chest expanded in slow, deep breaths against my hands as he loosened his hold, but didn't release me.

I felt his warm breath on my neck and his hand on the back of my hair. "You can't run now," he said, his voice soft and close to my ear. "The tree will just bring you back."

Chapter 17

A chill ran through my whole body at his words, at his touch. In a split second the last five minutes crashed together and started to untangle in my mind —the drug-like, intoxicating scent of the flowers, my gradual loss of will. I saw it all from the outside now that we were back on the ground, and the same submissive feeling came over me again standing in his arms.

So, of course, I ran.

Images of the yellow, horned snake striking at me flashed every time I blinked. Then his arm reaching out for me juxtaposed with the branch of the tree extending its fruit.

I shook my head to push the images away, but clarity didn't begin setting in until I almost ran straight over the edge of a steep, rocky hill, dozens of yards above the tree tops below. I skidded to a stop and fell backward, digging the heels of my shoes into the ground to stop my forward trajectory. I grabbed the grass under my hands and finally stopped sliding.

"OK!" I said out loud, panic pushing in on me from every direction. "*OK...it's OK...*" I caught my breath. The rest of the way down was nothing but rock face, steep and dotted with random, strangled looking shrubs. But at the bottom there was a clearing with three women, two of them gesturing wildly, and the other staring up at me. "Mae!" I shouted, finally realizing where I was. "Mae, I'm here! Rita!" The other two women looked up, then began climbing the rock.

"Frankie! Stay there. We're coming!"

"I think I can make it!" I said, inching my way down. "It's all right. Stay with Mae!"

I slipped twice, scraping the backs of my legs, but I made it to the clearing in one piece. Gia threw her arms around me, then abruptly pulled back and squared my shoulders.

"Your eyes!" she said, then turned my palms up. "And your hands? Your plants really work!"

Rita nodded. "She cured Mack, like I said."

"No, it wasn't the yarrow, listen," I started, but Rita cut me off.

"She saved her, otherwise she might have wound up like Burgess," she continued.

Gia took a deep breath, apparently already informed about exactly what happened to Burgess. "How did you even get up there?" she asked, shading her eyes as she looked up toward the top of the huge rock.

I glanced at Mae, whose wide, dark eyes were twinkling with a smile that just didn't reach her lips. "Sssssalamanders..." she said, flicking her tongue and rattling the shells in two handfuls of her hair at me.

I took a step back from her, startled. "I—I don't know," I said. "We were coming back from the beach. I just got turned around somehow."

"Next time just stay where you are," Rita said. "I doubled back for you and you were gone. We need to stay out of sight for a few days."

"Why would they come for you if they thought you or Mack infected Burgess? You'd think they'd stay as far away as possible," Gia said. "I think Poppy's wrong this time."

"It doesn't have to make sense," Rita said. "The quarantine is just to buy us all some time until we can figure out what attacked Burgess and Mack on the beach."

"Wait, you said Mack was fine?" Gia said.

Rita nodded. "Now, after Frankie did her plant voodoo. But she doesn't remember anything other than Burgess and the rest of those assholes on the beach. She saw something, though. She thought it killed Burgess."

"So, she just forgot?" Gia asked.

"It could have been a fever dream," I offered. "Do you ever replay something in your head the way you wished it would have gone?"

Rita narrowed her eyes at me. "You were there, Frankie. She wasn't sleeping."

"She wasn't totally awake though, either."

"You're sure Burgess said that something else was on the beach?" Gia asked. "You're sure those were his words?"

"Sssssalamanders..." Mae interjected again, and this time, we all stopped and looked at her.

"Why does she keep saying that?" Rita asked. Gia shook her head. "Mae, why are you talking about salamanders?" Rita took a step toward her. "When have you seen salamanders in the last decade around here?"

Mae only flicked her tongue at us again and rattled the shells in her hair.

"She's getting worse," Gia said with a sigh.

Rita nodded. "Just make her happy. That's all we can do for her."

"Come on, Mae. I brought you some new shells." Gia led Mae back through the cave opening, and Rita started pacing.

"Do you remember anything from the beach?" she asked me. "Gia watched you come off the boat and pulled you out of there right away, so I know you didn't have much time."

"Just that woman and who took my jacket. Gia was there maybe two seconds after that."

"Bitsy?"

"Her name is *Bitsy*?"

"That's just what people call her," Rita said dismissively. "We need to go talk to her."

"How do you plan to do that?" Gia said, emerging from the cave without Mae. "We can't go back into their camp with the quarantine."

"What about the girl?" I said. "Burgess and Mack both said there was a girl. Cara, I think?"

Rita and Gia exchanged glances. "Burgess said the thing that was on the beach took her..." Rita trailed off.

"But didn't Mack just say he let her go when she screamed?" I asked. Rita nodded. "We need to talk to her."

"It'll have to wait," Gia said. "The sun is half down already, and I'm worried about Mae. She keeps singing about salamanders and *bloodfruit* trees—weird shit."

"The tree!" I blurted, surprising myself as much as Gia and Rita. "After we got separated there was—"

Mae came running out of the cave with a fistful of shells in one hand. She grabbed the strap of my tank top and pushed me to the ground, shoving the shells into my mouth.

"She won't give them back! She won't give them back!" Mae chanted hysterically.

"Mae! Stop! *Stop*!" Rita and Gia shouted as they pulled her off me. I sat up and spit out the shells, but the metallic taste of blood washing through my mouth just kept returning. I brought my hand to my lips and saw the dark red smears covering my fingers, quickly followed by burning sensations all over my lips and cheeks.

"Mae, what the hell?" Rita shouted, holding Mae's bloody hands. I didn't know if it was her blood or mine.

She brought her fingers to her lips. "Shhhhh... shhhhh... She won't give them back..."

"Mae! Mae, calm down," Gia said, trying to bring Mae's bloody hands away from her face.

"She won't give you back. She doesn't give anyone back... Shhhhh... Shhhh."

Gia brought Mae back into the cave, and Rita hurried over to me and helped me up. "Are you OK?" she asked. "She didn't mean it. She's old."

"I know," I said before I realized how much it would hurt.

The insides of my cheeks felt raw as I tried to spit out the blood again, and I could feel grains of sand between my teeth.

"Stay here, I'll get some water and you can point out what I should pick to heal it up, OK?" Rita said, taking steps toward the cave. "Just stay here, and I'll be right back." I nodded and closed my eyes against the incessant burning that covered my mouth, my cheeks, even my nose. I spit out more blood, but swallowed a little too, which made me feel nauseous, so I leaned forward and just let it drip into the grass.

I thought of the cool water in the cave, how it had stopped the burning of the cuts on my legs...how it just stopped all the pain all at once.

In the same moment, the faint, sweet smell of the flowers floated through the air. It got thicker, filling my head and my chest.

You can't run... I heard the dark-eyed man say somewhere in the distance, and yet, all around me. I could smell him, all woodsmoke and sea and heat against my skin. I closed my eyes and saw his broad chest, his arms, lined with veins weaving around the muscles, which faded into the long, reaching roots of the tree as they disappeared into the rocks. *The tree will just bring you back...*

"Frankie!" Rita's voice was cold and biting like a sudden winter rain. She pulled me up by my shoulders and started splashing my face with water.

Water that smelled like iron and earth, not the sweet, cool water from the spring. I moved back from her, sobering.

"You passed out," she said, showing me the blood covered blades of grass she was peeling off my face. "It's not bad. The cuts are small," she continued. "Here, drink this." She handed me a wooden bowl of water and dipped her cloth in another one.

I swished the water carefully around my mouth and spit it out, taking most of the metallic taste with it.

"Thanks," I said gingerly.

"Do you want to chew on those yellow flowers?" Rita asked. I started to laugh, then thought better of it when the pain seared across my lips all over again.

"No...aloe," I said, trying to use as few words as possible. I nodded to the edge of the clearing, and

Rita helped me to my feet. I broke off a leaf and motioned to go inside.

"You sure?" Rita asked.

"She didn't mean it," I said, the words coming out boxed since I tried not to move my tongue or lips to better form them.

A fire was blazing in the cook pit when we came in, and Gia was washing Mae's hands with another bowl of water. I broke off the fat end of the aloe and handed it to Gia.

"What's this?" she asked.

"Aloe," I said. "The gel is good for her cuts." She nodded at me apologetically, and I held up a hand. "I know. It's OK," I said, hoping that was enough to make her understand that I didn't blame Mae, who was humming now and staring into the fire.

The burning feeling of my cuts had faded enough that I decided not to go back out for more willow bark. I just bit the end off of the rest of the aloe and pushed it around my mouth, then dabbed the remaining end over my lips, nose, and cheeks. I lay back on the furs of my bed and tried to remember my life before this.

It seemed like something I'd dreamed a long time ago. Something in pieces now. And like all dreams remembered in the waking world, I knew, deep down, that I would never again find my way back to it.

Chapter 18

A bright flash woke me, but it was the deafening crack that made me open my eyes.

Rain began pummeling my skin, and the stone was cold beneath my hands and bare feet. I heard tree branches swishing and shaking not far in the distance, the steady tattoo of drops growing like approaching war drums.

Another staccato flash illuminated the jungle around me, and although I knew it was coming, the earth shaking thunder nearly made me lose my grip on the rock I was clinging to.

"What the hell is happening?" I said into the night, unsure if this was reality or a dream.

Hands gripped my wrists and pulled me up, out of the rain, but just as quickly released me. My heart hammering in my ears competed with the ringing from the crash of thunder, and a soft glow emanating from several feet away began to brighten.

The sweet smell of almost-jasmine, almost-honeysuckle filled the air, and my stomach leaped.

"I told you that you couldn't run." His voice was clear and close. "Not on your own."

Another flash of lightning outside lit the small stone enclosure. He was crouched over the trickling stream between us gathering water in his hand. He started to cross to me, and the thunder shook the floor.

"Stay away from me," I said, shivering with fear, frozen where I stood.

"I'm not going to hurt you." He stepped into the glow and reached for me. I flinched away from him. "*I promise* I won't hurt you. Please." I didn't move when he took a step closer, and I didn't breathe as he ran his wet thumb over my lips and cheeks until they tingled the way my hands and legs did earlier. "Close your eyes," he said, but I hesitated. He nodded again, the heat radiating from him, my exhaustion, and the smell of campfire and sea melting my resolve. I closed my eyes and soon felt cool water pouring over my face. It ran into my mouth, finding its way into every corner, bubbling until I didn't think I could handle the sensation anymore. Not a second later, it was gone.

I blinked to clear my vision and knew the cuts from the shells were healed. He nodded and smiled a little as he cupped more water and trickled it over my knees, shins, and feet, which I didn't even know were scraped until I felt the tingling.

He stood again, inches from me, and turned my palms upward in his hand. With the other, he trickled more water, and I watched the new scrapes wash away. The lightning and thunder had moved on.

"*How…?*" I started, then changed my mind about which question I wanted answered first. "Why did you bring me here?" I asked, feeling a little drunk with the growing floral smell filling my head.

"The tree brought you," he answered quickly. "I came so you'd be able to leave."

"I don't understand." I shook my head at him, confused, but the wind howled across the rock opening before he could answer, casting a sheet of freezing rain over us. I clenched my teeth to keep them from chattering and instinctively moved toward him, away from the cold. I took a deep breath of the perfumed air and again wanted to fall into it. His arm wrapped around my waist, steadying me as warmth pushed through me all at once. His dark eyes met mine, the intoxication of the tree and the heat between us nearly paralyzing. I cleared my throat and took a sobering step back.

He caught my hand. "Come with me?" he asked. I hesitated, and he arched his brows in that inexplicable way again. "It's not safe for you here, and it has to be your choice or the tree will shriek like before. That will make others come." After another beat, my head was starting to spin again, so I reluctantly nodded. He brought my hand to his chest, drew me close, and jumped into the night.

Like last time, I heard the rushing tree limbs, and in the second before I braced to hit the ground, everything stopped except the deep, echoing thrum of a heartbeat. The wind and rain hit us from every direction, but we were out of the weather again in what only seemed to be a few seconds.

After my next blink, a fire was blazing in a hearth, which was made of stones pressed into a tall, earthen wall. The room seemed carved out of clay, each of the other three walls smooth with the shadows of dancing firelight. The floor was covered in furs except for just in front of the fire.

Lightning flashed in the distance, illuminating the sea outside the opening we'd just come through.

My breath caught in my throat as I turned to him. "*How*…did we get here?"

He walked toward the back of the earthen room and brought me a T-shirt—tattered, but clean and dry, then turned around and removed the cut off button down he wore with the bloodstain on the shoulder. The light from the fire flickered over his broad back, deepening every shadow and groove. He unfastened the waistband of his shorts and glanced over his shoulder. A ghost of a smile tugged at the corner of his mouth when he saw me watching him, and heat flushed my cheeks and throat. I turned away quickly to shimmy out of my own wet clothes into the T-shirt he'd given me. It was long and soft, and of course, smelled of woodsmoke and sea. My chest swelled as I slowly took in the scent.

When I turned around again, he wore only a dry pair of tattered gray cutoff shorts as he draped his wet clothes on a rack next to the fire. The light danced over his tanned skin as he held out an arm to me, the muscles weaving and wrapping from his shoulder conjured an image of the thick tree roots from the other cave in my mind. I startled and took a step back from him.

"I only want to hang your clothes," he said evenly, furrowing his heavy, dark brows in that way again—pained, but sincere.

"Sorry," I nodded, still feeling a little woozy and now, ridiculous as I handed him the clothes like he was some kind of wild animal waiting to snap at me. There was nothing he'd ever done to threaten me, but I felt it on a primal level—he was a predator. I just didn't know yet if I was prey.

He hung my tank top and shorts next to his and sat on the fur several feet away from the fire, glancing at me every few seconds.

"I know you have questions," he said. "I'll answer them, but you might want to get comfortable first," he gave a small nod to the fur covered floor and risked a small smile.

I sat down against the wall and gathered one of the furs close like it was some kind of shield as I searched for the snakebite wound on his shoulder, but there wasn't a mark on him. I let my eyes travel over the curves of his arms, shoulders, and chest as the firelight played over them. Everyone on this island I'd seen so far had scars, except him.

"You don't have a bite wound," I said after several seconds. "I know that snake connected with you. And then I watched it die in that clearing a few minutes later. You said it would kill me."

"It would have. It wanted to." He risked another glance at me, and I knew he was stalling, playing some kind of game, but I didn't know why. He sighed when I just glared at him. "That snake wasn't what it seemed," he finally said after several more minutes. "There are a lot of things on this island that aren't what they seem."

"Like you?" I said, letting the irritation and impatience slip into my voice.

He nodded, pained again somehow, and stared into the fire. "*Like me.*"

My head finally began to clear, and a bubble of fear rose in my chest. "How did we get here so quickly? And why do you keep helping me?" I asked. "How do you always just…*show up?*"

The man sighed and dropped his gaze to the floor. The muscles tightened in his jaw, and his dark brows pushed inward again. "I can hear you—like the tree hears you," he said, glancing up at me just for a second. He quickly turned his gaze back to the fire, apparently not finding the expression he was hoping for on my face.

"*What* does that mean? You said you would answer my questions." I let more of the impatience I was feeling lace my voice, but if I was honest, now it was more fear than impatience.

"I'm sorry," he added after another pause. "There's just so much, and I don't even know where to begin."

The rigidity I'd been feeling softened at this. He scrubbed his hands over his face with a groan and pushed them through his loose, dark hair.

I took a deep breath and decided to be blunt. "All right. Well, my name is Frankie Mason." He looked at me quickly, surprised.

A smile threatened to break free in the corner of his mouth. "I'm Knox," he said, briefly clearing his throat. "Knox Ryder."

I nodded at him. "Now we've begun," I said after a beat. He returned my nod, and this time, didn't hide his smile.

Several more seconds passed like this before he spoke again, but the warning tone was back. "You can't go to the tree again. At least not without me, all right?"

"Why? What is it? And the water…"

"A woman runs crates of that fruit and sap back to the mainland. It's not a normal tree." I blinked at him, not sure if I'd heard him correctly. "The water only works when it's in contact with the living roots; that's why she doesn't ship it too."

"What is it used for?" I asked, realizing the water was likely how he healed the snakebite wound and any other mark he may have otherwise earned here.

"I've never seen fruit like that before, and my job is literally to know about plants." Knox's jaw tightened again as he listened to my questions. "And why doesn't she use the fruit to grow a whole orchard of the trees on the mainland? This climate spans well into Florida."

At this, he met my eyes again. "The harvesters used to try to plant the fruit near different waterfalls so they'd have more harvest sites here, more sources for the water, but nothing ever grew," Knox said. "In fact, it killed all the other vegetation growing near it. They said it just had a *bad seed*."

"No one ever said what kind of tree it was?" I asked, puzzled.

"No, but it's the only one on the island like it. Mama Luz's team seems to be the only other people who know about it."

"Did you say, *Luz*?"

Knox's expression hardened. "Why?"

"Mae just said *Luz got me* when I told her the ship I was on changed somehow. That it wasn't the one I boarded."

"Did you talk to her on the ship?" Knox asked, seeming impatient now.

"No, only someone named Albert—wait, *Alistair*. We'd just put our bags away and were already in the middle of the ocean in the time it took us to go back above deck—" I started.

"*We?*"

"Scott... We worked together." I sighed, remembering it all over again. "We were sent on a field assignment that turned out to be a set up—he was there to kill me." I added flippantly, cynically, then explained the rest of the story about how he fell to the sharks, about the folder with Monroe's information, and how I thought I'd been drugged and moved to the prison ship. He listened to all of it without judgement, at least none that registered on his face or in his voice.

"Unbelievable. I'm sorry," he said several beats after I'd finished.

I forced a laugh, feeling awkward for disclosing so much. "No, I am. I didn't mean to go into it all."

He shook his head adamantly. "If it makes you feel better, I used to be a doctor. At least, I almost was." He turned his whole body to face me, his dark hair dried now and falling in loose curls to his wide shoulders. "But three years ago Mama Luz brought me here, too, she just didn't know it." He chuckled weakly and then let his dark eyes wander back to the fire. "This is exactly where I should be, though. But not you."

I watched the muscles in his hands and forearms work as he retrieved a carved stone bowl full of water from the fire and poured it into two more carved out stone bowls. The scent of mint filled the air as he handed me one of them. I was unsure of what to say —what to ask him first because I had so many questions now. I didn't know what he'd done to wind up here, but after what he'd just said, I needed to find that out first.

Chapter 19

"Why do you think you belong here?" I finally asked, not wanting to come right out and ask him what he'd done out of fear he might shut down. He looked at me cautiously for a beat, like he was trying to decide what to say next. Like whatever it was might change everything, and I knew my instinct to be indirect was right.

His gaze fell to the ground. "Because I didn't know what I really was until I got here."

"What does that mean?" I pressed as much as I dared.

He shook his head and looked back at the fire, noticeably uncomfortable. "I've seen things since I've been here, Frankie. I've done things. And I don't know how much to tell you because it all sounds insane."

"I've seen some insane things since I've been here too," I said, daring yet again to move closer to him. "I saw you walk away from a deadly snakebite. I saw you basically teleport us through the jungle, and I saw a man turn into some kind of demonic animal and then burst into flames on the beach. Then there was—" I stopped when Knox's face contorted like he was suddenly overcome with grief. "What's wrong?"

He crossed to put another log on the fire. "Nothing," he said without looking at me. "Just the image of that. Do you know what caused it?"

"He'd been bitten or stabbed by something on the beach the night the boat arrived. I think whatever it was infected him with Red Fever, " I answered, then quickly realized that he might not know about the variant if he's been here the last three years. "There's a mutation of the wasting sickness now. It started about three years ago."

He nodded slowly, still arranging the fire. "You think that's what made him…*change*?"

I shrugged. "Maybe. If he was infected after that wound, it would answer a lot of questions about this disease. All we know for sure is that it's transmitted through direct contact with the blood—and just the blood. It really doesn't make sense."

"So, *everyone* who gets violent changes first?" he asked, his voice laced with desperation as he took a step toward me.

"No. I mean, I don't know," I got to my feet, confused by his sudden intensity. "We've only had one real avenue for testing. Those who manifest the full blown disease are like ghosts. They just disappear… or maybe…" I trailed off, my mind numb and racing at the same time. Why hadn't I put this together? What if something about the Ferals' mutations made them combust like Burgess, and that's why none could be found alive? Would that have happened to Donovan if the Sweeper droid hadn't shot him?

"Are you all right?" Knox asked, startling me back into the moment.

"Sorry. I just thought of something, but I don't have any way to research it now that the man from the beach is gone. Unless we can find what gave him that wound." Knox moved close to the fire again and sipped the mint tea he'd made. I watched the muscles move in his arms and chest in the flickering light.

He was well built, strong, but not alarmingly so. And that was just it—he was *too* strong, too fast for a man. I remembered the bartender from Ivy's who threw men across the room, and my blood ran cold.

"I didn't mean to scare you," he offered, taking a step back from me.

"You didn't." I lied. "But you did say you'd answer my questions," I started again, forcing each word into the world. "How did we get out of that cave, Knox? How did you bring us here so fast?" I pulled in a deep breath and held it for a second before letting it out again.

"The tree messes with the way you experience things. It gets in your mind somehow and warps time until the effect wears off," he finally said. I raised an eyebrow at him. He tensed again as he met my eyes. "It brought you out there in the middle of the night, didn't it? You weren't the first."

"The floral smell..." I thought out loud. "Like a pheromone? Because it's carnivorous? Are you telling me that tree *consumes* people?"

He looked at me soberly. "That tree won't stop calling to you, now, Frankie. It's a chemical thing, I don't know. Like a drug. I've tried cutting it down, but it won't die—it self-heals with that water. Nothing stops it, so I finally gave up trying. It always takes who it wants in the end no matter what I do."

"But why not you?" I asked. "Why did the snake die after it bit you, Knox?"

"I don't think it died." His voice grew firmer. "They play with you, too, Frankie. They get in your head. Their bite is only part of what makes them deadly."

"So this whole place is just one big psychedelic trip or something? These aren't answers, Knox," I insisted, no longer so concerned with being indirect. "You said it would have killed me."

"And it *would* have."

"But not *you*? Why not you?"

Knox sighed. "Look, after three years here, I know what they are, and they know what I am, all right?" he said impatiently, aggressively, but a second later he blew out another breath and seemed to abandon his agitation. "I've just built up an immunity to it all. To the snakes, the tree…"

I didn't believe him, and something in the way he avoided my eyes, something in the new edge to his voice made it clear that he knew I didn't.

"Why did you help me if you'd given up on trying to stop the tree?"

The question seemed to take him by surprise, and everything about him relaxed. He genuinely smiled, even if it was just at the fire.

"You were trying to help people," he said quietly. "That's all I ever wanted to do. I guess I thought if I could help you, I could..." He trailed off.

My chest swelled again as another wave of heat rushed up my throat and into my cheeks. I took a sip of my tea and felt the fumes burn my eyes, but I kept the rough, warm stone bowl close to my lips anyway just so I could catch my breath.

When I finally managed to look up at him again, he was studying me with that same desperate expression—a push and a pull, a warning, but also a plea. *Who was this man, really?*

"Why don't you live down there with them, Knox? They could use a doctor. Why are you up here on your own?"

Another flash of lightning illuminated the small cave, followed immediately with a deafening explosion of thunder that seemed to shake the earth itself. I spilled what was left of the hot tea over my hands, then dropped the stone bowl. I watched it roll toward Knox's feet, but in the next second, he was inches in front of me.

"Are you burned?" he asked, taking my hands. His fingers were strong and deft as he examined me.

Immediately I felt the hairs on the back of my neck standing on end as goosebumps rose over my skin. His touch was warm, and at the same time I felt pulled into the heat of him, everything in me also wanted to run straight out into the night...where I instinctively knew it was safer. I couldn't explain it—that tug-of-war in him, the irresistible allure and the fear of not only being hunted now, but *caught*.

"You're like the tree," I whispered before I realized it. The thought was in my head and then suddenly in my ears. He exhaled as if the air had been forced from him by a blow as he dropped my hands, and with that, all the warmth drained from my body. "I'm sorry," I said abruptly. "I didn't mean to say that. I just…I felt…"

"It's OK," Knox replied, the shadow of a smile crossing his face in the firelight. More lightning flashes lit the room as the wind began to howl. Cold rain peppered my back in a sudden gust, taking my breath as I arched away from it. He quickly traded positions with me as a cacophony of thunder echoed around us again and reverberated through the floor. I could feel it radiating through me, and this time, through him as my chest pressed against his ribs. My breath caught, and my heart was beating so hard that I knew he could feel it too.

His fingers pressed into my lower back like roots burrowing in, steadying me…grounding me. I inhaled and couldn't seem to fill my lungs enough with the scent of him. The heavy rain and wind lashed in at us again, the shock making his body rigid against mine as I felt his fingers pushing up to my ribs for just an instant. He took a measured breath and swallowed, then released me to drag a thatched door in front of the threshold where he tethered the corners to ties I hadn't noticed before. I heard the rain beating against the makeshift door as he turned back toward me, his chest wet with rain and heaving, the muscles in his stomach contracting with each heavy breath. As the fire danced over his skin, I noticed the draft was gone.

"It was stupid to bring you here," Knox said shaking his head, seemingly angry now. "I can't take you back to the old woman in this storm, but we'll go in the morning." He crossed to the fire and pulled a folded leaf from a small ledge, then unwrapped it. Several strips of what looked like dried fish fanned out after he set it on the ground between us and pushed it toward me. "You should eat something."

I couldn't read him anymore, if I even really could in the first place. He was guarded now, tense, and with each passing minute it seemed he was increasingly resentful of my presence. Was this really because of the tree comment I'd made? I wasn't even sure what I'd meant by it.

"I'm really sorry again…" I said quietly. "About saying you were like—"

"Don't be. It's accurate." He cut me off and bit off a piece of the dried fish as he lowered his eyes to the fire again, his thick, dark brows and lashes, every rounded and angled edge of him outlined in shadows like a charcoal drawing come to life.

He finished eating and moved to the far side of the room—as far away from me as he could manage, it seemed. He stretched out on his back and threw an arm over his eyes, and I knew there would be no more conversation tonight.

I curled into one of the furs and lay by the fire watching him, wondering what raw nerve I'd stepped on with the tree comment, and then it occurred to me. He'd said he was immune somehow...he could heal himself in the waters, but without paying the price with his life like the others. Like those he couldn't save. If what he said about the tree being predatory was true, maybe he felt guilty, especially as a doctor.

But if he couldn't stop the tree, why didn't he just warn everyone about it? Why did he just stay here in this hole all by himself and let it all go on? *Why wouldn't he help them?*

Chapter 20

The fire was out when I woke up the next morning, and light was darting into the room through the thatched door. I'd forgotten where I was at first, the clay walls and the stone hearth all seeming smaller in the daylight somehow.

The furs were all straightened against the other wall. Knox was gone, but his clothes were still draped over the small rack next to mine.

I got dressed and folded the T-shirt he'd given me the night before, then made my way outside. The sky was streaked with wispy clouds, and for my perusal, I nearly toppled down the sudden, steep stone path cutting through a blanket of seagrass.

The sea was calm, expanding forever beyond the white beach. It was calming until I saw the ship dock, or rather, what was left of it—the lines of wooden pilings jutting out from the water.

I was on the other side of the island.

Knox appeared at the bottom of the long, steep path holding two pear shaped, green fruits and a large fish at the end of a spear he had propped on his shoulder. The breath caught in my chest to see him standing in the sun wearing only his gray shorts, which were hanging from his hips, a size too big. The notches of muscle there contracted as he walked like an ad for an island vacation playing out in front of me.

"Fish and fruit for breakfast," he said, making his way up the makeshift steps.

I cleared my throat. "Choco?" I asked once I got a better look, though I was almost sure I already knew that's what he was carrying. I hoped the conversation would force me to focus on the items tucked into his forearm rather than on his body in daylight.

"Bless you." He took the final step to stand in front of me, squinting a little as a smile pulled at his lips.

"Clever," I said, trying to mimic his almost smile. He laughed, and I felt like I'd won some kind of contest. "It's not a fruit, actually," I said, arching an eyebrow. "Choco is a squash." He nodded with exaggerated interest. At least his mood was better.

He took a step closer to me, crossing over the neutral, invisible barrier that was in place between us, which short-circuited my confident pretense. Just like a shift in the breeze, reality seeped into me all over again. He was still a predator, of that I was sure. But despite my heart suddenly pounding and the cool prickle that had started racing over my skin, I tried to convince myself again that I wasn't prey.

He took another step closer to me, so close I could feel his warm breath on my collarbones. After another few seconds, he cleared his throat and glanced at the glowing embers in the hearth directly behind me. "I need to get over there."

"*Sorry...*" I almost tripped trying to get out of the way as fast as I could as heat rushed into my cheeks.

He was smiling broadly as he crouched in front of the hearth and set the speared fish and squash aside. He threw in some kindling and blew on the coals until the flames caught again. I grabbed a few of the smaller logs stacked in the corner and added them while he put on the cutoff button down shirt he'd draped over the rack the night before. Several of the buttons were missing, which I supposed was why he wore it open.

He tossed the shorts that were also on the rack onto the fur bedding behind him, making room for the squash. Once they were in place, he moved the speared fish over the flames and sat back, rubbing his hands together nervously now that he was out of things to do.

"Your friends will be wondering where you are," he said abruptly. "I'll take you to them after we eat."

And just like that, his easy mood was gone again.

"Thanks," I said, surprised by the melancholy feeling that came with the thought of leaving. "What will you do then?"

He shrugged casually. "What I've always done I suppose."

"And what's that?" I asked, watching him turn the fish and the squash, both of which started to fill the room with a rich, hearty aroma.

"Keep the peace when I can. Keep to myself when I can't."

Irritation percolated inside me again. Everything he said was just a veil on the truth, on the real answers that I could tell he *wanted* to give me, but wouldn't.

"You said last night you used to be a doctor... *almost*. What did you mean?"

He heaved a sigh. "I was in school, but I didn't finish."

"Why not?" I pressed.

He flipped the fish again and poked at the squash. "There was an accident. People got hurt, and I wound up here."

He was clearly uncomfortable again, but it seemed he was going to be that way despite my questions, and I didn't see any other way of cutting through his vagaries. I wanted the truth about why he was immune to the tree, about the snake charming, and if any of this could possibly have something to do with the man-turned-monster who burst into flames on the beach. I was a scientist, damnit, and there *were* answers for everything. I just had to keep digging until I found them.

"How did they get hurt?" I asked, this time regretting how abrupt I sounded.

"They *died*, all right? I told you I'd answer your questions about the tree, not this." The edge in his voice returned, and he shot me a dark glare that made everything inside me want to run.

"I want to know what really makes you live out here all by yourself," I said, forcing calm.

He took the spear from the fire and dropped the fish onto what looked like a piece of bark, then used the tip to knock the squash from the rack onto it too. He tossed the spear to the ground and sat back, passing one of the makeshift plates to me before he began blowing on his food to cool it.

Several seconds went by like this and the tension was becoming impossible. There was nothing else I could say that I didn't think might make it worse, so I walked outside to the first step and looked out on the sea.

To my surprise, the wind had shifted and I smelled the faint scent of lemons, though I hadn't seen a lemon tree on this island yet. I turned to face the mountainside to find the large, grassy bush, and when I picked a few blades, the pungent smell filled the air before I could even bring them to my nose. Satisfied, I brought them in and started tearing them into small pieces over my fish.

"What's that?" Knox asked, notably calmer. "Lemon?"

"Fever grass," I said, offering him the rest of it. "But it's called lemongrass too. It doesn't really taste like lemons, but it will be good on the fish."

His lips quirked, and he gave me a small nod as he started shredding the clippings over his fish, then cutting the squash with the edge of a long shell.

We spent most of the meal in silence, which I used to arrive at the conclusion that this variety of choco squash tasted like a mix of cucumber, apple, and potato. I was about to announce my revelation, but Knox spoke up first.

"I didn't kill them," he said, again without meeting my eyes. "Not directly anyway. I didn't murder the people who died." I hadn't expected him to say this. I wanted to ask him follow up questions, but the climate suddenly felt like a rare butterfly had just landed, and if I so much as breathed, it would fly away. "There were four of us, and there had been an accident—a *mistake*," he continued. "I was trying to fix it. We were trying to get on a boat and leave." He shook his head, staring into the fire like a confessional. "I shouldn't have let her go back. I should have left Donovan in the car and taken her to the boat with Pritchard. Then I could have come back and dealt with the rest..."

"Did you say *Donovan*?" His dark eyes snapped to mine filled with equal parts confusion and suspicion. It was a long shot, but I had to know. "Not *Marcus* Donovan?"

Knox put down his food and stood up, which prompted me to get to my feet too. "Who are you?" He narrowed his eyes at me.

"Knox, listen. Where are you from? Before you were here—what state?" He just stared at me. "Was it Maine?" I asked. "Was it Portland, Maine?" He took a few sharp breaths and pressed his teeth together, making the muscles in his jaw jump.

"Who *are* you, Frankie?" he asked, his voice level, calm, and menacing.

"I worked at The Citadel. The Pathology Center," I started, holding my hands out as a gesture of assurance.

"The *Citadel*!" Knox laughed loudly, obnoxiously, and gaped at me in pained amazement. "Were you one of them? Did you make her add that fucking gel to the serums?" He grabbed the spear from the ground, like he needed that to scare me.

"Serums? No!" I moved back from him, holding my hands up higher. "I've spent the last six months trying to find a cure for a new strain of Red Fever...which is what Donovan had like I told you. We never had any serums."

"What did you do for Wu Fong Pharmaceuticals?" He moved toward me, holding the spear on me with one hand.

"Who? I don't know anything about them. Knox, I was a botanical consult for the Pathology Center, that's all. I ran organics; if you'll just listen!" I started to explain, but bile rose in my throat. I turned toward the door, but he was there in three strides blocking my way out.

"I'm listening," he said through his teeth.

"I started asking questions about Donovan, about his life..." I continued, backing away from him and feeling about a mile outside myself. "I was trying to figure out how he got infected so I could find a treatment."

Knox was quiet for a several seconds before I heard the spear clatter to the floor, making me jump. "You were going to cure him?" he asked.

I wanted to answer his question, but I didn't know how yet. "What kind of serums, Knox?" I asked instead.

"There were three of them—three colors...yellow, red, and blue," he said. Tears welled in my eyes as I remembered the microscope slides in Scott's travel folder. Knox's voice sounded distant after that. "They were supposed to give you unlimited years, strength, immunity, speed," he added. "But there were...*side-effects*."

"Was Donovan a side-effect?" I asked carefully, even though I already knew the answer.

"You were going to cure him?" Knox repeated hopefully, his voice tired and thin.

I shook my head at the sea and knew I was out of time. I turned back to face him. "No," I said, swallowing hard. I pressed my cheek against the cool clay of the doorway. "I was trying to, but he was killed six months ago by a Sweeper droid. He'd...*changed*, Knox," I added gently. "Worse than Burgess."

"*Six months* ago?" Knox's expression fell as he found the wall and slid down it slowly, his arms resting slack over his knees. He stared absently out to the sea through the open doorway for a long time before he finally whispered, "*Feral*."

Chapter 21

It was well past sunrise, and I didn't want Gia or Rita going out looking for me because they thought I'd lost my way again. Knox accompanied me, as promised, but we didn't go through the jungle this time. There was enough on our minds now without having to worry about djin snakes and predatory trees.

Wispy clouds lined the sky as we walked along the beach, the dark, brooding mass of the storm last night already far out on the horizon.

Knox told me the rest of his story as we walked— about how he knew about the Ferals, about his accident working as a longshoreman with Donovan. How the pallet from Mama Luz's ship had broken, sending the crates crashing down over his legs there on the docks, and how another unauthorized medic in The Grind, *Nyssa*, treated him.

My blood froze when he said they were caught and blackmailed for the illegal medical treatment. Knox's pace quickened a little as he talked. "Work for Wu Fong Pharmaceuticals, or sign away the next few decades of your life in fines," he said. "They promised us scholarships to The Citadel so we could become Authorized. We'd be legal doctors," he added, seeming far away. "Donovan and Pritchard could go to the engineering school instead of working on the docks, all we had to do was make a delivery once a week for Wu Fong—a briefcase full of the serums," he went on. "Nyssa packaged them in the Medical Arts building, but she was like a prisoner there with all the security."

"That's my building," I said, in disbelief. "I can't believe all this was going on right under my nose every day. Do you know how Donovan got infected?"

"He got the codes to one of the briefcases from a night custodian who worked in Nyssa's lab," Knox continued, scanning the water. "But he got stupid and injected himself with one of the serums on a delivery run. That's when everything started falling apart."

"So, something in that serum *gave* him Red Fever?" I asked.

Knox clenched his teeth, then nodded. "First his whole body changed—like within minutes after the injection. He got massive, bigger than Pritchard, and twice as strong." Knox scrubbed his hands over his face and pushed them through his hair. "So, then Pritchard came back after dropping off the payment for the case all in a panic because Donovan had changed into this...*creature*. He'd killed the woman who gave him the codes, and afterward Pritchard found him back in their dorm. By then he'd changed back to...*human*, I guess is the only way to say it, and we knew we all had to get out of there before something else happened."

"What did Donovan say when you saw him?" I asked, nearly breathless.

"He was unconscious in the car when I got there," Knox said. "Once I got all the information, I made Pritchard let me out so I could go back for Nyssa while he drove to the docks." Knox paused and almost smiled as his eyes briefly skimmed the wide expanse of shore in front of us. "We were going to meet there to finally take Mama Luz up on her offer to join her crew," he said with a small chuckle, then abruptly sobered. "But Wu Fong's people found us... They shot Nyssa, and Donovan pulled Pritchard off the ladder of Mama Luz's barge. He wasn't human anymore."

I was speechless, but at the same time felt compelled to say something, anything to beat back the ominous silence that seemed to have fallen over the entire beach.

"I'm so sorry," I offered, though it didn't seem to do anything more than remind me of how helpless I was to offset anything involving Red Fever, even someone's grief.

Knox closed his eyes in a long blink and shook his head. "How did he live like that for three more years?" he said to himself. "How could he have had any kind of life?"

"Someone must have helped him," I said. "Maybe keeping him off the radar until...they couldn't anymore."

Knox pinched the bridge of his nose, and I was lost again for something to say. My mind was spinning with this new information—that Donovan had become a stage four Feral, but then changed *back*. I'd thought after seeing his legacy chip logs that maybe our eight-hour onset timeline had been wrong, that the infection lay dormant for three years, but *this*? He was also killed in daylight and hadn't burst into flames like Burgess... His had to be a different strain. My heart nearly pounded through my chest at the idea that there could be any number of strains of Red Fever now.

"I never should have gone to her for help in the first place," Knox said after several minutes. He seemed to be avoiding saying her name. "Better to be fired, or even lose *fifty* years of my life to medical debt at the Authorized hospital. They would all be alive today if I'd just—"

"Knox, none of this is your fault," I said, reaching for his forearm. I stopped walking, which made him face me. "I know you've probably been convincing yourself that it was for the last three years, but there's no way to be sure that would have saved anyone. You know what it's like in The Grind, and it's twice as hard for a woman. Trust me..." He met my eyes expectantly, sympathetically, but this wasn't about me. "You can't live like this, hidden in a hole away from everyone. You were a few weeks from being a fully credentialed, *Authorized* medical doctor. You have a skill set that can help people."

"I know what I am, Frankie," he said without hesitation as he started walking again. "And I'm not that person anymore."

"*Why* not?" I insisted. "What are you, then?" I moved into his path so he couldn't keep evading the question.

"Frankie, you just don't know what—"

"I know it's bullshit that you think you can't help people now because your entire world turned upside down three years ago." I chided. He shook his head, his dark eyes wide with surprise, astonishment that I would dare... "Knox, look—" I started calmly, hoping to reduce the tension, but that's all I got a chance to say before his mouth suddenly moved over mine, stopping my scramble for words. His hands moved up my back, pressing me hard against him. As abruptly as the kiss started, it stopped with his fingers wrapped in my hair, his forehead against mine, and both of us heaving for breath.

"I'm sorry," he whispered, letting his hands fall to my shoulders and slide down my arms. He took a step back and let out a long, controlled breath. "I'm sorry..."

"It's all right." I took a step toward him, but he only stepped back, his eyes turned away to the sand below. "Knox..." I caught his hand in mine so he couldn't retreat anymore. "It's all right," I whispered, moving in slowly to kiss him again.

His body relaxed as his hands traveled back up my arms and stroked my neck, my face. His skin was warm under my hands, his heart seeming to pound harder with each breath he took. I felt compelled to hear it, so I let my head fall against his chest as we looked out on the sea. The sound of it was certain, and I knew I'd been under no delusion, no botanical hypnosis when he brought me out of the tree cave. There was something he still wasn't telling me, but right now, I didn't care.

"Stay with me for the next few days," he said, combing his fingers through my hair. "Tomorrow is the full moon, and another boat will be coming in the middle of the night to harvest the tree. It won't be safe for you."

"Why not for *me*?"

"The tree can sense the workers—their movements. It emits that pheromone, but they're always wearing masks," he continued in an even, quiet voice like he was telling a bedtime story. "It just keeps pumping it into the air until someone comes, usually someone from the beach who's predisposed because maybe they caught a whiff on the breeze once," he paused and met my eyes. "The tree devours them, Frankie. And in its distraction, the workers gather the fruit and the sap without issue. Then they leave like nothing happened."

I shuddered under his arm, and he held me tighter. "You've *seen* this happen?"

"Many times," he said quietly. "The more I fought the harvesters, the more people came from the beach, lured by the scent that all the commotion produced," he explained. "So I had to stop fighting. I just made it worse."

"On the night the boat comes, I could burn the tobacco to mask the pheromone," I said, frantically trying to figure out how I could stop this.

"That won't be enough. It has a taste of you now, and it will just keep trying to bring you back."

"We have to stop it before it takes *anyone* else. Rita, Mae, and Gia are in the cave just below it."

"And they've been there for years without issue. It doesn't want them. The tree hasn't called to them, or anyone else except on the night the harvesters come, and that's only because they provoke it," he said, stroking his thumb over my cheekbone. "It called you on its own, though, Frankie. It wants *you*. And I'll be damned if I'll let it take you."

My chest tightened, and I suddenly felt out of breath. There were too many unexplainable things circling in my head now. I *could* explain the strange, exotic tree that emitted pheromones to attract prey. There were countless species of carnivorous plants in the world that did that. I could even explain the healing water if I had a chance to study it more, but I didn't have an answer for how Red Fever made its way here from The Citadel, or if maybe instead, it originated here as a byproduct of the tree itself. There was only one way to find that answer.

I turned back to him. "You said the boat belongs to Mama Luz, and it brings the fruit and sap back to the docks in The Grind? The boat goes back to Portland, Maine?"

"Frankie..."

"We need to get on that boat."

"Stop, no."

"You've been gone awhile, Knox. There's a Feral attack almost every other day now in The Grind. There was even one behind The Citadel walls, but I was shipped out on that bogus field assignment before I could prove it."

"Frankie, listen—"

"Don't you see? Luz, this island, they're the common denominators. We need to get samples from the tree: the bark, sap, leaves, and of course the fruit. If any of that is somehow being turned into the serums you were talking about, then we can stop this. We can reverse engineer them and cure Red Fever. We can *stop* the Feral attacks for good."

"It's insane, no," he shook his head adamantly.

"I'm not asking for your permission," I said, pushing past him. "I'm getting on that boat, I'm taking some samples from that tree, and I'm going to find a way to stop this." He grabbed my arm and spun me back, and I could have sworn I saw fire in his eyes.

Chapter 22

Knox took a step toward me, his grip on my arm loosening, but not enough to let me go. "Do you think you can just swim out to that boat and stowaway in the cargo? You're going to get yourself killed!"

"Then at least I'll die trying to make a difference in the world. I can think of worse ways to go—as the victim of a Feral attack for one." I pulled my arm out of his grip and turned away from him.

"Frankie!"

I kept walking, not even knowing where I was going or how close I was to the other side of the island, but I'd heard enough apathy, enough rationalizing about why we hadn't been able to cure Red Fever. This was a real lead.

"We have a chance now," I called back to him. "We can finally stop this, Knox!"

"Yeah?" He caught up to me again and squared my shoulders. "Look out there, just beyond the pilings."

"I don't see anything except the ocean."

"That's right. Come on."

"Where?"

"*Come on!*"

I followed him to the edge of the shore, where he waded into the water. "Knox...?"

"Just stay there."

He hoisted himself onto the first piling and jumped to the next one like a practiced athlete. Then to the next, and so on until he was well beyond the breakers.

"*Knox!*"

He took off his shirt and dangled it over the water like a fishing lure, bobbing it up and down, then back and forth as he seemed to grow more impatient.

"*Where are you?*" he shouted, crouching down to thrash his shirt around in the sea. Almost immediately, he launched himself upward again, nearly losing his balance as he pulled his shirt high out of the water.

What jumped after it wasn't a shark, though it was just as big.

It was silver-skinned, silver-*haired*...until it shifted to jet black and crashed back into the water with a shriek that made me cover my ears.

"*What the hell*?" I whispered, watching him hop back down the pilings and onto the beach. His tanned face was flushed, his breath ragged, and I could see the wildness, the fear still behind his eyes.

"Nothing is the way it seems here, Frankie. Do you understand now?" he said, moving a hand over my face. "Those things sink every boat except Mama Luz's. Every raft. I've watched dozens of these people try to leave this island, and every one of them was dragged under, screaming as they were torn to pieces. No one can leave."

I had no explanation, and without some research, it was pointless to try to scramble for one right now. "I don't know what that thing was," I said simply. "But you just said they don't attack Luz's boats. That's what's coming here tomorrow night."

He tossed his shirt over his shoulder and pressed the heels of his hands to his eyes in frustration. "This isn't why I told you about the boat. This isn't how it was supposed to go."

"I know, and I'm sorry, Knox, but someone has to stop what's happening. Why don't you see how important this is?"

"Frankie, I just need you to—"

I kissed him, stopping whatever restriction he thought he was going to put into place next. I didn't think beyond the next second as my hands moved over his chest, down the grooves of his abdomen until I found the indentations of his hips and pressed my fingers into the curve of muscle there. Knox sucked in a breath, surrendering the fight, and pulled me into him.

"You need me to what?" I breathed against his lips.

His hands found their way under my shirt, drawing it up as his lips traveled down my throat, his breath warm and heavy over my shoulders, collarbones, sternum.

"I need you to take this off," he said, his voice low and urgent. I gripped his hair and arched into him as he slid down the straps of my bra, the cool breeze igniting my skin everywhere his warm mouth had been. I felt dizzy with the sensation, which tightened the knot low in my stomach until it turned into an ache that radiated, then pulsed through me.

"Knox…" I whispered. He moved like the waves over me as he lowered me to the sand, his hand cradling my head as I felt the muscles in his stomach pull taught. His other hand slipped under my lower back, over my hip and down my thigh until I felt the cool sand under my skin in place of cotton. His fingers traced a path along the inside of my knee as the tide crashed over us, through us, until I was suddenly afraid the swell would soon drown us both. Water suddenly pushed through his fingers, sweeping strands of my hair over my chest, and I flinched this time at how fast the tide was rising. As if reading my mind, he interlaced his fingers with mine in assurance as his lips made their way up to graze my ear.

"They can't reach us here," he said, his hand anchoring my hip just as another breaker crashed into us and made me gasp for breath. The water rushed under my shoulder blades, pulling me against him as it receded. I felt weightless, as if I would drift for eternity were it not for the weight of his lips on mine. I heard nothing but the all encompassing sound of his heartbeat thrumming through me, and I knew from this point on one thing was certain.

I would *never* be prey.

***

Knox held me close to him as we walked the rest of the way back to the camp, his eyes scanning the horizon, the shore several yards ahead, or the jungle to our right. Always scanning.

"Do you know what those things in the ocean were?" I asked, watching the haze collect again over the water. The storms weren't over yet.

"Up close..." he started, seeming to struggle to find the words. "Up close, they look like they were people. Once, anyway." I turned to look up at him. "I know," he said. "I wouldn't believe it either if I hadn't looked into its eyes. From a distance, it's easier to talk yourself into it being just the refraction of the sun on the water...the mirage on the horizon, like now." He angled his head at the sea.

"It looked like it had arms...*huir*," I said cautiously.

He nodded. "It did. And needle teeth like one of those deep sea nightmare fish—anglers, I think?"

I shuddered. "Do you think they're a product of one of the serums? Another strain of Red Fever?"

"Maybe."

My mind flooded with implications, but I drew them back. We had to get off this island before I could think about anything else.

"What kind of boat comes to harvest the tree?" I asked. Knox took in a breath and sighed, which made me laugh a little. "Did you think I forgot?"

"Well, I'd hoped I'd given you something else to think about. I mean, it's only been what, an hour?"

he said, checking his wrist for a nonexistent watch. "Speaking of that…" he started. "How long did you work at The Citadel?"

"Four years, why?" Knox audibly exhaled. I raised an eyebrow at him, confused, until he gave me a knowing smirk. "*Oh*," I quickly smiled back at him. "The Citadel's birth control mandate. No, I'm not eligible for reversal for two more years. But I don't suppose that matters now," I added, looking at the jungle to our right and the ocean to our left.

"It would have been the same for me," he said. "But I think mine may have been reversed already from…the cave water. I just wanted to be sure we'd be *OK*, you know…" he trailed off.

"That's right, you weren't on the prison boat where the men were sterilized."

"Where they were *what*?" He jumped a little as he turned to look at me, shock evident on his face.

I laughed and curled into him, though part of me still wasn't sure why I'd let any of this happen between us in the first place. I'd never let it happen this quickly with anyone in the past. Maybe it was a waste of time to analyze it because I felt better now… steadier somehow, though the wariness I'd felt in his presence wasn't entirely gone.

I needed to refocus. "Anyway, if I let myself get lost in all *that*, we'd never get off this island," I said, leaning playfully into him as we walked.

"*We*?" he said after a beat.

I slowed our pace until we stopped and met his eyes. "Why would you stay here?"

"Frankie..." he looked over my shoulder at the horizon.

"That's your world, too, Knox. You can't just let them take it."

"Take what?" he said with a laugh, but then sobered quickly and started walking again. "Anything I had worth taking is already gone. They can have the rest."

"Then what about the innocent people? What about the people like Pritchard and Nyssa who—"

Knox stopped again and shot a dark glare at me, his whole body suddenly rigid like a coiling djin snake. He took a slow, deep breath, and his expression relaxed.

"I can't help them. I can't even help the people here."

"You helped me." He sighed again. "And together, we can help the people in The Grind, Knox. You're a *doctor*. If I can get to my research, we can stop what Wu Fong is doing with the serums," I said, reaching for his hands. "If you could have stopped what happened then, I know you would have. We have another chance now."

"You don't understand," he said, shaking his head at the sand.

"Then tell me why. Why are you so intent on just accepting things as they are? Why won't you fight?"

"*Fight*?" he asked, the word filled with incredulity. He chuckled to himself and nodded at me. "Frankie, you have no idea how much I fight on a daily basis. How much I'm fighting *now*, this exact second—" he said, biting off the rest of the sentence with clenched teeth.

"Fighting *what*? Come with me, Knox. Come home with me."

"That, Frankie! That's what I'm fighting! It's so easy to think this—us…going home—could happen. But trust me, it won't end up that way."

"Why not? How *would* it wind up? You're not making any sense."

He threw his hands out to either side of himself and took a step back from me. "I belong here, Frankie. I told you."

"That's an excuse. This is a prison island, but your prison isn't in that jungle. It's in here." I said, bringing a fist to my chest.

He shook his head at me, then looked down the beach. "Poppy's camp is another few hundred yards up there. Stay on the beach until someone can take you to Mae's."

"Knox…*Why*?"

"Because there are snakes in the woods," he said, walking toward the brush and disappearing into the jungle.

Chapter 23

Knox was right about one thing. I had no idea how I was going to get on that boat now that I knew what was in the water just beyond the pilings, which was likely close to where the boat would dock. I didn't get a very good look at the rest of the barge Scott and I boarded, but if it was one of Luz's, then maybe the one coming tonight would be similar, with netting hanging over the side. If it docked near the pilings, I might have a chance.

As soon as the plan gelled, my stomach sank with the dread of impending failure. If I slipped, the things in the water would eat me alive. If I managed to get to the nets—assuming there were nets—how long would it be until the crew left the deck so I could make my way over the railing and hide? I would be racing daylight.

My heart pounded with fear and anticipation of it all as I rounded the corner of the beach and saw a few small, half-built shelters at the base of Poppy's camp, though I didn't see anyone from the prison boat working on them. I made my way up the timber ramp, which wound up and up through the pruned back trees.

At the top, Rita was sitting on a bench with Poppy and a few other people I didn't know.

Rita stood. "Where the hell were you? Gia and I were all over the jungle trying to find you this morning."

"I'm sorry," I said, trying to figure out where to begin without divulging anything about the tree now that I knew motion caused it to emit the pheromone. I didn't want anyone trying to find it. "I think I had a sleepwalking episode last night." I told the truth as best as I understood it because they would have seen through anything else. No one on the island would venture out into the jungle at night alone.

"Oh great," Rita said with a shrug. "That's a good way to get yourself killed. The boas out there would love to have you for a midnight snack."

"Them, or the things in the water?" I asked, not knowing exactly why I was bringing that up, but I knew it needed to be said. Poppy and Rita both stared at me, stunned.

"What things in the water?" Rita asked cautiously.

"The silver fish who change to black...and look like *people*."

"You went out past the pilings?" Poppy asked, narrowing her eyes at me. "No. I saw one of them jump. I heard it screech. What are they?"

"Security? We don't know," Poppy said. "Some of the older ones here have voodoo explanations for them—island spirits." She shook her head dismissively. "Probably some kind of pollution-mutated sharks."

That made sense. There's a logical answer for everything, I thought. *If you ask enough questions...*"How's Mack doing?" I looked out toward the open deck area and felt a flutter in my stomach when I saw the treetops. It was easy to forget how high up we were.

"She was still asleep when I got here," Rita said, making her way around the corner.

I started to follow her, but someone started yelling from the beach below. "*Popppppy*...come on down!" the woman's voice sounded drunk. "Bring Mack. We just want a little word."

"*Bitsy*..." Rita said.

A handful of people came running up the timber ramp as another round of yelling rang out below.

This time, a man's voice. "Or we could come up!"

"Shit, that's Ross..." Rita said. "Hey idiots, did you forget about the quarantine?"

"I told you not to engage when you went down there," Poppy chided.

"Stay here with Mack and the others," Rita said to me as she and Poppy made their way down the timber ramp to the beach.

Several of the people who had fled the beach now crouched along the interior wall that led to the open deck where Mack was sleeping. One of them looked familiar, but I didn't know why. She was blonde, like me, maybe five years older. She met my eyes, and it seemed like she wanted to say something.

"I've seen you before," I said, thinking out loud.

"*Maaaack!*" Ross shouted from the beach again.

The woman shuddered against the tree-trunk wall and hugged her knees.

"I told you…" Mack said weakly from her pallet bed. She turned toward the woman. "We won't let them take you."

Tears spilled from the woman's eyes.

"You were on the boat with me?" I said. "You were on the beach?" The woman looked at me knowingly now, a confidant instead of a potential antagonist. "Did Mack protect you from the men on the beach?"

The woman looked at me for another second before she finally nodded.

"We won't let them take you, Cara," Mack said again, her eyes still closed.

"Your name is Cara… I'm Frankie," I said, moving across the floor to sit closer to her, stopping when she flinched. "It's OK. Nobody is going to hurt you."

"Bring that bitch down here!" Ross shouted from the beach. Cara started visibly shaking.

"Hey… It's all right. They won't let them come up here. You're safe," I said, holding up a hand to her.

Mack sat up in her bed and tried to get to her feet. "Fuck off, Ross!" she called out blindly, her eyes still closed as she swayed. I rushed over to her before she fell to the ground.

"What happened? I thought she was getting better?" I said to Cara and the woman with rotted teeth who was next to me on the boat.

"She got bad again this morning. Bleedin' black," the woman said, making a hissing sound through her broken teeth.

"What?" I turned back to Mack and eased her back down onto the bedding. I moved the poultice of yarrow from her wound and saw the black, viscous grease seeping from it. "Oh, no..." I whispered. "Mack, can you hear me?"

"He wanted to kill him..." she mumbled, her forehead and cheeks beaded in sweat.

"Kill who, Mack? Burgess?" I asked.

"Got between us, gnashing..." she continued.

I took a step back from her when she started biting at the air, grinding her teeth and then biting again.

"Hope you're decent, Mack! Company's comin'!" Ross yelled from the beach, and Mack's mouth opened beyond what seemed humanly possible. Her canine teeth started to elongate just like Donovan's , and I nearly fell backward.

"Shit...*shit*! Let's go—we need to get out of here," I said to Cara and the few others who were gathered near Mack's room. I could hear fighting break out on the timber ramp with several more hostile voices calling for Mack. "Under the benches!" I whisper-yelled to them, grabbing up several palm fronds from the ground to conceal us.

"No…not again…" Cara sobbed. I held a finger to my lips to quiet her, then gripped her hand in mine. A loud crash startled us both, but not nearly as much as the blood curdling yell that Mack emitted when Ross, Bitsy, and what must have been half-a-dozen others flooded into the room.

Cara started to whimper, so I let go of her hand and reached around her shoulders, pulling her close to me and covering her mouth.

I could only partially see through the palms, but it was enough to see exactly what I feared. Mack's teeth were inhuman, and her eyes had also turned black like Burgess's as she intercepted Ross and his crew. They ran her through with a spear, slashed her with various axes and knives, but it was like she didn't feel anything at all. Ross tried to impale her again with the spear, but she lunged at him, her teeth tearing at his throat just like Burgess had done. Just like the bartender at Ivy's had done.

Cara started to vibrate with sobs as Mack tossed Ross to the ground, twitching, and went after Bitsy.

The others scrambled back down the ramp, pushing and clawing at each other as Bitsy flailed and screamed in Mack's grip.

"We gotta go! Ain't no help for her!" an older man with us yelled, then bolted toward the ramp.

He was right. There was nothing we could do to free Bitsy from Mack's grasp if being impaled, stabbed, and slashed with knives repeatedly had no effect already.

"We're going to run, OK?" I said to the others. "I'll go first. Just follow me, and run as fast as you can down the ramp like he did. Ready?" I said, releasing Cara. "*Ready*?" They all nodded. We threw aside the palm fronds and at my nod, sprinted across the bloodstained floor.

The guttural screams were enough to nearly paralyze me with fear as we ran past Mack and Bitsy, but the pinch of Cara's grip on my arm was enough to keep me moving forward.

We got to the opening to the ramp and nearly slid down the length of it. I got my feet under me and waved Cara and the woman with us ahead. "Hurry!"

The screaming had abruptly stopped as they ran ahead, both slipping and nearly tumbling down the ramp until the foliage started to clear. I watched them fall onto the sand and felt a wash of relief, which was soon replaced with terror when Mack came sliding toward me.

She was covered in blood and *pieces of my jacket,* which sent rivers of ice through my veins more than the sight of her fang-like teeth or completely black eyes. She quickly righted herself and began clinging to the support ropes and intermittent trees that flanked the ramp. She moved like an animal, jumping and pulling herself sideways toward me even faster than she had been sliding.

"Frankie!" I heard Rita call from the beach, her voice shrill and desperate.

"What is that? What the fuck is that?" a chorus of others shouted, and the shrieking began all over again.

Mack outpaced me and leaped from the side ropes a few yards ahead, catching my left leg and pulling me off my feet.

"Mack! *Mack*!" I shouted, hoping there was some part of her that was still able to hear me. She bared her teeth, and I kicked as hard as I could with my other leg, managing to connect with her nose. It was enough to make her lose her grip on my leg as I tumbled onto the sand and was lifted to my feet.

"Frankie!" Knox shouted. Everyone scattered except Rita, Poppy, and a few others I didn't recognize. He ushered me behind him as Mack fell from the raised ramp onto the beach, her dark hair stuck to her face, chest, and shoulders, which were all smeared with blood. She lunged at Rita, but almost immediately fell to her knees, consumed by an ear-piercing screech. Seconds later, she burst into flames.

"What the fuck was that?" the tattooed man who had been with Bitsy earlier said, his white-knuckled grip on his spear forcing every vein in his arms and neck to stand out. Several people tried to kick sand over the flames, which did nothing at all to reduce them.

"It was you..." Cara said as she abruptly backed away from me.

"What? Cara, are you OK?" I asked, extending a hand.

She flinched and shook her head, her face flushed. "You stopped him..."

"Let's go," Knox said, ushering me backward from the growing heat.

"Who?" I asked her. "Cara, he stopped who?"

"Frankie, *come on*." Knox's voice was low and uncompromising as I stumbled back, unsure of my footing.

"You're the man from the beach..." Cara continued, the flush from her face having drained away in what now seemed like terror.

"That man right there?" Rita asked, gripping Cara's arms and leveling an eye at Knox.

"He stopped him. He made him let me go..." Cara crumpled bonelessly to the sand.

Rita scooped her up and gave Knox a murderous glare. "It was you? What did you do to Burgess? To *Mack*?"

"He's the one who attacked Burgess and Mack!" Another voice sailed overhead, and the crowd began shifting toward us.

Knox grabbed my hand and set us running into the jungle, but once we reached the threshold, his arm locked around my waist. Branches immediately started whipping past so fast I couldn't even open my eyes widely enough to see where we were.

"Knox!" I shouted, but we just seemed to move faster until he finally slowed down and my feet touched the ground again. We were deep in the jungle —barely any light breaking through the trees—but I could still hear the waves crashing on the shore.

He held me in front of him and looked me up and down. "Are you all right?" he asked, only slightly out of breath.

"I'm—*what*...?" I gaped at him, my chest pounding, and my mind full of so many questions that none of them came out.

"You're cut..." He winced, examining my arms and legs.

I looked down at myself, the sight of the multiple scratches, sobering. "Knox *what the hell* is going on?"

He looked up suddenly and gripped my hand hard.

"We have to go."

Chapter 24

In about twenty steps we'd arrived again on the beach, only it was deserted. I was confused until I saw the pilings of the old boat dock, which were nearly submerged. The faint smell of lemons filled the air, restoring enough of my clarity to process that the jungle lashings weren't exclusive to my arms and legs. My forehead, left cheek, and the bridge of my nose all started to burn as Knox and I climbed the hidden stone path that I *thought* led to his shelter. But when we got to the top, there was no doorway.

"Where are we?" I asked, looking around.

Knox scanned the beach and then cautiously moved what looked like a panel of the mountain away—the back of it, a grid of bound, thick branches packed with clay and small stones.

"I'll get some water..." Knox said, replacing the panel behind us. Light shot through the sections that weren't covered in clay, creating a mottled pattern over the ground and walls. He helped me sit in front of the hearth, which was cold, and I watched him move across the room, pacing like a big, caged cat.

He dipped a coconut shell into a large, hollowed out stone that I hadn't noticed before, nor had I noticed the leaf-lined trough built into the wall that disappeared into the ceiling above it. He knelt in front of me and dipped a tattered piece of cloth in the collected water, then dripped it over the scratches on my arms. I expected the tingling sensation, and then to see the scratches fade away, but this was not *that* water.

"*OK*, it's all right." I winced, taking the cloth. Knox moved the earthen panel again just enough to reach out, returning with a large stem of aloe.

He knelt again next to me and half smiled. "I'm no botanist, but I know a few things. If you're wondering about the wall—"

"Knox, I don't care about your stupid door!" I nearly shouted. "Tell me what's happening. Tell me what you are."

"Frankie…"

"Damnit! You just ran from the other side of the beach *carrying me* in what could only have been ten seconds. You seem to be everywhere and nowhere at the same time. Snakes die when they bite *you*, and Cara just said *you* saved her from Burgess?" I stared at him expectantly.

"I didn't kill him, Frankie," Knox insisted as he approached. "You watched him die yourself."

"I know! He died from what has to be Red Fever!" I pushed him back from me, spilling the water in the shell. "Were you on the beach that night? The night my boat came?" He stared at me with equal parts fear and contempt, but I didn't care. "Were you watching it come in from your perch up here, and did you come down when you saw there was trouble?"

Knox's eyes were locked with mine in some kind of standoff for several more seconds before he finally spoke. "He was trying to hurt her," he said, the fear leaving his eyes. There was only contempt left now as his voice dropped and hollowed. My heart started pounding in my ears, and I moved back from him. His face transformed to reflect exasperation, pain. "Are you *afraid of me*, Frankie?"

"What did you do to him?"

"I got Cara away from him, just like she said."

"How? And what happened to Mack?"

"Mack thought—" he closed his eyes in a long blink and shook his head, exasperated. "I don't know what she thought, but she got in the middle of things and pulled Cara away from me the second after I threw Burgess."

I squinted at him. "Why didn't you say any of this when I told you about the attack on the beach? You were *there* and said nothing?"

"I had nothing to add," he said, weakly.

"Knox, those people back there think *you* put those holes in his throat," I pressed. "They think *you* turned him and Mack into those Ferals!"

"And is that what you think?" he asked, his eyes softer now, the small creases forming between his thick, dark brows betraying the neutrality of the rest of his expression. "Because that's all I care about."

"No," I said after a long pause, but I wasn't sure if this was because I really believed he wasn't to blame for what happened to Burgess and Mack, or I just didn't *want* to believe he was. "But you *were* there…on the beach."

He nodded. "I was trying to help."

"Well, did you see anything else?" I asked in desperation. "What made those marks? Mack even had one on her shoulder. It doesn't make any sense." I put my face in my hands, exhausted, and jerked back quickly when I felt the sting over my forehead and nose. "*Damnit!*" I closed my eyes and took a very deep, slow breath to hold back the tears I felt tightening my throat.

"Hold still. Just lie back and close your eyes," he whispered. I moved to one of the furs reluctantly, but the exhaustion was starting to sink in. After another few seconds, I smelled the aloe stem and felt the cool gel over the scrapes on my cheek and forehead. Knox's fingers grazed my collarbones, brushing my hair from my shoulders as he trailed the aloe over the scratches on my nose and throat. Slowly, the burning faded, and my head started to feel heavy with the relief. I let it fall against his hand as he moved it through my hair and applied another pass of the aloe to my face. He dragged the stem slowly down the center of my mouth, and then followed it with his lips.

He broke the kiss too soon and moved back to apply more of the aloe to my arms and legs.

I opened my eyes to ribbons of light falling over us through the panel door. They danced over his tanned, unblemished skin, and I waited to let the thought come to the front of my mind. It sat patiently in the background as I let my eyes wander over his hard, rounded shoulders and chest, the muscles weaving and tightening in his arms as he applied the aloe to my skin. I knew that the second I let the question into the world, this moment and maybe all potential moments like it could be gone. He was beautiful, brave, and mysterious, but there was also something he wasn't telling me, and were it not for the needle-like thought that pierced my mind, pierced the constructed fantasy that everything was just fine, I may never have come back to the real world.

I watched his strong hands, his long fingers gracefully apply aloe to the last scratch on my arm, and then I met his dark eyes. "Knox," I said quietly. "Why don't you have any scratches?"

Chapter 25

Knox's expression was unflinching. He swallowed after several seconds and then dropped his gaze.

He took a deep breath and set the aloe down, resigned. "When Donovan shot himself with that serum, he didn't know what it would really do."

"*Knox—*" I said, unable to keep the impatience with his continuous question evasion out of my voice. "Can you just give me a direct answer *for once*. We didn't go near the tree water this time. Why don't you have any scratches?"

He fixed his eyes on mine. "I'm getting there," he said with an eerie calm. "The crates that crushed my legs—the ones that fell from the pallet on Mama Luz's boat—there was only so much that could be done. The prosthetics I had were good, but they—"

"*Prosthetics?*" I interrupted, surprised. Knox's gaze darkened. "I'm sorry," I said quietly. "I just didn't know the damage was so bad."

He sighed. "So *Donovan* heard that the serums could regrow limbs, and after he injected himself, then doubled in size right there in the backseat like I said..." he trailed off, shaking his head to reset. "He injected me. I didn't ask him to do it. I didn't even know he was going to do it."

The breath in my lungs seized at this, but I forced down the panic and again found the scientist. "So, your legs just...?"

"No," he answered, understanding the rest of the question before I could ask it. "Nothing happened. Not at first anyway. We thought the serum was a dud because sometimes the they didn't work. The clients would just get a replacement briefcase if that happened—no big deal because Wu Fong was trying to get his name out there. But when I got to this island, things started happening."

I couldn't stop myself from looking at his legs, which in no way resembled appliances. His dark hair, the well toned muscles, there was nothing prosthetic about them.

"How…?" I said under my breath, marveling.

"The synthetic skin from my knees to my ankles was damaged, welling up with fluids, but when I got to the island, it started healing—changing from synthetic skin to actual skin. The rubber and coils were swallowed in muscle and bone," he continued, his brows drawn together in what seemed like pain. "I thought I was losing my mind, but ever since that first night, I've never had another scratch that didn't immediately heal."

I ran my fingers over his shins, his knees, and paused between the grooves of his thigh muscles as I tried to picture where the prosthetics had begun.

"There's no mark at all, no indication whatsoever that there was ever anything else here," I said.

"Wu Fong updated the prosthetics after I started working for him," Knox continued, stroking a finger over my forearm as he watched my hand. "I could run faster than a car, jump from ground level to a ship deck…and even when everything healed over, or whatever happened after Donovan shot me full of that serum, I could still move that way."

"Why did you tell me I must have had some pheromone trip from the tree when you jumped out of that cave?" I asked, pulling back my hand. "You *did* jump from that cave to the ground."

He nodded. "I didn't know what else to tell you then. I'd hoped I wouldn't have to tell you any of this."

"Knox, do you know how much easier it would have been if you just *would have* told me? I was afraid that you…" I trailed off and closed my eyes, exhausted.

"I'm sorry," he said, wrapping his hand around mine.

I met his eyes again. "They think you're a monster now. Rita, Poppy, all of them… They won't stop hunting you." I squeezed his hand and remembered about the harvester boat. "You said the tree won't stop calling to me either, so get on that boat with me, Knox. It's coming tomorrow night; isn't that what you said?"

He let out a long, arduous groan. "Frankie, you don't understand how much danger you'd be in… *please.*"

"No more danger than staying on an island with deadly snakes, a carnivorous tree, and some kind of toxic waste shark mutations surrounding it," I said adamantly. He raised a dark eyebrow at me as his lips quirked. "Get on the boat with me," I insisted again. He studied my face for several seconds, seeming to be contemplating something. "*Knox…*"

"All right," he finally said.

I gripped his wrist. "Really?"

"*All right.*" He laughed, nodding.

I threw my arms around him, knocking him backward, and regretted it immediately.

"Ow…*ow!*" I yelped, forgetting about the cuts and scrapes all over my legs, arms, and face.

"Oh god, Frankie…" he said, trying to contain his laughter as he deftly switched positions with me. "Tell me what hurts the most."

"Everything," I said, squeezing my eyes closed and trying to imagine that my skin *wasn't* actively on fire.

A minute later I felt him dabbing more aloe over my legs, and then the frigid coolness that followed as he blew over the cuts. He repeated the process all the way up my arms, neck, and my face.

"Better?" Knox whispered close to my ear. I nodded slowly, too comfortable even to speak. He laughed, then kissed me gently, careful not to mar any of his handiwork. "If we're going to do this, we'll need some supplies," he said after several minutes.

I opened my eyes and raised up to my elbows. "Like what?"

"Food, water—I don't know how long the trip will be...if it will be time warped or not like the trips that got us here—I won't be fifty steps from this door, don't worry."

"You're going out *tonight*? Knox—"

He shook his head. "They won't be out looking for me tonight," he said quietly. "They'll be planning to set out tomorrow, early. That's when we'll have to stay hidden."

"Then I'll go with you."

He tilted his head at me and just blinked for several seconds. "I'll be all right. They don't know how I can move," he said, a slow grin starting in the corners of his mouth a second later. "And come to think of it, there are still a few ways you don't know about yet either."

"Knox..." I shook my head and tried to keep from laughing. "There's nowhere that's not scratched."

"I'm sure I could find a few places," he said as his grin widened, and he slowly leaned in to kiss me. "Like here..." His hand moved under the base of my neck, cradling my head as he guided me down. He brushed his lips along the underside of my chin, his breath warm, tickling me as he whispered, "And here..." He blew on the scratches along my collarbones, trailing kisses somehow in between them as he raised the hem of my tank top. "Absolutely here…"

I arched into him, the alternating sensation of his warm mouth and cool breath on my skin, sending electricity through my core.

I took in a long, slow breath and moved my fingers through his hair. His fingertips skimmed the sides of my ribs and folded under my lower back as his lips moved downward over my stomach. I gently tightened my fingers in his hair and felt the low growl in his throat against my hipbone.

"Is there anything else I don't know about you, Knox Ryder?" I said between halted breaths. He laughed again.

"Let me show you…"

***

My entire body felt like it was filled with sand as I tried to open my eyes. I couldn't remember the last time I'd slept so deeply that even lying awake, I still couldn't move. My last waking memory was of Knox curled behind me, his arm over my hips, folding me into him like a midnight sentinel, and his breath in my hair.

Beams of dim light broke through the makeshift door, filling the clay and stone room with a soft, orange glow. I stretched out my arm expecting to find him still there next to me, but the sharp sensation I felt instead commandeered all my focus to make it stop. I sat up with a jerking motion and saw several more aloe stems wrapped at the base with a strip of cloth, along with bundled yarrow flowers and pieces of willow bark. Next to these, a sharpened blade that looked like it was carved from bone. I double-checked my arm and was relieved to find no new wounds as a result of nearly impaling myself before breakfast.

I got to my feet and went to the door cover, peering through to see if Knox might be just outside. He wasn't, so I slowly moved the door just enough for me to slip through. Knox was on the other side of the seagrass at the base of the rocks, his head bent over whatever he was doing. I took a few steps down the stone path, but stopped abruptly when he looked up at me, his hands and chest covered in blood.

My hands flew to my mouth, stifling any possibility of a scream.

"It's not mine," he said, dipping his hands in a large coconut shell full of water and splashing it over his arms and chest. He grabbed a folded, bound leaf about the size of his forearm and moved quickly up the path toward me. "It's snake meat. I just finished curing it with sea salt," he said, holding out the leaf package. Water dripped off his hands, chest, arms, and shoulders, but when I blinked, it was replaced with the blood from a few seconds ago. I blinked several more times to clear the images, and when that didn't work, I pressed the heels of my hands against my eyes. "Frankie, are you all right?" Knox said now in front of me as he carefully touched my elbow.

I flinched and dropped my hands. "I'm OK, yeah," I said, relieved to see him again slicked with water instead of blood. "That was just a surprise," I added, trying to laugh. "Was that a djin snake?"

Knox's eyes widened, "Ah, no…" he said at the top of a breath, then exhaled quickly. "A boa."

"Those are really here?" I asked, remembering Rita's warning about one of them dragging me off in the middle of the night.

"They outnumber the people," Knox smiled. "Even the djin snakes."

"I saw the medicinals—the yarrow and the rest," I said, desperately needing to change the subject. "How did you gather those already?" I asked, the sky still filled with bright moonlight.

"It's right here," he said, glancing around at the vegetation not more than twenty feet from where we were standing. "The sun will be up soon. I'm going to finish cleaning everything up, and then we'll get organized for tonight."

Chapter 26

We spent the day packing what was useful into the shoulder bag I made from Knox's old button down shirt and a belt holster with front and back pockets from his spare pair of shorts. He wore the T-shirt he'd given me that first night he pulled me out of the rainstorm, and by nightfall, we were ready to leave.

He paced the room, again reminding me of a caged cat.

"When the boat docks, we'll have to wait for the harvesters to disembark. There will only be a few left aboard," he said. "After they go through the brush, we'll move."

"How will we get aboard?" I asked. "Does it have a fishing net over the side? A rope ladder?"

His eyes darted to mine. "No net, it's a cargo ship," he said, pacing again. "There will probably be a rope ladder, but it won't be overboard. We'll have to go up the ramp."

"Won't they be watching?"

"No, the lookouts will be watching the jungle. I've never seen anyone else stay on deck. We'll just have to be fast. This will work," Knox said, seemingly to himself more than to me.

"It should be here in a few hours," I said, peering out the cracks in the door thatching. "Knox..." I whispered, all the breath in my lungs leaving me when I saw Poppy and Rita leading a group of people from both camps down the moonlit beach. I recognized a few of them from Poppy's shelter, and a few from Burgess's group. The large, tattooed man who had been asleep with Bitsy a few days ago walked near the front with Poppy and Rita, Ross's axe in one hand and a long spear in the other. Knox moved quickly to peer through the doorway next to me. "They're all together," I whispered.

"Enemy of my enemy is my friend," he said.

They scoured the edge of the jungle and were moving past the front of the mountain without issue until Rita seemed to hear something. She held up a fist and stopped abruptly.

"Oh, no," I said under my breath. Knox's arm moved over my stomach and shifted me behind him as Rita began climbing at the base of the rocks not a dozen feet below us. She found the stone path behind the long beach grass, and I couldn't breathe as she began climbing.

"*Fuck*," she hissed when her foot lost traction on one of the stones. She slipped, then grabbed onto a bunch of fever grass that was growing just outside the door.

Knox slowly removed the bone knife from his belt and inched away from the thatching. If she stepped on the door, it wouldn't support her weight. She'd fall through and I didn't want to think about what would happen after that.

She passed the door and after a few more seconds, we heard her descending. She hopped from above the door down to the stone path, then followed it back to the beach. "Nothing," she said to her crew, and they pressed on, disappearing down the shoreline.

Knox and I both exhaled audibly. He closed his arm around my waist and pulled me to him. My heart hammered against his chest, but his was steady.

"I'm sorry," he said close to my ear. "I should have heard them coming."

I shook my head at him. "Everything is all right, Knox. This is going to work."

He faced me, his thumb stroking my cheek, just under the scrape. "If something happens—" he started, then seemed to think better of it.

"We're going to get to the ramp after the harvesters go into the jungle. We'll find somewhere to hide once we get aboard," I said evenly. "And I will kick anyone's ass who tries to stop us."

"You're a scrapper..." He smiled at me, his dark eyes softening.

"I am what I've had to be." I smirked, but then tried to hold back the truth of it—the memory of Scott's screams, the image of his anguished face as the sharks tore him apart.

***

Knox and I sat in front of the door, my head leaning back on his chest. I didn't realize I'd dozed off until he kissed my shoulder.

"It's time," he said close to my ear. I blinked and peered through the break in the thatched door to see a barge that was much larger than the one Scott and I boarded. Men were moving through the water onto the beach as others followed them down the ramp, each of them holding a large crate. There must have been twenty, thirty, *fifty* men.

Adrenaline hit my bloodstream. I didn't know why I only expected a handful of people aboard. Panic swelled in my chest, and I took several deep breaths when it started to feel tight.

"I didn't realize there would be so many," I whispered as we got to our feet.

"They all bring back a full crate from the tree," Knox said evenly, his voice eerily steady. "They won't see us if we're behind the pull-housing on either side of the ramp, but we'll only be able to stay there until the last of the harvesters are aboard," he said. "By then, they should have a few rows of pallets loaded, and we can hide between those for the rest of the trip."

"That's the same kind of boat that brought you here, isn't it?" I asked, remembering the night he told me his story.

"The same."

"Are you all right?" I asked, noticing how everything about him had gone rigid.

He glanced at me, the beginning of a smile starting at the edge of his mouth.

"We're getting the hell off this island," he said, then peered again through the door. "They're gone. Let's go."

He moved the door slowly and crouched low. I followed, and we moved quickly down the stone path.

The white sand seemed to glow in the moonlight, which sparkled on the water about two hundred feet from us. The lap of the surf was loud in my ears, along with the jungle noises that all seemed to be coming from two inches away. Everything was louder, sharper.

The smell of almost-jasmine, almost-honeysuckle settled over me just for a second, melting away the tension in every muscle in my body.

"The tree…" I whispered.

He gripped my face. "Open your eyes," he said firmly, then shook me. I looked at him, unaware I'd even closed my eyes in the first place. "They're at the tree now, Frankie. Listen to me, we're going to run… *Frankie*!" He shook me again, and finally, the heaviness in the back of my head started to clear. "Right now, we're going to run to the ramp. Hide behind the pull-housing as soon as we get aboard— it's a big, wooden box. One on each side of the ramp once we get on deck, OK?" I stared at him, understanding all the words he said, but I couldn't feel the urgency he so clearly intended. "*Frankie!*" he hissed, and for a split second, I saw tiny flames in his eyes.

I flinched, the new jolt of adrenaline washing away the heavy film blanketing my mind. My heart pounded in my chest as he loosened his grip on my arms.

"OK…I'm OK…" I said, everything, every sound, sharp and clear again.

"Let's go!" He gripped my waist as soon as we were both on our feet. We were at the base of the ramp in an instant, and it took me a second to regain my bearings. I'd forgotten about his legs.

"*Knox…*" I shook my head as the cool water on my skin helped me clear a new rush of fog for an instant, but the floral scent from the tree that washed over me again was even stronger than before.

I felt my body relax against Knox's, and in an instant he was shaking me again. "Stay with me, Frankie! Fight it!" I heard him say, but it was what happened next that gave me the jolt I needed. "*Shit!*" Knox growled as Rita and the tattooed man came running toward us from the brush. Knox pulled me deeper into the water, underneath the ramp as two guards came running down onto the beach.

"Go, go!" I said, thinking he would climb onto the ramp, but instead, he wrapped an arm around my waist and *jumped* onto the deck.

I didn't have time to react as one of the guards now on the beach gripped the tattooed man's throat with one hand and punched *through* his chest, with the other. The gaping hole immediately filled with blood that began spilling onto the sand.

"Frankie, *there*," Knox said, gesturing to the pull-housing he was describing, which was an open-backed box that covered a wound coil of rope. We maneuvered toward it as Rita screamed a war cry and charged the other guard with her spear. He reached for her, but she ducked and ran him through the stomach, the momentum forcing them both to fall into the water.

She pulled out her spear and turned toward the other guard, who had a head start rushing her. He ran directly into it, impaling himself, but he kept coming at her. She let go and stumbled backward, watching the guard pull the spear all the way through his side, then turn it on her.

"No!" I shouted before I could catch myself. Rita glanced at me, both confusion and understanding fighting for dominance in her expression.

She seemed to find a middle ground as she turned her attention back to the advancing guard, shouting another war cry as she charged him.

"Hiiiiide, Fraaaaankie!" she shouted as the guard launched the spear through her chest, knocking her off her feet and into the ocean.

I collapsed behind the coiled rope, and Knox pulled me against him, covering my mouth.

I heard heavy steps on the ramp, then another set after that. *How could they be alive? How could they still be coming?* I thought frantically. No one else had come from the brush, and the harvesters hadn't returned yet from the beach. It could only be the guards.

Knox took his hand from my mouth and met my eyes as the footsteps reached the top of the ramp. He shook his head almost imperceptibly, an assurance that we wouldn't be found, but a hand gripped my hair and pulled me straight up into the air so fast I didn't know what had happened until I felt the bony, cold flesh of the guard's forearm under my hands. I was suspended in the air kicking at him wildly, but all this did was tighten his hold on my hair. His eyes were sunken, expressionless.

I heard a growl behind me, an inhuman, animal sound that moved through my chest and froze my blood with fear. The head of the other guard rolled under my dangling feet, and a second later, I crashed to the deck. I scrambled to my hands and knees and saw Knox's back to me in the moonlight. He lunged at the guard, who pounded his fists into Knox's ribs in vain as dark blood spilled onto the deck.

"Knox!" I shouted, pulling myself up to the other pull-housing box.

He lowered his hands to his sides, the limp, headless body of the guard in one, and in the other, the guard's head and spine. His throat was gone entirely. Knox threw the entirety of the carnage into the water as the shrieks of those sea creatures filled the air. Tears burned my face and I wanted to run, but I was frozen in fear. Knox turned to face me, his eyes were alight with fire, his mouth, chest, and hands covered in black gore as the moonlight illuminated his bared teeth…his four elongated, blackened fangs, a nightmare set against an otherwise perfect face.

I screamed without making a sound, my body racked in silent sobs as he walked toward me. He gathered the head and body of the other guard and threw them into the sea over my head, a new wave of banshee wailing answering. He met my eyes for an instant, the flames dimming before he climbed onto the railing and jumped overboard.

Chapter 27

I was paralyzed. My hands shook uncontrollably and everything seemed several layers away. The primal growl—*Knox's* growl—echoed somewhere in my chest, somehow it was inside of me, chasing me from within my own body.

Get to the box, I heard in my head. It was my voice, but different. Present. In control. *One thing at a time. Get to the box.*

I found the pull-housing just a few feet away and scrambled to it, wedging myself against the inner side wall. I squeezed my eyes shut to block out the sight of the rope, which slipped into flashes of a coiled djin snake.

Footsteps sounded again over the ramp, and I pressed my fingers into my arms trying to make myself as small as possible. I heard the heartbeat again, the strong, deep thrum from the base of the tree cave. From Knox.

The floral scent of the tree found me, loosening my grip on my arms, intensifying the bell-echo of the heartbeat and making it reverberate through me. *I could make it if I ran. I could make it to the tree...* I thought, a faraway whisper in the back of my mind.

I startled with the sounds of crashing on the deck. One crash after another that just seemed to get louder.

It's the crates...just the crates... I heard in my head. My voice again.

The one in control. The scientist. The *scrapper.*

I couldn't think about Knox. He'd jumped into the ocean, and out here, past the pilings, I knew what waited for him. I couldn't think about it. I couldn't think about what I'd seen. What he was. I needed to wait for the last of the footsteps, and then I could run to the pallets. I could find a small space and crawl into it and get the hell off this island. Away from the tree that reached for me again, the scent, like fingers wrapping around my throat, forcing itself into my lungs. The heartbeat was deafening.

I wedged myself between the pallets, forcing my arm between two of the crates despite the burning because I knew if I didn't, I would run to the tree regardless of the harvesters. I would dive off the side of the ship and swim back to it, oblivious to the monsters in the water.

I couldn't think. I couldn't breathe. The scent was everywhere, pulling, drowning me. I felt the pinch of the wooden pallet on my arm, the last vestige of what I knew. I grasped onto the pain in my mind because I knew *it* was real. It was the only thing that was real in the blackness and shards of moonlight. My head swam, the shrieking of the tree, the growls in the recesses of my mind, all of them drifting until there was only silence.

***

Shooting pain in my arm roused me. Everything was still moonlit when I opened my eyes in search of the source of the throbbing pain in my arm.

My fingers and wrist were numb and my forearm was swollen and purple. The shock of seeing my forearm wedged behind a piece of wood and pressed against the decking wall sent a rush of panic through me. There was no way to pull it free without taking off the first layer of my skin.

I tried moving the pallet forward with my other hand, but it wouldn't budge. I tried again, this time, also stretching my legs and pressing my feet against the front of the pallet as I tried to pull my forearm out. The wood dug into the skin of my inner arm, but I'd pulled it out a fraction of an inch. The unrelenting pain was enough to motivate me to pull again, gouging my skin more deeply, but at least it was enough to release some of the pressure. I felt blood rushing through my veins to my hand, which soon prickled with a million fiery needles.

I clenched my teeth and pulled one last time, feeling a distant burn over my numb skin. The pain in part of my arm was excruciating, and the blood welling up in parallel lines from my inner elbow to my wrist confirmed this was more than a scrape. It was a bargain price to pay for the relief of being free.

I let my head fall against the wall as the prickling numbness in my arm faded and more pain set in. I risked another glance at the damage, my eyes falling over the bag I'd made from Knox's ruined shirt.

"Oh, my god," I whispered, rifling through it for the medicinals. I tore off a piece of the willow bark and chewed it, placing the rest of it pulp side down over the gouges. I spread the yarrow blooms gently into the welling blood, biting down to keep from crying out. When this was in place, I used my teeth to tear a piece of the makeshift shirt bag free and wrapped it around my forearm, then I ripped the end so I could tie it off around my wrist. My arm throbbed. My head throbbed. I dug through the rest of the back and found the aloe stems, which I'd forgotten about, but there was more willow bark. I chewed another strip of it, and very slowly, the pain started to recede.

Ocean sounds filled the air, but there wasn't a single voice. Even the one in my head, my strong, resolved, somehow *other* voice, was gone.

I thought about Knox and wondered how much of what I'd seen was real. How much was the exaggeration of the tree's pheromone? But I knew better. He'd killed the two guards that should have already been dead after Rita impaled them.

My heart pinched at the thought of her. At the knowledge that the last thing she did on this earth was try to save me. My throat closed with tears, which came hot and fast to my eyes, blurring everything. The pinch in my chest spread to an ache when I thought again of Knox.

He *had* bitten Burgess on the beach that night while trying to save Cara. Mack must have been an accident if she got between them because she only had one puncture wound. I couldn't think of how else both of them were infected with Red Fever soon after. But it didn't matter now.

"Yer home now, Knox Ryder..." a woman's voice said in a thick, tropical accent, which sounded hollow like an echo. "Come out, come out, boy... I feel ya in me bones."

Knox? I thought.

"Hey-O!"

"Line her up!" Men's voices filled the air in the distance, and the boat groaned as the engines downshifted.

"Run along home witch'ya now..." The woman laughed, a rolling, deep laugh that seemed to shake the floorboards. "And soon we show old Djin how it always shoulda been."

A bright light flashed overhead, and it wasn't until the bone rattling crack of thunder sounded that I realized it was lightning. Heavy, slow drops began pummeling the pallets, creating a cacophony of echoes between the slats. The woman laughed again, the sound folding into the rumbling thunder as the same haunting growl from back on the beach ripped through the air. If Knox was somehow aboard this ship, he wasn't the Knox I'd known. Not anymore.

The boat came to a jarring stop and after a few more minutes of random clatters, a pallet of crates lifted into the air several yards away.

"Get clear! Storm's gonna make it slick!" a man's voice called out again as beeping noises joined the chorus of beating rain and roaring skies. The second pallet lifted into the air, and it wouldn't be long before the ones in front of me would be next.

I got to my feet and discovered that the harvesters from the island looked like the guard who grabbed me, their sunken eyes and leathered skin sending a river of chills down my back. They were silent as they methodically hooked the pallets to the crane.

I darted to the back of the boat and peered over the railing. It seemed like a twelve-foot drop to a small fishing boat that was docked next to the barge. From this far back, I could easily land in the water, or worse, on the railing below, but there was no other choice. The rope ladder was too conspicuous, and the wall of pallets was quickly coming down. Soon, there would be nowhere to hide.

Lightning peeled overhead as I climbed onto the edge of the barge and positioned one foot on the railing, gripping it with both hands. Thunder shook the sky, sending reverberations through the wood, through the bones of my hands. I startled at the sensation, which was enough for my foot to slip on the wet surface.

I felt myself falling freely overboard, the force of gravity pulling me down until the wind was knocked out of me and the rolling thunder above condensed and deepened to an all encompassing heartbeat that silenced every other sound.

When it stopped, the ships were gone. The ocean was gone. I was suddenly surrounded by buildings and empty streets. Cold rain lashed my skin as I put my back against the closest building.

He was here somewhere. It was the only way I could be here instead of in the bay.

"Knox!" I called out, feeling the tears burn my eyes. If they fell, I couldn't feel them in the driving rain against my cheeks. "Knox…*please*…" I sobbed, the visceral fear that any second he would come from the shadows and tear my throat out paralyzing me. *He would have done that already…* I heard my other voice again. The scientist. The scrapper. I got control of my breath. I focused on the logic… If he was going to kill me, I would already be dead. "*Knox!*" I called out again, pushing the fear out of my voice. Finally, he appeared in the alley across from me and took a step out of the shadows.

His T-shirt was stained in the guard's rain-washed blood, streaks of black covering his chest like he'd been clawed. But his fangs were gone and his hands were clean.

He looked at me with wounded eyes, pleading. Pained. I could only stare at him for several seconds, frozen where I stood. My chest grew tight and my stomach churned. It took everything in me to push aside what I'd seen. To see him as I had before. To at least try.

I nodded to him, and after a few seconds, he took a few more steps toward me. He approached with his hands held open at his sides like a guilty thing. A desperate, broken man soaked to the bone in regret.

I pressed my back harder against the concrete wall, willing myself to stay. To let him come. Every nerve in my body was electric with the urge to run as he made his way to me one slow, tentative step at a time. Each one measured, patient, bracing for rejection.

His dark hair was pressed to his throat as the rain streamed down his anguished face. I wanted to look away before my mind even had the chance to remember the blood dripping from his mouth or the savagery in his eyes.

But I clenched my chattering teeth and stared back at him, my whole body shaking with the effort as he took a final step toward me and closed the distance entirely.

He pressed his palms against the wall on either side of me and bent to kiss my forehead. I felt his body rock with sobs, which began washing away my surface level fear. I slowly touched his back, and his body seemed almost to collapse under the weight of it. I let my arm wrap around him, then the other as I stepped into him, pressing my cheek to his shoulder. His arms closed around me as the lightning flashed and thunder rolled, and the rain washed all his sins away.

Chapter 28

Knox and I didn't talk as we walked the abandoned streets in The Grind. The digital display over The Citadel gate read half past three in the morning, and the inhospitable rain was still driving.

My home outside these gates was long gone, a swallowed up shanty lost to looters and vagrants when my parents got sick.

I stayed with my neighbor right after they died, until she got sick too. They called it contact disease then—not full blown Red Fever—it was just the wasting sickness. A slow, graceless death.

No one could afford an Authorized hospital visit or the risk of legacy debt fines if they were caught seeking treatment from an Unauthorized medic. Debt that would transfer to their living family members if they died anyway. After no one was left, I wasn't going to wait out there to die too. I wasn't going to wait while no one did anything about the criminals behind The Citadel wall and their disgusting entitlement. I would find a way inside if it was the last thing I did. I'd find the cure because I had no other choice.

Knox led me through the streets until we came to a windowless, brick warehouse with a broken ocular scanner outside a heavy, iron door. My stomach sank, but then Knox pulled the broken cover off and looked into the hole. To my amazement, the door clicked. He replaced the broken cover and turned a series of handles until it opened.

It was dark and smelled like dust inside, but it was dry. Lightning flashed again, illuminating the room through a large, barred skylight high in the ceiling. It, combined with the moonlight, was enough illumination for Knox to find the crank lamp next to the door. He turned the handle several times, smiling in relief when it worked.

The room was sparse, but solid. Brick walls two stories high enclosed a large, open room with an industrial sink near the back, an ancient bunsen burner connected to a steel tank, and a series of metal cabinets and counters that surrounded a plastic covered hospital gurney.

A small refrigerator was on the floor next to a partitioned wall, and closer to the doorway, a coffee table sat in front of a dark, angular couch. In the corner, four wooden pallets stacked on the ground supported a mattress, the dark blanket over it tucked neatly underneath. A rack of clothes hung against the wall next to the bed, and there was a visible layer of dust on everything. The cement floor was cold through what was left of my soaked shoes, but there were remarkably no bugs or vermin in sight.

"When I got the dorm room at The Citadel," Knox finally spoke, his voice hoarse and quiet in the thrum of rain outside. "I never thought it would last. Pritchard and Donovan thought I was crazy, but I just squirreled away what I could here," he added, looking around. "I put the bars on the skylight, rigged the door, and illegally tapped the water and gas lines. Donovan actually helped me do that," he continued, a sad smile touching his lips. "No one will bother us here."

He walked into the partitioned area and came back with two towels, each of them embroidered with a letter C, which I recognized from the student dorms. He handed me one of them and then crossed to the rack of clothes, clapping the dust from a T-shirt, a pair of socks, and a set of soft, cotton overalls before handing them to me.

He toweled his dark hair and went back to the rack where he started taking off his dripping shirt, the shadows from the low light dancing over the lines of his muscles just like in the hollowed out cave on the island. I stepped out of my wet shoes and peeled off my wet clothes, wrapped the towel around myself, and already started to feel less numb.

"Do you have antiseptic?" I asked, eyeing the rag wrapped around on my forearm. I was afraid to see what was underneath. Knox turned to me, his eyebrows flinching before he nodded, almost gratefully.

"Over here," he said, glancing at my arm. He removed the plastic cover from the gurney and helped me onto it. "Lie back," he said, then hung the lamp on an IV stand to my left. He opened a drawer and took out a pair of medical scissors, iodine, and bandages and put them all on the metal table next to me. "Ready?" he asked before cutting away the fabric of the old shirt I'd used.

He removed the willow bark and mangle of crushed yarrow flowers and dropped them in a bowl on the metal table, along with the rest of the makeshift bandage. The wounds were jagged and edged in pink, but not infected. I smiled in relief.

He cleaned and bandaged the cuts, dabbing iodine over the ones on my face and a few on my other arm and leg, which he also bandaged.

The grip of fatigue was too hard to resist, now dry and warm and lying on an actual mattress, albeit a thin one.

I closed my eyes for what I thought would only be for the duration of the doctoring Knox was doing, though, like so many other things I'd come to learn lately, somewhere inside, I knew better.

But I didn't care.

***

The morning light spilled everywhere, and my whole body ached. Knox was on the couch across the room tinkering silently with a tablet, his wet and tattered clothes from last night replaced with a faded denim button down shirt he'd left open and dark pants that hung off his hips. A few seconds later, a smile dawned on his face. He looked up, startled, as I slowly inched my legs off the gurney with an involuntary groan.

He started to cross to me, but then stopped himself when he saw my expression. His smile withered, and the tablet behind him started talking.

"—three-week search and rescue mission has been suspended for Scott Jeffries and Francesca Mason, Citadel researchers whose ship was last seen off the coast of Florida on its way to a remote tropical island. Head CPC Pathologist Blake Bingham informed News Seven that his colleagues were pursuing a promising botanical lead in the fight against Red Fever when they missed their check-in. Coast Guard officials believe Jeffries's and Mason's barge fell siege to Hurricane Faye as they made their way to Snake Island, a Caribbean outpost. Hurricane Faye remains contained over the Bermuda Triangle for now, but is expected to reach the coast over the next week. Eric Lewis of our sister station in Miami has more on how they're battening down the hatches. Eric?"

The feed cut out, and all the blood had drained from Knox's face. "The video feed wouldn't sync, but I got the audio to take my headline alert with your name," he said carefully.

"Alistair must have told them about Scott, then." I thought of the man who greeted us on the barge leaving Florida, who also must have been the one who drugged me and put me on the boat with Monroe. "Why didn't he just throw me overboard when I was unconscious? Why go through all the trouble to put me on Monroe's prison boat?" I asked, my chest tightening with the memory.

Knox shook his head. "If Wu Fong was involved, I'm sure there was an agenda."

I swallowed, unsure where to begin. Panic stirred in my stomach, but this wasn't an unfamiliar feeling. In battling Red Fever, I'd sat before data, overwhelming data, and felt the same thing. This was no different, I decided. So I began with what I already knew.

"They tried to kill me," I started listing. "They must know Scott didn't make it back since he was listed as missing in the feed report too, and they must know I went on to Scrapper Island."

"Luz knows I'm here, but not you," Knox added. "That means Wu Fong won't know you're here either."

"*Luz* knows you're here?"

Knox pressed his lips into a hard line and nodded solemnly. "Almost right after I jumped over the railing, I was somehow back on the deck again, in and out of consciousness just like I was on my way to the island the first time."

"So she wanted you to come back here…" I said, speculating. "Was she the one who said something about showing *Old Djin* what we could do now?"

Knox looked up at me, surprised. "You heard that too?"

I nodded. "Isn't *Djin* what they called the snakes from the island?"

"That's why I thought I'd dreamed all that," he said, beginning to pace. "They were arguing, Mama Luz and another woman. Only it wasn't a woman. Those lightning crashes *were* Djin somehow. I know that sounds insane, but when the lightning flashed, I heard her voice, *Djin's* voice. She was telling Luz there would be a *reckoning for her interference*. In what, who knows," he added.

"I didn't hear that part. It doesn't make sense," I said, feeling flooded by everything he was saying. "But…all right…" I nodded, feeling collected enough to finally take a full breath, and enough to remember the more immediate issue. "Tell me. From the beginning…" I started, unsure how to even finish the question, so I just inserted another one. "Your strength, speed, and healing ability have been with you since you were injected with the serum?"

He took in a long breath. "Soon after," he said, his voice hesitant. "I started feeling something just before getting on Mama Luz's barge. It wasn't until I got to the island that I saw the physical changes with my own eyes—my legs, like I told you."

"Had you had any Feral episodes before those guards?" I asked without pretense. Clinically. Clean.

He blinked a few times, unprepared, then cleared his throat. "It was the first thing that happened when I got to the shore. Three guys rushed me. They tried to drag me off, and I don't know...something lit inside me." He looked away and shook his head.

I gripped the edge of the gurney tightly and tried to keep my voice steady. "Did you decapitate them?"

"*No!*" he almost shouted, but quickly regained his composure. He scrubbed his hands over his face and pushed them through his loose, dark hair. "No," he said quietly this time. "I threw them off of me, but in one of them...I just saw power, or at least his belief in it. Control." He shook his head again. "I just saw that he felt it. He felt like he had power over me. So, I took it."

I gripped the gurney until my fingers went numb, but it was the only thing that kept me from following every synapse in my body telling me to run.

"And then?" I asked, forcing the words.

"There was a vein in his throat. It's like I could *hear* it..." he said distantly. "I bit down and..." He took a deep breath, then another. "I just kept drinking, feeling that power running into me...and when it was gone, I threw his body into the waves. Far out into the waves."

My throat started closing with tension as I gripped the gurney more tightly than I thought was possible.

"What happened to the other two men?"

"I sat on the beach for a while. The boat had sunk, but looking back I know it must have been a harvester ship because those three guys were the only ones on the beach. They were there waiting for it," he said. "I smelled the tree not too long after they ran. I followed the scent and found them both in the cave splashing some of the water on their faces to heal whatever I'd done to them—I didn't remember then. And after they were healed, the tree took them."

"That's what it would have done to me…" I said distantly. Knox nodded and dared a tentative glance at me, which was a reminder of what I needed to find out from him. "You bit Burgess? You sensed the same feeling of control when he tried to take Cara?"

His expression hardened as if the question hit him like a fist. "Something like that. But I *stopped*. I didn't want to feel that pull again, which I did for weeks after I'd drained the first guy on the beach."

"That's why you dug out that hole in the mountain on the torrential side of the island?" I asked. "To cut yourself off?"

He sighed, nodding again as he took a seat on the couch and leaned over his knees. "I couldn't be around them. Not until I got myself under control."

"Why did you bite Mack? She was only trying to help."

"I didn't try to," Knox answered defensively. "She was wrestling Cara away from me and in the jostle, she must have tried to hit me with her shoulder or something. I don't know. But I know I *didn't* go after her."

He looked at me like he was waiting for me to argue with him.

"And you didn't...*drink* from the guards on the boat?" I asked carefully, not exactly sure how to sanitize it.

"No. There was no sense of control or power running through them." Knox answered, rubbing his hands and starting to bounce his knee. "When he grabbed you, though, Frankie I just wanted—" he paused and took a long, measured breath. "I just wanted to stop them, and there was no other way to do that. You saw them get up from being speared."

"How did they do that? What were they?"

He sprang to his feet and started pacing again, unable to be still anymore. "I don't know. They've always been with Luz—always part of her crews. But I never saw them violent before."

And then I remembered the bloodstained shirt he'd been wearing last night. I scanned the room for it and found it dried on the rack near the wall. "So you were aware before you'd turned," I said, looking around for the imager he must have had here if this place doubled as his surgery. "You saw them attacking and just *changed*?"

"It wasn't like a decision I made, Frankie," he said adamantly. "What are you looking for?"

"Do you have an imager here?"

Chapter 29

Knox looked at me blankly. "An imager—do you have one?" I repeated impatiently.

"An ancient one, why?" he asked, gesturing to the back counter. I cut a piece of his bloodstained shirt with the scissors that were still on the counter, then pulled off the sheet covering the device and searched for the power.

"This is their blood, right?" I asked flatly, holding up the shirt. "From the guards?" He winced, but nodded. "When I saw you on the boat, your teeth and this shirt, were covered in *black,* not red. I thought it was just the dim light, but those guards didn't die after being speared, and neither did Mack."

"*What*? When was she speared?"

"In Poppy's shelter, when Ross and his crew stormed in," I said. "But afterward she just kept coming like the guards. Knox, I don't think that black substance that appeared on Burgess and Mack was the byproduct of an infection, at least not the way it seemed." He shook his head at me, puzzled. "I think it was their *blood*." I stepped back from the imager and gestured for him to come and look for himself.

He blinked as if he'd been slapped, but after a beat he sobered and made his way over to peer through the scope.

"Those aren't...*what the*?" he started, then adjusted the lenses. "No, they are blood cells, but they aren't like any I've ever seen," he said, straightening, his dark brows knitted. "If their blood was corrupted, other systems had to have been well on their way too," Knox added.

"Absolutely they were," I agreed. "Mack was able to grip the walls with her bare hands, and what Burgess did to his henchman at their camp was just… *inhuman*." Knox's gaze swept the floor before he turned away from me, and my stomach knotted when I realized that while I was rather intentionally not fixated on what he did to the guards on the boat, he clearly was. "Knox, I didn't mean…"

He turned back to me abruptly and waved it off. "So what's your point, that they weren't human? That Mack and Burgess were on their way to becoming something else too?" he asked quickly, folding his arms over his chest, and I knew his real question was one he refused to ask.

"I saw you bleed when that din snake bit you, Knox," I said evenly. "You're not like them. *Donovan* wasn't like them." I took a quick breath when his only movement was the muscles tensing in his clenched jaw. "OK, we can find out exactly what they were. Can that magnify for DNA?" I asked, doubtfully since the imager looked older than both of us put together.

He shook his head. "No, it's not strong enough."

"We'll have to get this sample back to my lab then," I added as Knox crossed to the sink and began soaking a dishtowel. He wrung out the excess water and began to wipe the dust off of the surfaces in the kitchen. *The water…*I thought, remembering the rag and bowl of water next to Mack's bed, the bloodied water in the bowl next to Burgess's. "Knox, wait—do you remember when I told you we learned that Red Fever is somehow *only* transmitted through direct contact with blood? What if there was something in the seawater surrounding the island, another strain of Red Fever that also needed direct exposure to be transmitted?" I speculated. "Both wounds for Burgess and Mack were irrigated with that water. What if all you did was provide access when you bit them?"

Knox stared at me intently, wordlessly until he started pulling materials from one of the drawers behind us: alcohol swabs, a lancet, and another slide. "Give me your finger, Frankie," he demanded, then took my hand and tore the alcohol swab open with his teeth.

"What are you doing?" I asked as he scrubbed the side of my index finger, then snapped the lancet. The drop of blood bloomed and dripped onto the slide he'd positioned underneath.

"Finding something out. Here, press on this to stop the blood." Knox handed me a cotton ball and unwrapped a sterile metal instrument with a curved edge. He put it into his mouth, then dragged it through the blood on the slide and tore a cover off another machine.

"How do you have a miniature bio simulator but not an imager from this century?" I asked, incredulous.

"Did you think towels were all I took out of The Citadel?" he said as he loaded the slide, then smiled briefly and shrugged. "The imager was too big to fit in a backpack." He keyed in an incubation timeframe and stepped back to watch the reaction digitize. The screen flooded with code instead of a 3-D rendering like the simulator in my lab, and I held my breath as he crossed to read it. He turned to me, his face blanched. "NEP..." he said quietly. "No evidence of pathogen. Your blood is still clean, Frankie."

I exhaled all the breath in my lungs and gripped the edges of the towel I realized I was still wrapped in from last night. I looked down at it and laughed as Knox tried to close the distance between us, but I stepped back reflexively. I might as well have struck him...

I rubbed my eyes—clinical is what I needed to be now. Clinical is what I could do. "Let's focus on what we know," I said, making a mental list. "Whatever that serum did to you, it hasn't killed you, even when you've had a Feral episode. Burgess and Mack died after their first change when they went into the sun... but not *you*." Now I began to pace. "Could it be that you're just a carrier of Red Fever, or only affected by some part of it?" I asked myself evenly. Distantly. Pulling back all my emotions and fears until I could start to see a clear, logical answer. "But it doesn't make sense that my blood would still be clean right now… We *know* the serum infected you, and you *could* have infected Burgess and Mack through the puncture wounds, which were deep like a—" I stopped abruptly and turned back to him. "Like a snakebite."

***

I was electric with possibilities. Actionable possibilities, not magical thinking. We knew the virus had to be in direct contact with blood, which both a syringe or…*fangs* would have accomplished. If Red Fever was then metabolized as a venom, even as a short-lived neurotoxin, then I could make an antivenin and pair it with an immunity booster. That just might reverse Knox's condition, and it *should* neutralize the effects of Red Fever in newly contracted cases.

I just needed samples of the fruit and sap the harvesters took from the tree. I needed to access my research to see if there were any traces of that fruit or sap in Donovan's system, then cross reference that with *Knox's* system, and of course, I would need the serums and a sample of Knox's…*venom.*

"If your teeth—" I started, but he cut me off, evidently having followed the same thinking. I'd forgotten he was a doctor.

"Antivenin..." He nodded. "But I don't know how to control it like that—how to bring it on...the teeth," he said awkwardly. "I've figured out how to stop them, but like you saw with Mack, it's not perfect."

I chewed my lip trying to navigate the next steps, but each path I speculated came with the same risk.

"You said power—threatening power, like someone trying to control you, provokes it?"

"I don't know. That's what I thought until the guards on the harvester boat tried attacking. They didn't *feel* like anything to me."

"But even though they were a threat, you didn't feel compelled to bite them—to...*feed* on them. *Sorry*," I added when he winced.

"Adrenaline," Knox seemed to decide. "One of the body's first physiological responses to a threat is to dump adrenaline into the bloodstream..."

"That must be what triggered the bartender back at Ivy's too—the heightened adrenaline from all the pressure that night?" I thought out loud. "That's something else I can cross reference with Donovan's cadaver file if I can just—" I stopped when Knox's expression hardened. "I'm sorry. I forgot he was..."

"A person?"

I gave him a solemn look. "Your *friend*. You know that I just want to stop what happened to him from happening to anyone else."

"He was an idiot." Knox shook his head. "And he was reckless. God, the *stupid* decisions he made.

Everything had to be right now, no matter the risk. He never thought of the consequences. That's all I ever thought about Frankie." He scrubbed his hands over his face. "Except once, but hell, I guess that's all it takes." He turned away from me, locking his hands behind his neck and looking upward as if the answers he sought would descend from the ether.

"He helped you tap the water and gas lines," I finally said. It was the first positive thing I thought to say to pull him out of this downward spiral.

Knox looked back at me as a laugh caught in his throat, seeming to surprise him. His brows crashed together as his dark eyes glassed. He briefly nodded, then laughed. "I guess he did do that."

I watched him struggle with how to feel, with where to put the new waves of guilt and loss that I now knew were years old. They were finally just too strong for him to keep behind the dam any longer, and even though I understood this, I couldn't find one logical argument to help me understand why he lied to me *again* even after I'd directly asked him what he'd done on the beach when my boat arrived.

"Knox…" I started, knowing I had to ask because if I didn't, the question would rattle behind every other thing he said to me from this point on. This was the crossroads, the point at which he had to decide if we would stay here, stranded…*lost,* or if there was some way we could move forward. "Knox…" I exhaled. "I need to know why you lied to me about Burgess."

Chapter 30

Knox took a deep breath and let it out slowly when he found a spot against the wall at my left. He leaned against it and put his hands in his pockets, his gaze focused on something across the room.

"Have you ever known you were going to be right about something, and then when it came true...that feeling..." he started as he crossed his arms over his chest, noticeably uncomfortable. "That almost arrogant feeling of, *see, I knew it*...and at the same time wanting nothing more than to have been wrong." Knox risked a glance at me.

"I think so," I said, remembering the countless Red Fever trials.

"The look on your face after I'd killed the guards on the boat, Frankie—I'd never seen you so afraid, not even after Mack chased you onto the beach at Poppy's camp," he said quietly. "It was everything I was afraid it would be, so I jumped overboard hoping those things in the water would just finish me off because I couldn't stand the idea that you'd always look at me with that much fear." Knox pushed off the wall and turned to me, he met my eyes briefly, then let his find the floor. "That's why I didn't tell you about Burgess or any of the rest of it when you asked. I didn't want you to look at me the way I knew you would... The way you're looking at me now."

Knox's brows crashed together as he focused fiercely on the ground. He pressed his lips together tightly, the muscles in his jaw flexing as I felt the rest of the barrier between us starting to fall away.

I wondered what I would have done in his position—being so sure that if the truth got out, it would be my biggest fear come true. I'd like to think that I'd have been honest anyway, be damned the consequences, but if I knew I'd lose him if he found out I was from the Grind…I'd hidden that from Scott, from Jack and Blake. I had no business being self-righteous when I had my own secrets.

I went to him slowly, not sure yet how I felt except to say that it was somewhere in the middle again. Somehow needing to feel his heartbeat encompassing everything around me, and at the same time, knowing with the most ancient part of my being that I needed to run. Maybe there was no way to choose. Maybe this, with him, whatever it was or would ever be, demanded that I find a way to accept both realities.

We stood like this for several seconds, inches apart. It felt like drowning, sealed inside a statue—fighting and struggling, but neither of us moving. I didn't want us to die here just because I wasn't sure yet how we would live like this, so pressed my cheek to his chest, closed my eyes, hoping to hear his heartbeat from the island cave.

His fingers moved through my hair and down my back as he clung to me.

"I'm sorry…" he whispered with what seemed the last of his breath, his arms wrapping around me even more tightly. "I should have told you about the beach that night. I should have told you everything even if it meant I'd lose you too."

And there, finally, the dam broke. I didn't think he realized the depth of this confession in this new deluge of pain and regret, which I realized had been building since he couldn't save his friends three years ago. I knew he hadn't forgiven himself for Nyssa's death, especially. That was obvious, but now, looking back on how guarded he'd been, on everything he'd hidden from me, I wondered if he wasn't trying to rewrite the past—to protect me in the way he felt he'd failed her—by keeping me as far away as he could from his suffering.

"I'm not going anywhere, Knox," I combed my fingers through his hair and pressed my cheek to his throat, trying to be as close as possible to him. "I'm not going anywhere."

I leaned back and ran my hands over his jaw, which was shadowed in dark stubble. His eyes were bloodshot, still brimming with fear and regret, but there was something else in them now. Something steady. Focused.

One of his hands moved to the nape of my neck as the other unfastened the towel I was still draped in from last night. It loosened as he kissed me slowly, held up by nothing more than the pressure of his body holding mine. Just like in the island caves during the storms, the sudden cool air on my skin pushed me against him. His hands were warm around my waist as his fingers again pressed into every dip and curve until I couldn't stand not being closer to him. I slid my fingertips down his chest, tracing the rise and fall of his muscles, the long, narrow valley that ran down the entire length of his torso. His breath came faster, more ragged when he broke the kiss, letting his lips travel down my jaw, over my throat. I felt the gentle scrape of his teeth against my skin, and a stab of fear ran through my core.

"Frankie..." he breathed my name as he gripped my hips, holding me at bay. Small flames danced in his eyes for just a second as he maneuvered me toward the wall. It was cold against my back, and I sucked in a quick breath at the shock of it, then another when his hand guided my thigh over his hip. The towel that was once between us fell away as his lips moved over my throat again, behind my jaw, and I thought I would never find my way back from the dizzying sound of his heartbeat echoing in my ears. "Are you still afraid of me, Frankie?" he said breathlessly, suspended between seconds that felt like an eternity.

I felt my pulse quickening, my blood heating in my veins. I held his face so he would look at me. So he would see me. His dark eyes were wild again, and his heavy brows furrowed in the same fierce, yet pleading way he had.

"I'm not afraid of you." I said quietly, but surely. His mouth closed over mine hard, making my breath catch as his fingers gripped outer my thigh, his forearm pressed to the wall as he cradled the back of my neck. I curled my fingers around his biceps as a swell of gravity pressed down on me, through me, reaching deeper and wider until it swallowed every clear thought in my head.

"*Knox,*" I said on the edge of an exhale and closed my eyes, lost in him, adrift, until he tightly wrapped his arms around my waist and carried me to his bed. The combination of his warm exhales over my throat as the soft, cool sheets touched my back made me lightheaded. I breathed him in as his mouth traveled over my skin, all traces of woodsmoke and sea washed away in the rain.

He pulled back slowly and combed his fingers through my hair just before meeting my eyes. "I would never hurt you, Frankie," he said, stroking my cheek. "I promise you."

I smiled up at him, the heat of him radiating over me, through me. "I know," I whispered, feeling the swell build low in my stomach again. It expanded into my chest when I heard his heartbeat like the rhythm of the entire world reverberating everywhere inside me. He pressed his lips to mine again, softly, but urgently, as was the contradiction of him. Everything about him was as intoxicating as it was terrifying, but there was nothing I could do, trapped in between those worlds. Trapped, it felt, between life and death—the split second decision to freeze or run, because there was no fighting him. There was nowhere either of us could hide here, and nowhere I would have rather been.

Chapter 31

I was truly astounded by the shelf life of the canned beans Knox heated over the bunsen burner. He'd been gone three years, but they were still perfectly fine.

"This is not a testament to my cooking," he said as I took another bite.

"It would be a testament to mine."

He narrowed his eyes at me. "And that fever grass you added to the fish?"

"Never would have occurred to me if you hadn't been making the fish already."

"I guess we're a good team, then, because I never would have thought to put grass on fish."

"Why not? Chives are basically grass. So is wheat…barley, oats, which are all used in breading," I said, smiling proudly when he looked at me like I was crazy.

"Nobody thinks of grass when they think of breading." He chuckled. "What kind of bait and switch is that?"

"Bait and switch…" I said to myself, feeling the idea gel.

"Frankie?"

"That's how we're going to get to my research," I said, my mind racing. "Can you get that tablet to queue a number? A personal number, anonymously?"

"Uh, probably. Why?"

"Because I need to arrange a little bait and switch, just to make sure I can trust Jack."

"Who's Jack?"

"One of the pathologists in my lab." Knox's expression hardened. "No, I don't think he was involved with setting me up, but I have to be sure. If we can get his girlfriend to meet me without knowing it's me, we'll have some leverage in getting the truth out of him. If he's not involved, he could help us get back inside The Citadel. She's jealous. Always teasing him about having a wandering eye," I said. "Jack has a boat at the docks. If you can get that tablet rigged, I'll get her to meet me there. And then I'll need your help again to…convince him to tell us what he knows. Do you have any syringes here?"

"I should," he said, crossing back to the kitchen/surgery area. He opened a few cabinets and came back with a packaged syringe. "There are more. What are you planning?"

"If he knows about the serums, he'll know about the risks too. Do you have any dye? Or something that will color water yellow, red, or blue?"

"Iodine is the closest I can probably get to red with what I have here."

"Perfect. How long will it take you to rig the tablet for an outside, anonymous queue? And we'll need a signal scrambler. Can you make another one?"

"I guess we'll see…" he said, moving back to the couch with a smile.

He worked for about an hour while I took a shower and then put together the iodine mixture, adding just enough to tint the water. I capped the syringe and brought it over to him.

"Does this look close to the color from the briefcases you used to deliver?"

He nodded. "Pretty close," he said, handing me a necklace that looked like a machine shop art project.

"Oh, thanks?" I said, trying to keep the confusion out of my voice.

He chuckled. "It's the signal scrambler. Not as elegant as the ones Donovan rigged on my lines, but it's what I could make with what was left of Wu Fong's gear. The tablet is dark now too if you're ready to queue," he added. I set the syringe down on the coffee table with a trembling hand, which surprised me. Knox folded his fingers around mine. "She probably had no idea about what they set up," he said, intuitively understanding even before I did.

I gripped his hand, then took the tablet from him and dialed Anita's number. It was early enough in the afternoon that Jack wouldn't have been home, but late enough that she would be done teaching kindergarten for the day. It rang once, twice, and on the third ring, she answered.

"Hello?" The sound of her voice was both comforting and haunting. A part of a life that didn't feel like mine anymore—one that was taken from me, and I was the only one who could get it back.

"Is this Anita?" I said, thinning my voice.

"Who is this?" Anita asked with an edge.

"Jack's girlfriend," I answered.

"Excuse me?"

I sighed audibly. "I can't do this anymore. Can you meet me at his boat tonight? I don't want any trouble. We've both been through enough. I just want to clear my conscience."

Knox's eyes widened, and Anita gasped. "What did you say?"

"Tonight at eight. I have some things that belong to you too. And come alone, or I'll leave."

I disconnected the queue and blew out a breath, my heart drumming in my chest.

Knox stared at me. "Do you think she'll come?"

"She'll come. But she won't be alone."

***

Anita hadn't come alone. It would have been stupid for anyone to come to the docks alone this close to dark, regardless of how close to The Citadel gates they were. This was still The Grind.

I didn't know how she managed to get a personal Sweeper droid to escort her, especially on such short notice. I'd expected she might ask a friend to accompany her, or maybe even Jack, which would have made things more complicated.

She wore her blonde curls tucked into a dark baseball cap, but there was no mistaking her bouncy gait. I hated to have to put her through this, but we didn't have any other options.

Send the droid away, or I'm gone. I messaged her.

A few seconds later she touched her temple, then turned to the droid. It retreated, and I messaged her again.

Get on the boat. Go to the galley.

Knox had turned off the alarm system and waited behind the door as Anita made her way down the steps. Once she was inside, Knox silently shut the door behind her.

"Frankie?" She gasped my name, all the blood draining from her face. "Oh, my God, Frankie!" She threw her arms around me. "We thought you were dead! They said your boat sank!" she babbled, then remembered why she'd come. "Wait… Why all this?"

"Anita, I would like you to meet my friend, Knox," I said, nodding to him. He grinned, his dark clothes blending in with the woodgrain until he took a step forward, duct tape in hand.

She startled. "I don't understand. Frankie, what the hell is this?"

"Have a seat, Anita." I told her how my field assignment was a set up. That Scott indeed was dead, not because our boat sank, but because sharks pulled him off the side of the boat he'd tried to throw me from. Once she was up to speed about Scrapper

Island, and once Knox had finished duct taping her hands and feet to the chair, I pulled out the syringe full of iodine. "You're going to queue Jack now and put him on speaker."

"Why are you doing this, Frankie? We were friends!"

"We're still friends, Anita. I'm not going to hurt you, but I need to know if Jack was part of this."

"He wasn't part of anything! He was upset when we got the news about your boat. I've never seen him so upset. In fact, I wasn't *completely* shocked to see it was you who queued me with that story about being his girlfriend. It all kind of made sense."

"*What*?" I gaped at her. "Anita, that's delusional. Get him on the queue."

"I can't," she said, glancing at her bound hands. I rolled my eyes and tapped her temple for her.

"Blink for speaker," I commanded, and she complied. The queue started pinging.

"Hey, babe," Jack answered.

"Hi, Jack. Did you miss me?" I said. Anita glared at me. "Fr—Frankie?"

"That's right. Back from the dead, no thanks to you."

"Frankie! Oh, my God! Where are you? Where's Anita?"

"She's sitting here taped to a chair," I said. "I'm about to inject this syringe full of red liquid into her neck. I suppose I could pick a different color, though. Care to guess what my other options are?"

"What the fuck are you talking about, Frankie? Where are you?"

"Would you have been the one they sent to kill me if Scott hadn't been the *low man on the totem poll*?"

"*What*?" Jack's voice was thin and tight. "Where's Anita, *goddamnit*? Anita!"

"I'm here!" She sobbed. "I'm all right. Jack, what did you do?"

"Nothing! I don't know what she's talking about!"

"What are the other two colors for the syringes, Jack? I'm about to inject this red one into Anita's delicate little neck." I said, taking the cap off the needle full of iodine solution and pressing it to Anita's throat. She started sobbing again.

"Jack! What did you do? Tell her!"

"Nothing! I don't know about any syringes! Frankie, I swear to God if you hurt her, I'll find you and kill you for real with my own fucking hands!" he shouted, his voice cracking.

"Download my research on Donovan and upload it to your research cloud," I said. "Then send the password to Anita."

"And you'll let her go?"

"Not yet. I need you to find out what shipments are coming to pathology from Wu Fong Pharmaceuticals and upload those findings too. Find out about any incoming botanicals from the

Caribbean and put it all on your cloud account. Do you understand?"

"Fine, yes. Are you going to tell me what this is about? Scott tried to *kill* you? Where is he now?"

"Somewhere in the digestive track of about a dozen sharks. If he's even still there," I said coldly.

"*Fuck…* Frankie. Listen to me. I had nothing to do with that, all right? I wanted to go with you, remember?"

"You *what*?" Anita hissed.

"Oh, Christ…with both of them. Her *and* Scott."

Knox's eyebrows pitched as he pressed his grinning lips into a line.

"I want to believe that," I said. "But right now I can't believe anyone. Someone in that lab tried to murder me, and when it didn't happen, they sent me to some upside-down prison island."

"*What*? Frankie, I swear to God. Let her go, all right. We can talk. I'll help you find out what happened. Just let Anita go."

"After I get my research and everything you can find on shipments from Wu Fong or the Caribbean. You try to track her, and I'll put this needle in her throat, Jack," I said slowly. "Did you know Donovan was infected with Red Fever because he injected himself with a serum? It was red, just like this one. Queue at six, and I'll have her line open again."

It wasn't safe to go through The Grind at night, especially since the rain had stopped. Knox had rigged the signal scrambler, but it wasn't a guarantee that Jack wouldn't be able to track Anita's communications chip eventually. We wouldn't be able to stay on his boat for much longer.

Chapter 32

I took the scrambler off at six, and right on schedule, Anita received the login and password to Jack's cloud account. All of my research was there, but there was nothing yet about Wu Fong or any shipments from the Caribbean. I downloaded my files onto Knox's tablet and scrolled to find the model of Donovan's stage one cell wall structure.

Jack's queue came several minutes after I accessed his cloud account.

Anita answered and put him on speaker again.

"That's all I could get from your research," he said. "There are chunks of it missing—all that peripheral stuff you gathered about his legacy debt at the tea shop. I can't find that."

"Who else had access to my work, Jack? You, Scott, Blake, and Beck. Is that it?"

"As far as I know. It's Beck's wing and Blake's lab."

I nodded, more confident than ever that they'd both conspired to kill me. "What about Wu Fong? The shipments of anything from the Caribbean?"

"Nothing except your field assignment requisitions," Jack added. "But it's weird because usually those have to go through Human Resources, especially with spending accounts attached to them," he continued. "But Blake just initiated yours and skipped underwriting altogether because the funds came from a private donor—*Raphael's Tea Shop*. You really liked tea that much that they sponsored your trip?"

"Jack, *oh, my god*," I said impatiently, the frustration with Scott's original idiotic story about our *one-day anniversary* celebration all the more biting now. "They must be connected to Wu Fong. A front business. That's why they were so dodgy when I started asking about Donovan's part time job there. The hover car tried to run me over right after Scott and I left there too."

"Shit, Frankie…" Jack said.

"The fruit shipments…" I thought out loud. "Jack, the old woman at that tea shop acted like she knew Scott. What if he was picking up the fruit from them to make the serums?" I looked at Knox. "What if he's the delivery person who replaced Donovan?"

"If you're both done playing detective now, do you think you could *let me go*?" Anita hissed.

"Cut her tape," I said to Knox, then turned my attention back to Jack on the queue. I needed my simulator, but there was no way Jack would be able to get that past security in the lab, let alone out of The Citadel. He would have to run the tests. "Jack, I need you to go to Raphael's and tell them you've had a breakthrough, but you need more of the fruit. Tell them you'll be coming from now on instead of Scott."

"Are you kidding me? What if they have no idea what the hell I'm talking about?"

"They will. They have to," I insisted. "When they give you the fruit, run it for organic matches against the Donovan data, and upload that to your cloud."

"Frankie, this is crazy."

"Do that, and we'll bring Anita to you. Write up two voluntary trial passes so they don't scan us at the gate. Then Anita can get us through."

"That will cost two hundred credits each, and I can't access the lab accounts on Saturday," Jack protested.

"I'll pay you back. Just do it." I said. "You can let us in the lab from there. I have one more test to run."
Anita was asleep on one of the bunks and had been for hours. Knox and I took turns sleeping in the other one until the tablet pinged with Jack's cloud update and woke me up. It was almost noon, and I nearly cried when I read the data.

"I was right," I whispered. "It's the skin—the same extract from the skin of that spiky red fruit was in every one of Donovan's mutated cells, Knox." I felt the tears welling in my eyes, spilling over and burning my cheeks. "We found it… We found the source of Red Fever—at least one strand of it." He smiled and was about to say something, but I was talking again before he could get it out. "We're not done, though. Your strand is different. He injected you with a different serum, right?" I asked, quickly wiping my tears away.

Knox's expression was equal parts concern and amusement. "The blue one. Donovan used the red one on himself."

"OK… there are other extracts here, one from the flesh of the fruit, and one from the seed." I read from the tablet. "We need to get to my equipment to run a sample of your blood against those." I set the tablet down and woke up Anita, who was already starting to stir. "Time to go," I said, slipping the signal scrambler over her head as we made our way up the stairs, off the boat, and toward The Citadel's infamously patrolled gate.

The rain hadn't completely left the area. Dark clouds hung overhead, heavy with the promise of another deluge.

"I'm sorry we had to pull you into this," I said as we walked with Anita. Knox held her arm, his other hand positioned under her hair with the syringe ready to plunge into her throat if she tried to run or scream.

"All you had to do was ask," she said bitterly. "You didn't have to hold me hostage. And he doesn't have to do *this*," she said, struggling against Knox as much as she could without jostling his hand.

"If you'd been through what we've been through, Anita, you wouldn't trust anyone either. After this is all over, I'll make it up to you. I promise." She huffed as we approached The Citadel's gate kiosk. I hadn't seen it from this side for a long time. The barricade was down, and a swarm of cylindrical, metallic Sweeper droids hovered overhead on both sides, waiting to electrocute anyone who tried to enter illegally. Anita dutifully scanned her palm on the gatekeeper's counter.

"Authorized. Anita Curtis," the droid voice inside the kiosk said. "You will be escorted to the Pathology Center with two voluntary trials. Please refrain from diverting off course, or force may be used to redirect you."

The barricade in front of us lifted, and two of the Sweeper droids dropped from the sky to escort us. One floated in front of us while the other followed several yards behind.

Knox's jaw was clenched when I looked up at him. "Are you all right?" I asked, almost slipping my arm into his, but stopped when I realized it would probably look strange the way he was holding onto Anita.

"Fine," he said. "It's just weird to be back here."

His eyes scanned everything like they did on the prison beach. Still looking for something that would jump out at any minute.

"What's a *voluntary trial*?" Anita asked.

"They're people," Knox answered coldly. "The Citadel tests experimental drugs and procedures on them."

Anita balked. "And people can just walk into The Citadel for that? Just from anywhere with no identity check?"

"They don't want to *scare off the applicant pool* with a bunch of paperwork." Knox's voice was low and menacing like when I'd first met him in the island clearing. "And they don't want a record of the names and faces of the people they test on linked to The Citadel. They pay the subjects a handful of credits and send them back to The Grind to deal with whatever was done to them. That's most of what I treated out there."

"What you *treated*?" Anita asked, clearly holding back her horror. "So you're an *unauthorized* medic? How did you know how to treat what happened to anyone at *The Citadel*?"

Knox leaned toward her. "I know how to stick this needle right into your jugular. But then I'd have to carry you up to the lab."

"I didn't mean…" Anita whimpered, confused until we reached the lab entrance, which fortunately wasn't far from the gate. She buzzed the Pathology Center door, and we quickly moved to the elevator and up to the lab.

I'd walked into this place each day for the last several years, but now it felt foreign, like everything else since I'd left.

"Babe!" Jack rushed toward us.

Knox jerked Anita's arm, pulling her back. "Stay right there."

"Frankie—I got you what you wanted, which was a *galactic* pain in the ass by the way," Jack said, his bloodshot eyes electric blue with fear. "Now let her go. You were right about the fruit and Raphael's. I'll help you, OK?"

"I said I have one more test, and then we're done," I nodded to him. "Just stay right there. Knox, come over to the simulator and sit her in the chair." He followed me, walking backward with Anita in tow. I grabbed a syringe from the drawer and opened the package, then set it on my work station.

Jack took a step toward us. "*Frankie!*"

"Listen to me," I said as calmly as I could. "I didn't want to think you were involved with trying to kill me…"

"I wasn't! For fuck's sake Frankie…*please,*" he held up his hands and took another step closer. "I'm an asshole, but I'm not a murderer."

"Stay there!" I shouted. Anita sat in the chair Knox had steered her to. I moved my hands under her hair, putting pressure on the needle against her throat as I took it from Knox's grip. She winced and whimpered again.

"Goddamnit, Frank!" Jack's voice cracked.

I took a deep breath. "Put your head on the desk, Anita, and lay your hands flat so I can see them." I said. She complied after I nudged her head forward to my workstation. "Knox is going to do a blood draw and put it in the simulator, and I swear to God if you try anything, Jack, I'll put this needle in her artery," I said through my teeth.

"Jack!" Anita cried. He took another step toward me, and I tightened my grip in her hair. She cried again.

"I don't *want* to hurt her, Jack, but you're making me! One more test, and then we're *gone*, all right?" I glared at him. "If you really weren't part of this, then you stay right there and help me sort this out when the test is done."

He nodded. "All right. You got it. OK," he said, finally stopping where he was with his hands lifted in the air.

"You got her?" Knox asked, eyeing Jack.

I nodded, "You know where to deposit it in the simulator?"

"Yeah." He let go of Anita's arm and picked up the syringe, sticking it expertly into his vein and depositing the draw.

"All right, he's done! Now let her go!" Jack said.

"Come over here and send those results to your cloud, Jack. Then, I'll let her go."

Knox stepped back from the simulator as Jack typed furiously into my computer. "There! It's done—it's done!"

I let Anita go and watched the data populate. Trace elements of the fruit's peel registered in Knox's cells, as did traces of the fruit's flesh.

"*Both*?" I said, confused, but then the seed data populated. It was an overwhelmingly dominant match to the material in Knox's cells. "Oh, my god," I breathed.

"They made the blue serum from the seed..." he said absently, staring at the highlighted areas of the cell model, and the data was *still* populating.

"We found the source of Red Fever," I whispered, feeling years of disappointment melt away. "We need the novel virus simulation queued to test these, too, but we can treat you, Knox."

"He's *infected*?" Jack asked, eyeing Knox. But I didn't have time to respond before the sound of clapping came from across the lab.

Slow, loud clapping.

Chapter 33

"*Blake…*" I whispered, then glared at Jack. "You called *him*?"

"No! I swear!" he said, blanching as Anita ran into Blake's arms.

"What?" I gasped. "No, she was wearing a scrambler!"

Anita glared at me. "I didn't call him, you psychopath!" she shouted. "But I would have!"

Blake clapped one final time and threw an arm around her. "You've always been able to think outside of the box, Frankie." He cocked his head and looked inquisitively into the distance. "Imagine my surprise to get a frantic queue from Raphael's today when their shipment of bloodfruit was being picked up by just one person," he said, looking like a demonic red-headed doll come to life when he casually pulled a gun from his waistband. "I'm impressed at your leap of faith with just sending Jack, honestly. You're usually such a pragmatist. For your notes, though…" he whispered. "I always send at least two additional security details on pick-up and delivery runs."

Two enormous, leathery skinned men walked up behind Blake from the corridor, flanking him as he walked toward us.

"Flat-nose…" Knox said under his breath, his hands turning to fists at the sight of one of the guards.

He glared at Blake. "You made Nyssa add that shit to the serums? It was *you*?"

Blake's eyes widened. "Nyssa… You don't mean Nyssa *Blair*, do you?" he started to grin. "Too bad what happened to her down at the docks, what, three years ago now? I never would have pegged her for a thief. She was always so…*giving*," he added, his grin shifting into a lascivious smile.

Knox lunged at Blake.

"No!" I stepped in front of him. "They have guns," I said quietly. "Remember how Donovan died?"

"What the fuck have you been doing, Bingham?" Jack asked. "Does Beck know about this?"

"*Beck*? What do you think? " Blake laughed as Anita clung to him.

"And you." Jack shook his head at her. "All your paranoia about me, and this whole time you've been with *him*?"

"Not the whole time," she said flippantly. "Just since it became abundantly clear that you were going to be a lab rat forever, Jack. Did you really think I wanted to be stuck in this hole spending all my time with a bunch of brats?" She sneered, all traces of her angelic kindergarten teacher demeanor gone.

"And you think *he's* your ticket out of here?" Jack laughed. "Where could you go, Anita? People are dying out there! *Everywhere*. Miami, Myrtle Beach, New York—Red Fever is even in *London* now. And it's *his* fault! Haven't you seen the feeds?"

"London… Now that was a particularly profitable acquisition." Blake nodded to Anita.

I narrowed my eyes at him. "You're sick…"

"Not at all, actually…" Blake pointed his gun at Knox. "And I never have to be now that a little tropical birdie told Mr. Wu that our favorite delivery boy was back in town…all grown up and immortal now. Well, *almost*."

"Blake, stop. You don't know what his strand of Red Fever does to people," I said, raising a hand as if that could somehow deflect a bullet.

Blake sighed as he turned his gun on me. "See, that's always been the difference between you and me, Frank. I don't *care*."

A beaker suddenly hit Blake in the head from Jack's direction as gunshots rang out. Another beaker shattered against the wall, and Jack raced toward us, crouching.

"Go! Go!" he said, waving us into the corridor. One of Blake's guards had already blocked the elevator, so we ran toward the stairs. "My car is close. Come on!" Jack said, leading us down the stairs, but another guard started coming up. "Shit! Go back!" We climbed flight after flight of stairs until there was nowhere else to go except the top floor corridor, where we only found locked offices and emptied trash bins.

"Fire escape!" I yelled. We went back into the stairwell and pushed open the small door to the roof, but nearly fell backward when a huge gust of wind ripped the door out of Jack's hands. The sky was roiling with black clouds as I ran in the direction of the fire escape housing. "Come on!" I yelled, tapping my temple in the hopes I would be able to connect with Citadel security, but like on the barge, the signal was only static. "Jack! Do you have a signal? Can you queue out?"

He tapped his temple, but we only made it a few more strides before Blake and his guards poured from the stairwell in pursuit of us.

Anita followed, remembering the signal scrambler and ripping it from her neck. She threw it at Knox, nearly missing his head as it bounced off the side of the building behind us.

"Asshole Grind trash!" she shouted through the rain, which poured down over us in sheets. A flash of lightning struck the fire escape housing, sending us to our knees.

"Knox, can you jump from up here?" I asked, feeling the vibration of answering thunder shoot through me.

He looked over the edge of the building. "I don't think so."

Blake's fiery hair turned muddy brown in the rain. He pushed it out of his eyes and raised his gun to me again. "Why do you always make everything *so difficult*, Frankie?"

"Bingham!" Jack shouted, holding up a hand to Blake as he stepped toward him. "Look, we can walk this back, OK? Just stop before things go too far."

Blake turned the gun on Jack and pulled the trigger without so much as saying a word. He fell backward against the edge of the roof, sliding motionless to the ground.

"Jack!" I screamed.

"All right, Frankie," Blake said, recalibrating his aim at me. "Please try to die this time."

I heard the shot just before a blinding flash struck behind Blake's head in time with a simultaneous, deafening crack. When I could see clearly again, everyone, including Blake, was on the ground. A dizzy feeling came over me in force as I noticed what seemed like diluted watercolor paint falling over my legs. Nausea replaced the dizziness when it started to gush through my fingers, thick and red and dark. My heart started pounding in my ears as everything else muffled.

"Frankie!" Knox shouted from far away. Another bolt of lightning ripped across the sky, splintering in every direction. The building shook with the roar of thunder that surrounded me as flames caught on Knox's arms and shoulders before finally igniting his hair.

"*No!*" I cried, the image of Burgess and Mack bursting into flames flashing in my mind. He opened his mouth in a scream that rivaled the thunder, his canine teeth elongating into fangs just the way they had when he tore apart the guards on the barge. The familiar, low, all-consuming heartbeat grew louder until it silenced everything else.

A wave of darkness pushed over me, the imploding tunnel vision hijacking my equilibrium until I wasn't sure which direction was up or down, save for the driving rain pummeling me like small rocks falling from the sky. Suddenly, everything was cold except for my hands, which were warm and sticky as I tried to focus on pressing them to the bullet wound I knew I had, but for some reason couldn't see anymore. My teeth began to chatter just before I dropped to my knees, only vaguely aware of the impact as another round of lightning and thunder filled my consciousness. I blinked several times until I could see at least the blurry approximations of everything. I looked up for Knox, but he wasn't where he had been.

"We have to get off this roof!" Jack said, stumbling toward me as he held his shoulder. "Oh my god, Frankie."

"*Jack…*" I smiled, relief settling over me even as the pain in my side flared and began radiating everywhere.

"Let me see, Frankie…just lie back," Knox said, surprisingly from my other side. He started moving my hands to my sides, and I let them fall.

"*Shit…*" Jack said.

"You're all right…You're here…" I found Knox's dark eyes, but only for a second before the tunnel vision started to return, threatening to swallow everything again.

"That's right, Frankie. Be still, you're going to be OK," Knox said again. "Just keep looking at me—Frankie…*Frankie*!"

A branch of lightning peeled across the churning, black sky. I closed my eyes because it was too bright, and the sound of the heartbeat in my ears was too loud to hear anything else except the palpable, growling roll of thunder that followed.

Chapter 34

When I opened my eyes in the hospital room, Knox was sitting next to me in a pair of scrubs, one hand clenched into a fist over his mouth as if he were in deep thought.

Thunder cracked outside, calling back what happened on the roof, or at least, what seemed to have happened. I tried to recall the vision of Knox on fire and realized it must have been shock, but the memory of Blake was as real as the pain that radiated through my whole body, and a weighted dread filled my chest.

"Knox..." I said, which somehow sent an even sharper jolt of pain through me. "How's Jack...?"

Startled, he looked over at me quickly and smiled. "Hey, scrapper." He glanced warily at the grandmotherly nurse who was adjusting the settings on the machine next to me. "He's fine, don't worry," he added as his fingers brushed strands of hair from my forehead, his other hand bringing mine to his lips. "Frankie, I'm so—"

An abrupt knock on the door interrupted him.

"Mason?"

"*Dr. Beck*?"

"Call me Howard, please," my boss said. He entered the room with a bouquet of sunflowers in a vase, which he set on the table at the foot of my bed.

"Howard Beck. I work with Dr. Mason at the CPC," he added with a nod to Knox.

"Knox Ryder. I'm…a friend."

"Ah, *Ryder*," Beck said, arching a white eyebrow. Knox's arm tensed. "I understand it was your quick thinking that saved my team. Where in the world did you find duct tape?"

Knox's face blanched. "In the offices there…on the top floor…um, when I broke into them," he stumbled, finally pressing his lips into a hard line as if to stop any further explanation.

"Well…" Beck chuckled. "The CPC is in your debt."

"Dr. Beck, you said he saved our *team*. Where is Jack?" I said, making a mental note to ask a serious question about duct tape later.

"Oh, he's fine, fine," Beck said, putting his hands in his coat pockets. "Bullet through the shoulder, but it was a clean in and out. They released him last night not long after you both were admitted, and he was back at the lab already this morning working on the Red Fever leads you managed to put together…even after what you'd been through." Beck shook his head, a shadow passing over his face. "O'Dell relayed the debacle that was your field assignment. I shouldn't have let Bingham run with that."

"Honestly, sir—"

"Please, call me Howard," he said. "Luckily, Mr. Ryder here was returning from *his* field assignment when he was. I'm sure it was good to see one of our own out there after what Scott Jeffries..." he trailed off, shaking his head again as he turned to Knox. "Anyway, the CPC is in your debt for bringing Dr. Mason home."

Knox and I exchanged confused glances. "Well, anyone would have done the same," he said, playing along.

Beck gave him a fatherly nod, then beamed at me. "So, as I was saying, O'Dell tells me you've had a breakthrough in Red Fever. A fruit enzyme you discovered at the tea place you like so much?"

"I *don't* like the—" I started, but pain shot through my torso again. I sighed. Whatever. Fighting it was too much work. "Yes, sir—*Howard*. It looks promising. Does this mean I'm not dead anymore in the eyes of the CPC?"

Dr. Beck chuckled. "Your bay is waiting for you, Mason. I'm hoping they can wrap the investigation with Bingham's back alley operation before too long, and you can get back to work in peace. Speaking of Bingham..." He looked back at Knox. "Have you done your boards yet, son?"

Knox blew out a breath. "Uh, no, sir. But—"

"I'll get them ordered. I suspect we'll have a residency opening in pathology, and I imagine completing a three-year field tour will knock off most of your internship obligation. That is, if you're interested in specializing?"

Knox's brows shot up. "Thank you, sir. But...I actually have a practice waiting for me *outside* the Wall." He glanced at me. "I just needed to find my way back to it."

"Ah," Beck gave him a knowing smile. "Well, it was worth a try. Good people are hard to find. We'll get your Citadel records sent to the panel for review next week and I'll find a way to add in the internship credit. I'll look forward to seeing you for your board defense so you can get back to work without interference."

"Wow, well, thank you again," Knox said, more than a little surprised.

Beck smiled. "We're all a team in this profession. You've more than demonstrated that, and I won't forget it." He offered Knox his hand, then turned to me. "And Mason, because of you, we can help a hell of a lot of other people now. You keep me posted on when to expect you back."

"Yes, sir—*Howard*." I corrected again. This was never going to become a thing. "Thank you."

"Knock-knock, Frank, I know you need your beauty sleep but we've got a problem..." Jack said, coming through the open door with his arm in a sling. "Oh!" he blanched.

Beck grinned. "Yes, we do, O'Dell. See if you can't snake charm our soon-to-be *Authorized* Dr. Ryder here to come work in pathology, and there's a European field assignment with your name on it." He chuckled, slapping Jack on his good shoulder as he made his way for the door.

"Really?" Jack froze as Beck walked past. "Is he serious?" Jack turned back to the door. "Sir, are you serious?" He waited for a second, then pointed at Knox.

I tried not to laugh. "What's wrong? Are you all right?"

Jack glanced at the nurse and gave me a wry smile. "Nothing a little *duct tape* couldn't fix."

"You duct taped his shoulder?" I squinted at Knox.

"*And* your gut, right there on the roof." Jack laughed, then glanced at the nurse. "True story, Frank? Good thing you were already out cold. This guy wore a trash can through the director's window and did some office supply field surgery shit. I think you still have paper clips in there somewhere."

"Shut up." Knox rolled his eyes and smiled.

"Hey, I'm not complaining," Jack said. "I stopped bleeding long enough to whisper a heartfelt *fuck you* to Anita *and* watch Blake's freckled ass get handcuffed to a field gurney. Worth every blindingly painful second it took to get the tape off." He smirked, but it wilted almost immediately when he saw the nurse glaring steely daggers at him. He cleared his throat sheepishly. "Apologies for my language, ma'am," he added like the good Catholic school boy I'm sure he never was.

"Visiting hours are almost over." She pursed her lips, quickly finishing her adjustments and leaving the room.

Jack let out a huge breath. "Finally," he said, sliding the door closed. "I thought I was going to have to start hitting on her."

"Jack, what the—?" I started to ask through another restrained laugh.

"Yeah, yeah, save all your *what the hells* until I'm done," he said. "I told you I'd help you sort all this shit out, so listen. The Crisis Management team is coming to debrief you, like, now, Frankie, and you need to tell them you wound up on *San Isidro Island* and *Miguel* gave you both a ride back here on his yacht. I know a guy who gets me cigars from an island off the Cuban coast—he's going to corroborate."

"Is that what Beck was talking about with Knox's field assignment? He didn't have one of those, Jack. They're going to pull his records and see that."

Jack's face froze as his eyes darted to Knox, then back to mine. He shrugged. "It's fine. I know another guy."

"OK…hang on," I said, squinting at him. "Why even say all that in the first place? We need to tell them about that penal colony. There's a tree on that island that is *literally* eating those people."

Jack shook his head vehemently. "I tried to look that place up, Frank. There's no record of anything called *Scrapper Island* or even any kind of penal colony island anywhere. But that's just the beginning. Those guards who got blown to shit by the lightning on the roof? Gone," he said. "Sweeper droids found no trace of them when they picked up Anita and Blake."

"*What*?" Knox asked.

"No," I said, shaking my head. "I saw them all on the ground."

Jack nodded. "That's what I'm saying. The Sweeper droids brought Anita and Blake down, both of them ranting about Ryder here spontaneously combusting to this woman from Crisis Management," he said, looking quickly over his shoulder. "I heard her tell her guys to *send them in for a work-up*, so of course, what did I say when it was my turn to debrief? That Blake was trying to be some kind of mad scientist asshole on the rooftop. *That's* what I said. And I was back home in my own bed last night while Blake and Anita were probably tucked in nice and cozy with a straight jacket." Jack swallowed hard and rubbed a hand over his dark stubble. "There's some other level shit happening here, Frank, and you need to tell the nice Crisis Management team what I just said so you can go home."

"What did *you* see up there on the roof?" I asked him, then held my breath.

Jack looked over at Knox abruptly and blinked several times. "Well, in addition to all the other *what-the-fuckery*, yeah, Dr. Duct Tape there was on *actual* fire. And by the way, I'd keep that under your hat with the crisis team too because people don't usually walk away from being struck by lighting." He leaned in and spoke conspiratorially. "And PS: we're going to have a long talk about how he was *not* struck by lightning when you're no longer an invalid."

Knox folded his arms as he crossed to the window, and the deep breath I took caught under my ribs.

"I have everything we need to start treating Red Fever now, Knox. I just need to get back to my research and I'll find the—" I stopped and reset. "*We'll* find the answers." I smiled at him when he glanced back at me. "The three of us make a good team."

Jack sighed and sunk into the chair next to me. "I think this might be bigger than Red Fever, Frank."

Knox sat on the edge of my bed and took my hand again just as there was another knock at the door.

"She's awake!" a cheery, middle-aged man announced as he stepped into the room. "I'm Dr. Garcia, and you are one lucky lady," he said, flashing a wide, white smile that creased each side of his tanned face. He tapped the panel on the wall and pointed to the projected scan it produced. "How do you feel?"

"A little sore, but good," I answered.

"Well, that's to be expected." He chuckled. "The bullet managed to miss all your internal organs, and since there was no trace of it other than this groove in one of your abdominal muscles *riiiight* there…we think you somehow pushed it out."

"What?" I asked, confused. "Is that even possible?"

Dr. Garcia shrugged. "If you'd have asked me a few days ago, I'd have said no, but I can't argue with these images," he added, gesturing again to the display. "You might have some scarring because of the lasers we used to cauterize and close, but according to these digitals, everything is already on the mend. If you promise to take it easy, I think we can get you out-processed before the sun sets. What do you say to that?" he asked, pressing a thumbprint into the bottom corner of the panel just before it closed.

"That would be great," I nodded. "Thank you."

"My pleasure, Dr. Mason. Get some rest at home before you try putting that hero cape back on. Someone will be up soon with your discharge paperwork." He gave me another smile and nodded as he passed a tall Mediterranean woman with cropped dark hair, who seemed to have appeared from nowhere in the doorway.

"Frank…" Jack said under his breath.

The woman smiled warmly as she crossed to me, her heels clicking on the tile. "Hello again, Dr. Mason," she said, her thick, dark eyebrows arched as she looked me over. "You may remember me from Ivy's several weeks ago—Eve Adams, Crisis Management." She showed me her identification, the inside of her wrist revealing an apple tattoo with a yellow snake through it.

"Yes, I remember you," I said. "Are you here to take a statement?" I asked, confused when two orderlies with rolling gurneys entered the room. Her smile faded until her expression mirrored the sympathetic kindergarten teacher countenance she wore at Ivy's that night.

"We can do that once we're on the road, if you like."

Chapter 35

"What's this?" Knox got to his feet.

"Listen very carefully," Eve leveled her intense green eyes as each orderly pulled back the sheet of their respective gurney to reveal a lab coat, lanyard, and clipboard. "In eight minutes, a team of three highly trained agents will be in this room to make your deaths look like accidents. To avoid that, gentlemen, you can either put on these items and walk alongside as we wheel Dr. Mason out on one of the gurneys right now, or we can wheel all three of you out under sedation. We're here to help you, but I'm afraid the details will need to wait. What will it be?"

The orderlies each reached into their pockets, but didn't pull anything out...yet. Knox and Jack both saw the action and exchanged brief glances with each other and me, but for some reason neither of them answered Eve.

"Give them the coats," I finally decided for them, unsure why this math was difficult—like it or not, we didn't really have a choice in going with these people.

Eve smiled and helped me onto the gurney while the two orderlies kept an eye on Knox and Jack as they slipped into the lab coats.

"Cover your hair with this." Eve handed me a thin, fabric shower cap, then helped Jack get the other side of his lab coat over the arm that was in a sling. "Mr.

Ryder, you will push the gurney while Dr. O'Dell walks at your side studying the paperwork on the clipboard. Both of you will follow Arthur," she added, angling her head to the orderly next to her. "He'll lead you to our transport while Angelo and I make sure no one follows." Both of the orderlies gave an answering nod, and I couldn't help but notice that neither of them looked like they were agents of any kind—no overt muscularity, no hard lines on their faces—but that was probably the point.

Jack slipped his lanyard on as he got into position, suddenly confused and oddly calm, given the fact that assassins were literally minutes from attacking us. *Was I the only one on edge here?*

"Want a clipboard?" he asked, confused. "I seem to have two." I turned to find him holding them out just before Arthur snatched one out of his hand on his way to the door. Jack's brows shot up as his eyes followed Arthur. "*Or not.* Sorry, Frank. You snooze, you lose."

Arthur hushed us over his shoulder before looking down each end of the hallway. After a few more seconds, he motioned for us to follow him out the door.

"Where are we going?" Knox asked.

Eve drew a finger to her lips. "Stay quiet. Head down. Follow Arthur to the ambulance bay."

And with that, we were in the hallway. Knox met my eyes, his heavy, dark brows drawn together in an expression I couldn't fully distinguish...anger or concern, or more likely both. He gave me a subtle nod, which I returned, and at least I relaxed a little.

In what seemed like seconds we were getting into the elevator.

Arthur let out a breath. "We might pass these guys here, so keep your heads down. They know your faces," he said to Knox. "There are two Caucasian men and one Asian, all average size, all wearing scrubs like mine—if we get separated, follow the hallway around to the left until you see the bay doors. Someone will be there to get you loaded up."

The elevator doors opened before anyone could respond, and again, we were moving. Jack watched the floor just ahead of us, but he didn't lift his eyes. Knox gripped the side rails of my gurney so tightly his knuckles were white. The tension radiating from both of them filled my brain with static, so I closed my eyes since I couldn't see where we were going anyway.

Everything got louder the instant the world went dark. The sound of quick, rhythmic footsteps, the swishing of the lab coats, the hum and occasional squeak of the gurney wheels. The air was also colder and seemed thinner on this floor, which I thought must have been the result of being so close to the outside main doors. *Why was it taking so long to get there?* Leaving my room and getting down here took seconds in comparison to this never-ending hallway.

And in the time it took me to have that thought, Jack swore under his breath as the sounds of struggle filled the air. I opened my eyes, but I couldn't see anything except the overhead lights and the tops of the windows in the corridor.

"Go—go!" Arthur yelled.

I gripped the side rails of the gurney as Knox started running. Cool air rushed over my skin, but the sensation was eclipsed by the startling sound of gunshots from behind us just an instant before we barreled through the bay doors. All at once, everyone was shouting.

"Get in!" A woman who looked *nothing* like an orderly with her black tactical vest and plainly visible, very large gun strapped to her back motioned repeatedly for Jack and Knox to get in the rear of the ambulance. She began running alongside us as a man in a similar uniform gripped the far end of the gurney I was on, somehow lifting and loading it into the vehicle in a single move. I looked around frantically for Knox and Jack, but didn't see them get in the ambulance before we started moving.

"Stay down!" the man said as he closed the left side of the ambulance doors and fired his own gun from behind it. "Come on! Jump at the turn!" he yelled to someone apparently following closely behind us.

"Knox? Jack?" I almost shouted. Knox gripped my hand.

"Right here, Frank," Jack said, startling me from near the front of the ambulance.

We hit a curb hard. Pain shot through my whole body, but whatever scream I was about to release fell apart when Arthur crashed through the remaining open door and collided with the gurney, the pain this time giving me tunnel vision.

"They were already embedded," he puffed, trying to catch his breath. "Doctors' coats."

"Eve?" the man in tactical gear asked.

"She got the two on my tail from somewhere in the wind. No trace of her."

The man nodded. "Are you hit? What's that?"

Arthur looked at his shoulder and found the fabric of the scrubs ripped and blood staining the edges. "No, just a graze. You three?" he asked, looking from Jack to Knox, and finally, to me.

"Are you all right? You got knocked around back there." Knox eyed my stomach. He exhaled and ran a hand through his dark hair, which was blown in every direction.

"I'm OK. Where are we going?" I asked.

"Somewhere with significantly less shooting," Arthur said. He exchanged looks with the other man, who drew a pistol and shot both Jack and Knox so quickly I didn't even realize what had happened until they both slumped over. I started to scream, but stopped when I felt a burning in my upper arm. I jerked my attention back to Arthur, who immediately started to blur before my eyes. "Everything will be all right now, Dr. Mason."

***

I heard classical music somewhere in the distance. *Für Elise*? The building, rhythmic notes made my insides feel like they were detached, floating, like I was approaching the crest of a rollercoaster climb where gravity doesn't seem to exist for a few seconds. I opened my eyes instinctively, but instead of the expected, unobstructed space and the ground far, far below, everything was close—even cozy. A fireplace was dark in the far corner of the room and books, as far as I could tell with my vision still blurred, lined the shelves from ceiling to floor in front of me.

"*Knox*?" I tried to call out, my voice cracking and quiet.

"Right here, Frankie," he said, approaching from behind me. "It's all right. Everything is fine."

"Why did—" I started, but was interrupted by a coughing fit. I braced for the searing pain I had come to expect, but somehow it never came.

"They drugged us," Jack said from across the room, *both* of his arms crossed over his chest. I rubbed my eyes to help clear my vision. "For *logistical* reasons, whatever that means." He squinted, his voice full of contempt.

"Jack...your arm?" I asked, but before he could answer, the door opened, filling the dim room with blinding light for a few seconds.

"First, I do apologize for the sedation." Eve said, the click of her heels on the floor echoing until she made her way to the large, oriental area rug I wouldn't have otherwise noticed. "Our calculations for evacuating the three of you while you were conscious were off by a few minutes. Not anyone's fault, but it was a chance we couldn't take again moving through the remaining checkpoints of the mission."

"Hang on," I said abruptly. "You drugged us because we were *too slow*?"

Eve just smiled at me. "As I said, it was strictly a decision based on correcting our calculations. But none of that matters. You're safe now." She smoothed her dark blazer and matching slacks before crossing to the large, wingback chair in front of the fireplace. "Please, sit." She motioned to Knox and Jack, then met my eyes. "You should also be able to move without pain now, Dr. Mason. Please, take a seat."

I sat up the rest of the way on the gurney slowly, against expecting pain that didn't come. I pulled open the cardigan I was wearing and lifted the hem of the loose t-shirt underneath. The bandages on my stomach were gone, and so was any evidence that I'd ever been shot.

"How is this possible?" I asked, glancing again at Jack. "It's the same with your arm?"

He straightened it, then pantomimed swinging a bat. "Ready for spring training. And let me tell you, this is the only reason I'm not looking for throats to punch right now after that dart to the jugular."

Knox took a step toward the chairs Eve had just offered. "Who were those people after us, how did you know about them, and how did you heal Frankie and Jack?"

Eve nodded as she tapped a tablet sitting next to her on the side table. Projected areal images of roiling smoke and flames pouring from the Pathology Center building filled the air above it.

"I'm afraid there's no sound because the network is still offline," Eve said. "But we managed to patch into the drone camera."

A cold dread settled over me. "*What happened*?"

"What is *happening…*" Eve corrected. "This is live footage. All three of your residences have suffered the same fate, I'm afraid. We believe Wu Fong is responsible, given their involvement in the black market immortality drugs, which we've been able to connect to them thanks to watching your research progress, Dr. Mason. Thank you."

"The cloud… Can I have that tablet?" I could barely keep myself from yelling. If all hardcopies of my research were destroyed at the pathology center and the tablet we'd downloaded it to at Knox's place was also destroyed, the only chance to salvage it was to download it again.

Eve shook her head solemnly. "We've already thought of that and used Dr. Bingham's login information to access the cloud. Unfortunately, your entries have been wiped from the servers. Dr. Bingham had a count down program installed, likely at the insistence of his associates at Wu Fong, to erase the research in the event he was compromised and no longer able to monitor it. Wu Fong likely has the only copies of your research now."

I heard what Eve had said, but the words wouldn't process in my mind. It was impossible. This was the *Citadel* Pathology Center. *Years* of work on novel Red Fever. "*All* the research?" I managed. "Even the wasting sickness data?"

"Unfortunately." She raised her brows in that kindergarten teacher way again. I felt sick.

Jack scrubbed his hands over his face and took in a deep breath, letting it out with a long, swallowed groan. "That's it, then. If the lab is gone, the work is gone. It's over."

"Not quite." Eve turned off the feed. "There is an upside to all this—a chance you can fast track your work again now that we know what the source material for the Red Fever infection is."

Chapter 36

Jack chuckled ruefully. "Fast track our work *how*? The CPC is on fire and the server is wiped. Why are these assholes even still after us?"

Eve took a deep breath and turned to him. "I'll need to start at the beginning..." She folded her hands in her lap. "In addition to my affiliation with Crisis Management, I work for an agency that keeps certain historical items out of the wrong hands. Those *wrong hands*—Wu Fong, and we believe others—are the ones interested in you and your friends." Eve turned her attention to me, her intense green eyes fixing me in place. "We've been following the Red Fever enigma for years now, like you, trying to determine its origins. As you and especially Mr. Ryder can *personally* attest, this is no normal pathogen."

"And why do you think I can personally attest to that?" Knox narrowed his eyes.

"Mr. Ryder, plainly put, we believe your...*condition* is the result of being dosed with an extract from the *Tree of Life*, as it's known—a tree we also believe to be located on the island from where both you and Dr. Mason have just returned."

Knox guffawed, his eyes wide as he looked to me like he wanted confirmation that it was the correct response, but I wasn't laughing.

"Sorry, the *garden of Eden* Tree of Life?" I asked before I could filter the doubt from my voice.

"Indeed, the same." Eve nodded, "I know how it sounds, but understand that many items of legend are actually quite real. The legends themselves are simply centuries-old attempts to explain what science had not. At least, not yet." She glanced from me to Knox. "Suffice it to say, I'm sure you can all understand the danger in this fruit being misused, as it is now with the so-called *immortality* drugs being distributed on the streets."

Jack held up a contemplative hand. "So this *Tree of Life* is *supposed* to make people immortal, but what, there's a glitch that turns some of them into werewolves or—" He glanced at Knox carefully. "Or gives them other abilities?"

"Not across the board, no." Eve shook her head. "We suspect that Red Fever presents differently depending on one's ancestry. For example, we've learned that those lacking significant levels of Denisovan or Neanderthal DNA developed the wasting sickness, while individuals with high levels of Denisovan DNA, such as the bartender from Ivy's, and Neanderthal DNA, such as Marcus Donovan, apparently react more...*dynamically*. Until your breakthrough work, Dr. Mason, we just weren't sure what was causing the different genetic responses."

"But Knox's reaction wasn't like any of those you mentioned when he was exposed," I said, wildly curious about what her explanation for that could be. She cleared her throat and turned to Knox.

"No..." she started. "And this is because we believe that you, Mr. Ryder, are descended from a different evolutionary line altogether. One of four yet unrecognized lines that also overlapped with Homo-sapiens for a brief time...the *First Bloods*, as they're called in many religions. And Ghob—*Mama Luz*, as you've come to know her—wants to restore these lines as the dominant species."

"Did you say, *Luz*?" Knox hissed.

Eve gave a subtle nod. "She is more than she appears, as I'm sure you've also suspected, Mr. Ryder. She believes she is the *Gnome Queen*—the leader of one of these four *First Blood* lines: the evolutionary line of Earth elementals...Mother Nature, in essence."

Knox chuckled, exhausted as he scrubbed his hands over his face. "All right..." he shook his head. "So you want me to believe that I'm one of her long lost *gnome* subjects or something? One of those little garden dwarfs with the hats?" Knox backed away and began to pace. "Because some crazy fruit drug woke it all up, right?" He nodded wearily as his heavy brows darted together. "Sure...makes sense."

"I assure you, this is no joke, Mr. Ryder. With more tests we hope to discover which of the four lines your DNA reflects, but I understand how farfetched this all sounds. Let's start with something concrete. Tell me, did you and Dr. Mason come into contact with any fresh water on the island, perhaps with restorative properties?" Eve asked, her voice tight.

"How did you know that? Is that what you used to heal Jack and me?" I asked, feeling hope spark in my chest until I remembered that Knox said the water didn't work once it was out of contact with the tree.

Eve tilted her head as if weighing her words. "Technically, yes. In short, we believe you must have absorbed enough of these waters to trigger what's known as an *adaptive response* at the cellular level. Your body was, in fact, able to then push out the bullet and immediately began repairing the damage," she said, her eyes darting to my stomach. "With that in mind, we extracted some of your plasma while you were all sedated, replicated the white blood cells, then returned the mix to you, save for the dose we also gave Dr. O'Dell. Our suspicion proved to be true—it has to be the same tree." She turned to Jack.

"Supercharged convalescent plasma," he mumbled to himself, all traces of humor vanished. "So, what is this island water?"

"Legend gives it many names," Eve said. "The Pool of Bethesda, the Fountain of Youth, though these were purportedly near Jerusalem, not in the middle of the Bermuda Triangle."

"And nobody knows why it cures people? No science on that yet?" Jack pressed, incredulous.

"I'm afraid not since it's been lost to the ages, but now, perhaps we can change that." Eve added. "Which brings me back to the upside I'd mentioned, Dr. Mason. The novel Red Fever virus—the wasting sickness—is likely now reversible with the convalescent plasma sourced from your blood. As for what has affected Mr. Ryder, Marcus Donovan, and the bartender at Ivy's, I'm afraid that's a bit more complicated because as I've eluded, we believe the cause there is not a viral variant, but rather—"

Jack blanched before interrupting her. "Something different in their cellular makeup." He met my eyes. "Frank, we thought those cellular differences in Donovan were *caused* by the virus."

I took a deep breath and nodded at him before turning my attention back to Knox. "So if this is a gene that was turned on by a reaction to that fruit enzyme, can't we just turn it off—or at least edit it?" I asked, turning to Jack. He crossed his arms over his chest again and pressed his lips into a hard line.

"If we knew which gene it was, maybe. CRISPR can isolate and edit DNA mutations in the cells, which wouldn't be any more involved than sickle cell treatment or cellular dystrophy therapy, even some kinds of cancer treatment. Piece of cake. But if we're talking about atavism here—human tails or chicken teeth or something—this could be…complicated."

"All right." I took in a sharp breath, my chest tightening with the realization that I was quickly drifting out of my depths. *Maybe I couldn't save Knox. Maybe it really was too late for him.* I closed my eyes and shook my head to keep that thought at bay. "All right," I repeated. "Then there's still hope for the antivenin. I can infuse it with jicambi and supercharge the antibody response. We just need to get another sample of the fruit so I can isolate the enzymes again, and I need some of those syringes if we can get them to cross reference…" I trailed off as I realized Jack and Eve were both looking at me with pity. "Look, I know it's a long shot, but maybe—"

"I'm afraid there are a few obstacles with that route." Eve sighed.

Jack nodded slowly. "Like I started to say, let's pretend that I believe Ryder's genome stems from some ancient line of humanity that doesn't exist anymore. If that's the case, Frank, we have no way of knowing what's normal for him. We thought Donovan's cellular differences were *caused* by the virus, remember? But now that we know better?" He shook his head. "We can run an immunity report from Ryder's legacy chip and maybe find which gene was turned on three years ago, but it's likely not that simple. Who knows if neighboring genes have been affected the last three years as a result. Hell, cancer is basically atavism, Frank. At some point in the progression, there's just no undoing the knots."

A vacuous hole opened in my chest, gripping and pulling at the fragments of hope I'd constructed. I couldn't let it. I couldn't just do nothing.

"All right, well, if you work on that, I'll work on the antivenin path. We'll find a way, Jack."

"Dr. Mason…" Eve began, but tapered off when I

glared at her—an instinctive reaction to the consolation lacing her voice.

"What? Do you have some other miracle water trick up your sleeve instead?" I widened my eyes at her, not even trying to hide my impatience and contempt as I beckoned her to finish what she was going to say.

She took in a slow, calm breath and smiled gently. "Regarding the antivenin...the concept may have merit, but you should know that the operation at Raphael's tea shop has been scrubbed—all employees were replaced and all inventory records were sponged within twenty-four hours of Dr. Bingham's arrest," she said carefully. "Wu Fong and Ghob— *Mama Luz*—are the only possible avenues left for acquiring more of the fruit here on the mainland. And even then, there is no guarantee that they actually still have it."

Everyone was silent for several seconds as Eve's last sentence hung in the air. My mind raced again. There was a chance. That's what she was saying, wasn't it? I turned to Knox, but he was already shaking his head.

"Luz is a ghost. I tried for years to find out more about her, both when I worked on the docks and even after I had access to resources at the Citadel—her boat had no shipping records, no home ports, she had no official business name. And Wu Fong?" He laughed. "It would be easier to *row a boat* all the way back to the tree on Scrapper Island than it would be to infiltrate their operation."

I shook my head adamantly. "There *has* to be an easier way. It can't end like this after everything, Knox. We're too close now."

Eve cleared her throat. "Actually, Dr. Mason is correct—there is an easier way," she offered, getting to her feet and smoothing her pants again. A small grin pulled at the corner of her mouth as she made eye contact with each of us. "The boat I have waiting in port is *fully automated*. No rowing required, and I'll have the lab equipment you'll need brought aboard."

"What...are you talking about?" Jack asked after a beat, the floor creaking in protest as he took a few hesitant steps toward Eve.

A woman in her late sixties pushed open the oak door and stood in front of it, her expression grandmotherly, yet fierce with her sharp cheekbones, dark eyes, long, straight nose, and angular jaw. Her silver braid hung to her waist, her warm, copper skin glowing under the chandelier light that illuminated her white house dress. She gave us a knowing smile.

Eve nodded at the woman. "Alma will show you to your rooms, and tomorrow, we'll prepare to return to Scrapper Island," she added, her green eyes alight with purpose. "Your research requires more fruit, and I need to secure that tree."

If you liked *Bad Seed*, please consider leaving a review! These go a long way to helping authors like me find cool readers like you.

FIRST BLOODS

- Prequel 1: *Feral*
- Book 1: *Bad Seed*
- Book 2: *Bitter Fruit* (Coming soon!)
- Book 3: *Killing Frost* (Coming soon!)

FIRST BLOODS Companion Series:

EDEN'S BLUFF ACADEMY

- Book 1: *Poisoned Garden*
- Book 2: *Thorny Gates* (coming soon)

ELEMENTAL WARS

- Book 1: *Nervous Water*
- Book 2: *Scorned Earth* (Coming soon!)

***

Did you like *Hunger Games, Maze Runner,* or *Divergent*? If so, check out my YA dystopian series, *The Elements*:

AQUA

TERRA

AER

IGNIS

About Tracy Korn

Tracy Korn is a USA Today bestselling sci-fi / fantasy author and all around science geek who may or may not have a "Lip Smackers" chapstick addiction.

When she's not inventing dystopian worlds (and subsequently saving them or wrecking them more), she reads about other people doing it, practices her newbie cinematographer skills, and dreams of someday meeting James Cameron.

To be the first to hear about new releases, giveaways, and if Tracy ever really does meet James Cameron, sign up for her VIP Readers list: **bit.ly/TracyKornNews**

And of course, stay in touch on Facebook, Twitter, Instagram, and other platforms found at **TracyKorn.com.**

Just want book release updates? Follow Tracy on the following platforms!

Amazon: **amazon.com/author/tracykorn**
Goodreads: **bit.ly/TracyKornGoodreads**
BookBub: **bit.ly/TracyKornBookBub**

Acknowledgments

Many thanks to my beta readers, who helped fine tune this series so far! I appreciate your keen eyes and quick feedback, but most of all, I love that you have as much fun in these made up worlds as I do. Thanks so much to Brian Busby, Karin Cleaves, Deb Commons, Jackie Denton, Alicia Hooley, Judith Johnson, Liz McMahon, Becky Myers, Margarita McClain, LaVerne Schaf, Jackie Tansky, Leza Weber, Billie Wichkan, Kathy Wortham, and Christian Yoder. Thanks for being part of my tribe. Many thanks also to my family for their undying support, especially to my husband, James, for his tireless patience with my cover tweaks. Love you guys!